To my friend Renée Vogel

Grove Press
New York

Locas

Yxta Maya Murray

Published simultaneously in Canada
Printed in the United States of America
FIRST EDITION

Library of Congress Cataloging-in-Publication Data
Murray, Yxta Maya.
        Locas / Yxta Maya Murray.—1st ed.
            p.   cm.
        ISBN 0-8021-1605-1
        I. Title.
    PS3563.U832L63   1997
    813'.54—dc20   96-44826

DESIGN BY LAURA HAMMOND HOUGH

Grove Press
841 Broadway
New York, NY 10003

10 9 8 7 6 5 4 3 2 1

Locas

Part One

1980—1985

Cecilia

My family's lived in Echo Park for my whole life. It's our home. We belong here. They must call it Echo because you can't hear yourself think around here with all the noise. The people here are crazy.

I was gangbanging like Manny till I was fifteen and I got pregnant. Anyways, I don't do it no more. I'm working at the good life now. But we've got the finest gangbanging blood in the Park. Manny started the Echo Park Lobos and all those boys would be nothing but an idea without him. Since I'm his baby sister that means I must have that blood in me too, somewhere in me like a wild horse. So I could be like Star Girl and Chique and Lucía. But that's not me. I fight it. I try real hard all the time.

* * *

Mama likes to say that we started here From Scratch. Like a cake. She's short and brown just like me, with flat hands and feet. We're so small they called me *Muñeca*, which means doll. She came over here from Oaxaca, pregnant and holding on to Manny's little fist so he wouldn't get away. He was *loco* even then. "I must have washed five hundred houses before we got our papers," is what Mama says. "Better than having nothing to eat but dirt." We're all legal now but I'm the real American. I was born here red white and blue. Mama was so afraid of what the INS would do when they caught her without her green card that she wouldn't go to the doctor until she was screaming with those labor pains and I was pushing out of her, small and wet and trying to be alive. She had me in the car, messing the seats and the dash and then rushed to Kaiser after. They took us. Then. I'm here now anyway.

Manny quit school quick. In the ninth grade? When he was fifteen years old, so that he could run with these *vatos* Chico and Paco and Beto. They'd scoot around the streets picking pockets and stealing small things at first. Pocket radios, junk jewelry from store counters, silver-plated *milagros*, anything that looked shiny and expensive even though they didn't know what things cost. Manny had this little dark body with bird legs, a skinny chest, and a steel-rod collarbone. His face was round cheeked and square cornered, and there was a line of tiny fur over his top lip like the pencil mustaches *vaqueros* wear in westerns. My big brother, he was just playing kid games but you could already tell that he had a taste for the bad. I'd see him pick off a pair of sparkle-stone earrings from a store and he wouldn't even blink while he slipped them in his pocket. Fifteen back then was still young, and he wasn't hurting nobody. That was 1980. Fifteen around here is different now.

I was ten when Manny was fifteen and he was like a prince to me. Mama would scream at him all day long for stealing and skipping school, she didn't even know that he'd stopped going until he was almost grown. She'd scream at him all angry with her wild hair but I just loved him. I loved him and loved him.

It was like we all grew up in a minute. One day he's stealing candy and the next he's the kingpin and every boy in town is looking his way. Manny was the first of his kind in these parts. No one in the neighborhood had ever seen a gangster like him before.

Twenty-five years ago the Park was just that, a park with regular joes walking around. In 1970's Echo Park, you had white families in tract houses with rose gardens and barbecues, and all of us Mexicans squeezed into the little spaces left over. We made our money by pumping their gas and bussing their tables and cleaning up after them with our hair wrapped up to keep cool. What were the vatos doing, zoot-suiting then? Mama talks about how in the old days you'd look outside and see hairy-chested greasers playing dice on the corners, laughing and yelling loud like music, playing boy games with their knives and their little stealing and running away from the police after puffing out their chests like prize turkeys. The *cholos* then were just posers who didn't have nothing better to do than bust each other up for pocket change. It was the downtown gangsters who had all the business, not the Echo Park vatos. Our boys were so busy showing off for each other with their big greaser hair and snaked-out suits that they couldn't decide if they were disco Latin lovers or penny mafia. There wasn't nothing behind it.

But Manny's an organizer. He's thinking money. When he was younger than I am now he was working on something bigger than playing craps on the corners and getting into knife fights over a couple of dollars. It had been done before. Even Mexicans had been gangbanging before Manny came in on the scene, but Echo Park, there was virgin territory. Manny looked at the Crips and the White Fence locos and the Bloods. He liked what he saw, and he knew he could do better. At sixteen he got our streets in a row and made his connections, starting small with a few boys pulling purses off *viejas* or knocking down liquor stores. And after that he dipped into the tough, dealing these tin-can Saturday night specials that could misfire and take off your face.

I remember being twelve years old and he looked as strong and beautiful as Pancho Villa must have been. He'd wear loose-cut blue jeans and these clean-press flannel shirts, stuff black and rose-red bandannas into his left-hand pocket. I watched the border brothers on the freeway with their faces like old leather and their bone-white teeth and their clip-clop huckster talk, begging the *gabachos* in their cars to buy their bags and bags of fruit or flowers. Not my Manny. He was always too proud to bend.

But he'd come back to the house with money. "Hey!" he'd say to us, walking in the door with mile-long strides, and the bronze in his skin would flash at me like a lantern. "You *know* I'm taking care of all you." And then there's the cash, a few big bills, crisp and flat like new leaves there on the kitchen table. "More than the rent." His smile.

Mama didn't know what to do with that. The first few times she didn't say nothing. She puts it in her pocket, quiet like, and figures when things ease up she'll ask what he did to get that money. Mama knew enough to be patient by then. By the time Manny was old enough to bring a little home she'd already put in a dozen hard years washing up after rich *rubia* ladies with smooth blond helmet hair who'd call her Maria even though her real name's Corazón. She's not an old woman, but a taste of that, and a whole life before fighting it out in Mexico will teach you how much some questions cost.

But after a while, "Manuel, where'd you get this?" she'd ask, her square face squinting up while she folded the money into her skirt. At first he'd answer, "Painting houses," or "Washing dishes." My mama had her heart full of love and smarts and none of us is dumb. Manny's leaving five hundred dollars on the table and he's not even seventeen.

She'd pray and pray, doing the rosary and sprinkling holy water on the floor like some old *curandera* but even after asking she didn't stop taking it. You'd be crazy.

I saw with my brother what it is to become a man. And I wanted to be a man like that. He got stronger, his skinny body moving up and the curves coming out in his arms. His belly hardened into muscle and even the points of his eyes got sharper and sparked like black diamonds. Mexicans ain't big people. The boys in Echo Park don't look like no Muhammad Ali. We're more featherweight boxing. So Manny grew up as tall as he could but he was still looking like a movie star.

And he was more than only pretty. He starts moving from picking pockets to stealing cars, and then sees how that money can *fly* in specials. Locals with a little rainy-weather cash start coming to him looking for a piece, and he'd reach into the back seat of his chopshop car and pull it out, make the nickel color wink under the street lamp light. He'd charge a hundred, even, and I know he'd grin when he'd slip the bills in his pocket. But it wasn't just the money he loved. He was learning how little gangsters would treat you like a *patrón* if you flashed them a fifty and showed them the pistol you had packed under your belt. *Señor* Manny, that's what he wanted to be called. And the boy knew what it took to be the boss.

He came home one day with his face bruised plum-colored and a thin-line slash curving up from his lips to his eye. You could tell he wasn't hurt too bad, though, from the tornado look he's got whipping across his face. But he doesn't jump or holler. He doesn't punch a hole through the wall. He just sits down in the easy chair, puts his feet up and smiles a little. We're bugging out at him like he's a Martian or grew an extra head. There's puffy blueberry smears over his left eye, that skinny mouth kissing his left cheek, but he wasn't feeling any of that pain. Mama had taken one look when he'd breezed through the door, then caught her breath hard up through her throat.

"What happened, *m'hijo?*" she asked him, her voice calm at first, but she got up fast out of her chair to see how bad the damage was. He was sitting there bloody and quiet and happy, and it wasn't normal, something wasn't right. He'd liked the hard fighting, and winning, and from how he's grinning out at us you could tell that he even liked showing off all the red on his skin. I saw how Mama's face got darker, and I started crying too, hiding in a corner while she starts screaming, "WHAT DID YOU DO? WHAT DID YOU DO?!?" her hands grabbing at the air and reaching toward him like he'll disappear and he didn't answer her because he didn't have to.

That was the day that Manny took over the specials business, not even a business yet, a trade-for-money operation run by some skinny man named Gato, which means cat in Spanish. Gato was named that way because he was skinny and slick like a pussycat. He had a connection from East L.A. and would get a couple guns a month and swap drugs and girls and cash for them with the cholos thinking he's the main tough man in town. Not tough enough. Manny got Gato's connection's name and when the cat man finds out he swaggered over to my big brother like a heavyweight gangster and tried to tell him what's what. It didn't take long. Manny chopped him up into raw meat with those fast fists of his. Featherweight.

He still had that fire in his blood when Mama won't stop. Her voice had tugged and looped like a knot, and then it starts booming longer and louder and snagging on us like barbed wire. Her eyes are as big as windows and her teeth are flashing and biting. I know she thinks he's killed somebody. But Manny decided he was sick of listening to what women were going to tell him. No boss man listens to an old lady, and no patrón lets his mama tell him what to do. His eyes got full and steady, and he stood up taller than he had to and watched her real careful.

"Watch it, Mama," is what he said, his left hand quivering down by his hip like a wild animal. She stopped yelling when she saw him there, how he would hit her like she was just any other woman. Her lip dropped and she shrunk back, ashamed and frightened. I waited to see, but nothing much happened after that. Manny didn't raise his hand, but he didn't soft the air with a smile, neither.

I'm sitting in the park, grabbing fists of grass and eye-balling my brother next to me. He doesn't just kick it in the park no more. He lords it. He'll swashbuckle over here, wander over there, swagger back to talk with a couple of his tar-headed vatos. Then he'll ease right down like he's got all the time in the world and stare at the scene out his slitted eyes.

He didn't even have what you'd call friends those days. He had a *clika*, and the gangsters in it were like his blood brothers. In six months he'd grown that specials business up so it brought in more money, five hundred dollars on the kitchen table started to become regular. He'd grouped three of his tightest boys, Paco, Chico, and Beto, and they'd made the suppliers start humming and the sales start jumping like a new machine. The other started answering to him after that. Every no-name in the neighborhood with some extra time or a bad temper was answering to my brother like it was natural, like there wasn't nothing else to do but plant themselves quiet and fixed to the ground in front of him, and then do whatever it was he said. Like soldiers, maybe, is what they thought they were. Soldiers for Manny. That's when the Echo Park Lobos were born, nice and small like a baby, feeding up on that gun money. And that's why today, Saturday afternoon in the park, he gets to stomp around the green grass like he's some king.

But I don't know why they're called Lobos, so I ask.

"Cause we're as mean as wolves," is what Manny answers after a minute, but he doesn't look at me when he says it. He looks up instead at a couple of homeboys who are standing by a bench, and they start high-fiving and hoo-hooing when he says that. This nasty part of me thought, Damn right, *pendejo*, I saw how you talk to Mama. But he didn't see any disrespectful look on my face when he switched his stare back and gave me one of his sideways smiles.

"Muñeca girl, I can make this a big place, see?" Manny waves his hand around like to show me something. "There ain't nothing here now but men. But I got eyes. I see where all this is going and how I'm gonna get it there." He was talking quiet but with something hard under his voice, and now his hand's a tight ball sitting on his hip. I softed up pretty quick then. You can't help but loving a man who says things like that.

* * *

I read the papers. People thought we started t
or any other gangbang because we loved seeing bloo
called us animals, made their little speeches. But it wa
just like anything else. My brother's a businessman, a leader.
Pretty soon he had fifteen, twenty, twenty-five boys working
under him. Paco, one of Manny's homies, got in on the jobs, then
his cousins wanted in, trying to get their cut. Beto's homie Chevy,
Rafael, their friends, till it's one big clika. They had their meetings in the park, all huddled together in the dusk by a picnic
bench, wearing their Pendleton wool shirts and their baggy black
pants. They got their specials business going and then moved on
to fancier deals and started selling to locals with deep pockets
and gabachos who didn't want to bother with the license. I don't
even know the name of all those new guns they got. They were
foreign sounding, black and shiny and wild, macho and pretty
like those boys. Mama was getting smaller every day with worry.

She used to say, "*Oye,* when I get you out of school I
go to school myself," her face lighting up with the idea of wearing those square graduation hats and the long black priest-
looking robes. "Like a business degree," she'd go on, "help me
get my own business. A restaurant!" and she'd pat her hands
together like she's making tortillas fresh. She had that American dream the same as anybody else. But she wasn't saying anything like that after Manny started bringing home that money
he gets from selling gangster guns. She just started squeezing
back into her skin like she wants to hide, doesn't want anyone
to notice her. That's shame for a Mexican woman, losing her
man and control of the whole *familia.* Her boy talking back to
her like that. "Mama, it's going to be OK. Manny takes good
care of us," I told her. But she just looked at me under her
eyelids and whispered her rosary, like I'm some *chingada* that
she doesn't really know.

* * *

The clika started running into problems pretty quick. Everyone's going to try and climb on top one day or the next, hoping they'll figure out a way to scramble right over my brother. Chico, who's from Oaxaca like us but light skinned and thin lipped, he'd been Manny's right hand from the start. But one day he sells a gun to a white man from Long Beach who gets scared. The gabacho calls the police, makes some story up like he ain't doing nothing wrong, and pretends he's giving the cops a tip. But it ain't Chico who gets it. It's Manny. Chico somehow slips the cops Manny's way and my brother goes to jail for seven months.

Lucía, Manny's girlfriend, told me how the policemen came and took him. The day after he'd got arrested I'd gone over to her house where Manny sometimes stayed, and we're in her ratty little room, shivering because it's January but the heat ain't on. From the hall you could see how the door's busted open, big splinters of wood sticking out and the handle's broke.

"Coming to my house to get him," she was saying, twisting her hands together. "We're on the bed, you know, and then they're all standing right there, what do you do? All of a sudden these blue suits are cracking my front door open like it don't matter, but it's *my* place they're fucking up, see what I'm saying? That's *my* door and who's gonna fix it. Nobody, that's who," she says, beautiful and tough but looking weaker that night. Lucía's almost like a rubia. She's got that thin long body that you see on television, and she dyes her hair shiny red, some green lights in her eyes, beautiful pale skin. Not like me. I'm nothing but looking like a dirt-dark Indian. But that girl could almost pass.

Her dancer's body stiffs when she remembers last night, and I can see purple shadows under her eyes.

"Manny jumps up like he's gonna take them boys down and I just stayed put, watching careful cause I know where it's at. Ain't nothing you can do with them cops, right? But he's yelling like Mr. Big Man. 'COME ON! COME ON *ESE*!' and I thought he's gonna pull a gun out of his pants and get both of us dead. Manny don't even have his shirt on. He's standing there half naked and screaming like a loonytunes, and the cops was digging it too. 'We can do it the hard way, Silvas,' this one says, I think he was a Mexican even, but all them pigs are the same. Took four to drop him, and then they start punching him in the face when he's flat down. I still didn't do nothing. They ain't gonna see me start screaming like some loser vieja."

"So he's just lying there?" I ask. I can't imagine it. Not my big cowboy brother Manny.

"After they beat him enough that vato couldn't do nothing but roll over like a dog. They pull him off the floor and he sees what it is. It's over, homes. He don't even look my way, his face and ears red, and bawling cause he's so pissed. Not me. Even when they drag him out the door and I see how he's still trying to walk like a man, I wouldn't let my baby see me cry." I notice then how her eyes ain't pink or wet, how she only looks bone-tired and angry enough to spit.

"You going to be all right, Lucía?" I'm still a baby face so I try smiling at her so she sees it's going to be OK, but she's doing this thousand-yard stare.

"That Chico bastard," she goes on. "He's gonna get it. Gonna get hurt, that vato. I know Manny's gonna do something about that, and I know he'd better." Lucía's a tight little spring. She knows with Manny on the inside nothing's going to be left on her table.

"Where's my money?" she asks then, still not looking at me but her fingers were gripping together like a lock. "Where am I gonna get my money?" But I couldn't say nothing. It ain't like the women are supposed to know where the money comes from anyways.

It took some time for her to bend back up. The girl had got used to the cash that Manny gave her every Friday night so she can go and buy her bread, her meat. So she can pay for her heating bill. She'd got used to it the same as we all did, but she doesn't save like Mama.

Me and Lucía and Mama went to go see Manny in jail a few days after he'd been taken away. They give you a little time to visit with your family, in a big room with all the other families, mamas and babies and sisters, women bawling and the men looking down at the floor, people angry and embarrassed and their faces turning pale as pearls. But you can't do much real visiting. The walls got ears. *La chota* think Manny's got the danger in him so there's fat-cat guards with button-popping beer guts and bloodless lips standing on the sides, watching over us. I don't like their looks. Legs apart like A-frames, caved-in chins, munched mouths. I don't like the rest of it, neither. There's a lady a foot away from me talking to her jailbird man, but she's doing more crying than talking and one of her arms is hooked in a sling. Another woman's bouncing a bubble-shaped baby on her knee across from a *veterano*-looking dude with healed-up jigsaw scars on his face. They don't talk.

I'm getting itchy waiting for Manny. We've been here for twenty minutes already. The three of us are sitting at a beat-up wood table and when I look down I see how people had scratched out their names and words in spiky square letters on the tables.

Pigs Suck.
Vatos Rule.
Spic Mexican Bastards.
Mexicans fuck you UP.
Zelda loves Alberto.

After I've read the whole table, he shows. Manny comes out looking the same but his face is messed up. He's wearing soft orange cotton prison clothes, and there's new cuts on his cheek and slicing down his lip. But the worst thing is how you can see in his eyes that he's getting bone-crushing mad because only women are coming to see him this time. This room is full of women coming to see their men.

"Where's Paco?" is the first thing he asks, and his voice is cracked like he drinks whiskey. Like he doesn't sleep no more.

"I don't know, Manny," Lucía said, *linda* looking with that red hair all done up, curled and sprayed, she's wearing purple eyeshadow and a pink dress, like it's a special occasion. But she toughs up a little when he just wants to know about his boys. "*Chale*, I'm not knowing about nothing they do." Mama's just sitting there with her face hanging down and her cross in her hands while she prays to the Virgin. Not even looking at her own son. I'm so excited to see him. His hands are spread out flat on the table like he's trying not to make a fist, but he's staying cool headed. From the low sandy sound of his voice he seems so sure of things even with them guards standing earshot close behind him.

"Well, then." Manny's keeping his face real still but you can tell he's figuring something out in his head. After a minute he gives her a wink. "You gotta make sure it keeps together while I'm in here, right?" he says to Lucía, and his eyes ain't black diamonds anymore. They're two clear dark stones. "That train's coming."

Gangs are mostly a man's business. The cholos don't want no sheep to ever get a taste of their action. But that's when women started getting some in the Lobos. Then, when Manny let Lucía help him.

Manny told us about this bag he kept in Lucía's closet without her knowing it before. "Don't look at it," he said. "Bring the shit to Paco, but watch him. Make sure he's still on the inside with us, and don't show him nothing till you're sure he ain't no cheater. I don't know how far this Chico thing goes." Manny's face shadows up because just thinking about Chico makes him twitchy. "If Paco's still a Lobo, give him the bag and keep your mouth shut till I get out." His face was darker than mine even, and there's early hard lines coming out around his mouth when he talks and the air around us smells like metal.

Mama couldn't take her boy's bad talk so she pressed up out of her seat slow and tired and when she left to wait for us outside her small face folded like paper. She didn't say nothing but I heard what she's thinking. *Qué lástima*, boy's nothing but a chingado like his father.

"Don't worry about her," Manny says about our mama. He looks at Lucía and then flicks those black eyes my way. "You listening to me now."

I was a seventh grader in pigtails but Lucía still took me along for her ride. I think she was afraid almost as much as me, but a girl like her doesn't want to be left empty handed. Now she was getting in on Lobo talk, and I could see how her brain had started going tick-tock and working overtime.

Mama was already back at the house. When we'd taken the bus back to the neighborhood she'd been boiling like a spitfire because she knew that the two of us think Manny's sexy, a hardbitten and cold-as-ice outlaw with that whiskey in his voice. But as soon as we got off at our stop we'd run back to Lucía's, aching to see what's in that closet, what he's been hiding. She was living in a one-room apartment, trying to keep it clean by wiping up the dirt and dust with her little rags and covering up the furniture with cheap blankets, but she couldn't hide how poor she was. There were cracks in the walls and tape on the windows, the busted front door wasn't fixed yet, and the refrigerator's empty except for some water. She was mostly making the rent from what Manny gave her, but that day, when she started helping the Lobos, she got an idea of how she could earn it for herself.

He'd hid the bag in the back of her closet, just like he said. It was brown, creased and folded up and full of heavy things. We dragged it up on the bed and let it sit there, looking at it for a minute like it was a birthday cake waiting to get sliced up and passed out to all the hungry kids at a party.

"What's this boy keeping in my house?" Lucía said, and she's all jumpy now.

She unrolled the bag with her fast hands, and the clanking of metal inside let us know that there's guns, like we thought the whole time, maybe fifteen of them all piled up like groceries and it looks like someone's getting ready for big war. But they're pretty. Not specials like before, these are dark heavy metal with clicks and knobs and sights, a puzzle of *cuetes*, lying there heaped on her bed as casual as laundry.

"Chingado," she says. "I'm in it now."

I felt it too. When I looked down at the bag with them fancy guns spilling out I thought, Yah, that's the life. Banging around with a stick of fire down your belt, making like Superman, these cholos got it going on. They can buy themselves a piece and walk around brave because they know they ain't bluffing. They'll take on any enemy that comes their way. But women, they ain't supposed to carry on. So when I saw them shiny killers I only got a little hungry, dreaming about what it would be like to live that *macho* life. Not Lucía, though. She was starved for it. I saw her running her hand over the pistols, then picking one up and looking through the sight like it belongs to her, like she knows how to use the fool thing.

"Hey, ésa," I say, getting all nervous because she's acting up. "Put it down before you get yourself killed."

But she wouldn't pay me no mind. That *chica* was already far out gone. "Oh, baby sister, I ain't putting nothing down," she says, making this low laugh. She bends over the bed and picks up three, four guns, so her hands are full of gleamy black gunmetal, then looks at me and shows me her big teeth. "A little sheep like you don't even know what I got here, do you? This is the bomb, girl! One hundred percent solid gold!"

I didn't say nothing more. I didn't snap my tongue at her or shake my head, I wouldn't say one wrong word to her at all. Because I could tell that them man games were going to make Lucía strong, the kind of strong where you don't care about nothing else. She was standing there, tall and pretty and them guns looked monster big in her hands, and she didn't look like no weak girl now. "The *gold*," she said again, stretching her hands out to me, and for a minute, under the yellow light of that naked bulb she had hanging from the ceiling, I could almost see what she means.

Lucía

Don't tell me I don't know what it is. When I got in the business girls wasn't doing shit in the clika. They could grin, sex, color up their faces, that's about it. A woman was a sheep. So he thinks he's the man, but he's not the man no more. I'm the one scoring.

Hey honey, you get some respect for this chola, see? When I was a kid we had nothing. My mami and papi would scream at each other in our little house, the sounds bouncing hard off the walls so that you couldn't get away from it no matter where you ran, he's hitting on her like she's a punching bag, making blood-red and dark blue marks over her little eyes and wet mouth, and there was those *rancheras* on the radio over his yelling making me crazy.

Well check out my clothes now, I'm doing fucking fine. I'm the one screaming in all your faces, I'll do anything. I'll do it all.

OK. I caught the taste for gangbanging quick when I saw those guns in his secret little brown bag. Just touching them was like holding fire in your hand.

When I finished bugging my eyes at them bombs on my bed I took the bag to Paco and I looked at him hard, toughing up my face and trying to make sure I was doing the right thing, but it ain't like these men could ever give you any answers. Paco used to be Manny's boy. He was a tall piece of chickenbone with no blood in him, and even if he slicked his hair back like a gangster the vato still had these empty eyes. I know he didn't see me as no real Lobo player who'd wind up sitting on top all fat and pretty like I am now. He just saw some girl, a *chavala* good-for-nothing, a piece of ass.

I'd brought him that bag at his house, just like Manny told me to. "Manny says to keep a lookout on Chico," I tell him, giving him my test. I put the bag down on his floor, keeping my hands real still, but I was shaking inside. Nervous like I had dynamite, like the cops are going to come tearing down the door again and take *me* away this time. There was something else there, though. My heart beat up all fast and excited.

"Mmmmmm," he said, and even if he didn't show me no respect he still eyeballed me in the face, so he got the bag. But I could see how he wasn't sure what to tell a woman, and I thought maybe he'd give me the story. I smiled at him like a stripper asking for a dollar, and I saw him warm up for a second, stretching his lips up smooth. But it wasn't no use. He wasn't gonna let a woman in the game no matter how sweet I look.

"Hey man, what you know about Chico?" I asked him, making that cheeky face.

"No, ésa, I don't know nothing. I got it from here." He shut me off, frowned his mouth back down, then carted the bag away without even giving me a nibble. No matter. To Paco I was just handing him some load and talking too much, but that action made me feel like a Superloca. It was the first time I'd ever been a player. Check it out, right? Check this old girl out. I remembered my stinking place with the cockroaches and rats that kept on scratching behind my walls no matter how hard I scrubbed. And I thought about my empty mouth, how I had to keep it quiet while the men get to make all the moves. My pitterpatter heart started punching and kicking then when Paco don't give me the time. I didn't wanna be a shut-up sheep no more. I wanted to yell out so everybody in town could hear me loud and clear.

But I didn't make a sound. Hey, *look* at me, ése, I thought while he's walking away. You tell me what it is. Don't be doing that.

When Manny first fucked me I was nothing but a cherry, thinking love was the biggest thing. He found me when I was just fifteen years old, a red-candy cherry girl sitting on the porch in my new dress with the bow, my curvy legs showing out under my pink skirt. I was getting sunburned out there by the Indian summer and I was bored sick out of my mind, waiting on them steps for my mami to finish up. That's when I saw him driving down my street in this coal-black Bel Air cruiser that was spitshined to a mirror, and I didn't never think I'd ever see something better than that. The vato was slick. Inky black hair buzzed up, dusk dark skin, white teeth shining out. He looked like a fairy prince to me.

"Hey, *chiquita*, what you say?" he said, pulling up by the curb and sticking his elbow out the window. *Suave.* He was the ticket. I loved him right away with his Valentino smile and his strong-looking arm waving me over. "What you doing, linda?" I didn't even stop to think. I ran right into them arms of his like they was gonna save my life.

My Manny had that sweet juice in them old days. Back then I would of spread for any old dude that came swinging with a smile, but I got lucky with him. That boy knew how to work his way around a woman. He would bring me daisies, hold my hand out in the park. Sing to me if he'd drunk some beer. And he'd take me driving in his lowrider by the beach at night with the moon shining out, the windows rolled down and the radio playing cheesy love songs, his hand up my knee.

"What you want, baby girl?" he said to me the first time, looking straight ahead at the road, but I could see him grinning like a fox. I played shy and kept my wiggly tongue still in my mouth. And what can a sheep say to a *don juan* anyways? I thought that boy was the *bomb*. When I see Manny now I think of a losing hand, cause that's what he drew. But I remember how he had these polished-rock muscles wrapped in blue zig-zag taks, a smoky cologne smell, and his voice was going down me like smooth warm wine. Manny was everything I wanted, a man any chica would of killed for.

"What you want?" he says again, fingers creeping up, and I stay real quiet, cause I was thawing, melting, and I'd never felt that heavy heat before. "You want me, eh? Cause I love you, linda, that's right. I'll take care of you, girl."

That'll pop any sheep's cork, especially a Tecate sheep that ain't never heard sweet words. "Oh Manny!" I start crying cause I thought he could make good on them promises. "I love you! I love you!" I tried to jump him like I once saw a lady do in a *telenovela*, wrapped my arms around his head and kissed his cheeks and his lips so he can't see the road, he's laughing and driving like a one-eyed drunk, and I never felt more happy in my whole life.

"This what you looking for, sweet thing?" he asks me, after he finally stops the car out by the road, and the moon's cutting a bright ring out of the night. You could hear the waves pounding and I had that virgin fever all over me. "Yah, I want you," I told him, trying to sound low and whispery, and he got this bad-boy smile on, then set down to that business of making me a woman. Reached his hand up and pulled on my bow like he was opening up a birthday present, and I was thinking of the daisies he'd gave me and the sea outside and the pretty moon up there. Yes yes yes, I'm saying in my head. Yes baby yes.

He sure knew how to fire up a cherry. Smoothed me down right, set me up in my own apartment, got me food, every-thing, a rabbit-fur jacket so I was strutting around the Park look-ing like a five-dollar piece. He showed me off to his homies and I stood swaybacked and batted my eyes. "See my beautiful girl?" he said, that's how I met Paco and Chico, with Manny hooking his arm into mine and telling them how pretty I am, and Chico looks at me funny and says, "Yah, ése, you did good. That's some sweet chica." It didn't matter there was rats in my place or that I was dressing like some whore. I didn't care how his homies didn't call me by my name. When we first got together I thought I'd won the sheep lotto, know what I'm saying? Everything Manny gave me was gold. I knew he saved me from hooking, from the gutter. I would of done anything for that vato. Any-thing he asks for. Manny was my *world*.

"Baby, you just stay put and I'll set you up in style," is what he told me in his best lady-killer voice, and I believed that boy like he was God Himself. I spent all my time putting on lip gloss, pumping up my hair so I'm looking like Charo, squeezing into skin-tights and five-inch heels. I knew I had to flirt and swing and show off my best parts to keep my man happy. And I *was* looking fine, check it out. "Come here, mama," he'd say, they'd all say it even if I was just walking down the street. I had a whole town of ten-second boys throwing me wolf whistles and telling me I'm sweet, but back then I was saving it all up for my Manny. I was a slick little jalapeña, pop me in your mouth, cause sex is in a Mexican woman's blood, it comes natural, and I gave it to him crazy, wild with lots of noise, for as long as he could take it so that he'd stay put by my side. "Love you love you love you," I'd whisper in his ear, and my eyes would fill up with them sheepy tears. But I wouldn't say much of nothing else. I thought I knew how to make sure things stay my way. Little quiet sheep's not gonna give any trouble, right? Not gonna say peep.

And he was worth it back then. Manny's *jefe* was even better than his don juan. You could tell he had it going on even when he was a puppy vato dealing guns, cause the homies treated him like a hero. "O, *sí*, jefe man," they'd say when he's walking the street. "Patrón, you got the *goods*." It made me so proud. I'd look over at him, see how he had these Indian eyes and movie-star mouth. A *man's* man. He didn't even have to beat on his gangsters to make them do what he says. "Go score for me, son, I'll set you up right, eh?" he'd say, giving a boy a couple of specials, and they'd come back with shiny smiles and a fistful of twenties. He was gonna make us all rich. Hey homes, just smell the green coming in, you know? Get this shit started. Paco and Chico and Beto, fucking greasers, them boys was like little stick men to me, Manny was the only real vato in town. I'd see him making cash money with his business, and I noticed how everybody on the street would high-five him, show him respect. That makes a woman's heart fill up and spill over. But it made me hungry, too.

You know when you find your ride? When you find that thing that makes you go zoom? Looking at Manny walk around here like some superstar got me started, in more ways than one. I was one of them sheep that might have thought I was queen bee just cause I got to fuck the patrón. Like them women that think if they get the main man's eye they got it all. Well, not me. Even when I was that baby chica, sometimes I'd look at myself in the mirror to see if I looked anything like a big boss. I had that fluffy sheep hair, long pony-girl legs, a round smooth face. But somewhere I thought I saw a little of Manny in me. "Hey, what you say?" I'd whisper to my face in the mirror, try and make a buffalo stance. At first I felt like that cause I loved him. I thought I wanted to have some little piece of Manny in me, fire-bright, red-coal hot, sitting down deep in my belly, making me strong and beautiful the same as him, so that Parkers on the street would see me and know. I wanted them all to think I was the bomb just like him.

But it didn't take too long before I was wanting them things for my own self. After he got penned I figured pretty quick that juicing the boss wasn't gonna make me one. And I didn't have time for romance then. Who's gonna take care of the sheep, right? After he's busted two days, three days, all of a sudden I'm hearing those rats nibbling behind my walls after dark. I had my rent due, my *refri* empty, and my hands turned cold and sticky when I'd think about how my money's locked up. There wasn't anybody leaving big bills on my pillow now. And for damn sure nobody was giving me respect on the street. I knew when he got out he was gonna be Mr. King around here again. A woman, though. A sheep ain't no good if she don't got a boss man behind her. Unless she gets herself a plan.

"That train's coming," is what he told me when he first got locked up. But once I got good and scared I wanted to do some of the driving myself. I wanted what *he's* got. And when I'd got hold of them guns he'd stashed in my room and had my words with Paco I started having my wild dreams, thinking maybe I could group as good as any man.

Manny didn't get out of the pen till seven months after Chico snitched him. Every time I'd go see him he was bigger and meaner looking. His cuts had healed, and I don't think it's cause he was making any friends. He'd grown these jail muscles that popped out bumpy and this brushy flat hair that stood straight up like the veteranos' he meets inside. But it's hard to look too strong behind bars. I was still his woman, but I was getting some ideas by then. Maybe I'm not gonna look to no vato forever, I'd think to myself when we're talking in that zoo-room full of cons and crying babies. He'd run his fingers through his hair and light up a cigarette, and I'd see how he looked foolish and dangerous in them pajama prison clothes. And it would run through my head again. Maybe someday a man's gonna be looking up to *me*.

While he was inside I kept an eye on Paco and Chico and found what was happening. Everything was still so small then. We only had a few boys running guns, but there was already the makings of *cabrón* C-4, the only enemy the Lobos ever had in these parts. Chico got that started.

One day I see Paco on the corner with his homies, standing stooped and hunchie like a question mark but doing that gangster shuffle dance that badasses do when they're together. He was duded out in a black ski cap pulled down low, baggy pants slung lowrider down on the hips, and then the shiny black shoes. Paco and Chevy was stacked together on the sidewalk smoking a little weed and laughing that low laugh, moving their hands up and scuffing their feet while they talked. Beto was there too, small like Manny and with the same cropped black hair sticking up with grease, a scar on his mouth from when he was eight and fell off his bike that made him look so tough.

"Hey, *Paquito*," I said, sliding up soft next to him, just letting the skins of our arms touch light, turning on that switch in his head so he gets loose. "You take care of what I gave you?"

"Uh huh," he answers, pink-eyed. He'd taken a couple hits already and the boy opened like a door as soon as I cuddled up to him. "I got those pieces sold right off and the money's waiting for what Manny wants to do with it."

This boy's a stupid, I'm thinking. I'd have that money and be gone with my fast feet.

"That's good, son, that's good," I say. I wanna laugh cause two tugs on some cheap reefer and he's giving it all up, but I just smile instead. I get braver and start to blink and coo and even paw him a little, stroking his shoulder with my finger just once, light like a tickle on top of his thin white t-shirt.

"You ever find anything out about that Chico?" I ask him, making my voice low, and I can feel Beto getting twitchy there. He's not sure why I'm asking questions, and he don't know how much stupid Paco should tell a girl like me. But Paco talked on, his mouth moving just cause I touched him like that.

"Chico man's got his goodies on the side, *ésa*," he said, and he's bragging now. He's got a load of front-page news stuffed in his head and why not tell the sexy thing with the tickle finger a thing or two? He smoothes and ruffles his feathers, grims up his mouth. "I think he's fucking with Manny's system. Scared the shit out of that Long Beach gabacho he was gonna sell to. He pulled his knife when he's just supposed to be doing a deal like Manny told him to, then made the dude tell the cops all about the Lobos, all about who Manny is. The man even gave him your address, Lucía."

"Shut up," said Beto. "Just shut the fuck up."

"Don't worry about it," I said, turning toward him and

looking at that kid scar on his mouth. I wasn't scared of them *vatitos* like I was of Manny. "It's OK I know a little. I'm just the jefe's." And I did know some then. I knew enough so that it's Manny who's gonna have to come to *me* with questions.

We called Chico *Rubia* for a nickname cause he's got blond hair like a whitegirl. He hates that. But he can't say we're wrong. The vato's pretty like a woman, with that corn hair and ocean color in his eyes instead of the flat black that so many of us have. He's lighter than even me, who used to walk around all tall and proud like I'm special cause I'm not so dark like all the others. But that Chico's just dying to be dark like a man, so he's the one trying to get famous. Pulling knives on a gabacho just to get Manny slammed up, that's cold. Still, it took a long time before we was finished with him for good. Chico and Manny had been friends since they'd been kids and it was gonna take more than something Paco said once to break that up.

I told Manny when he got out of the pen, after I hugged and kissed him so hard I thought even a strong thing like him would break.

"Baby," I said, slipping my little tongue in his ear, holding on to him hard like he's gonna float away. "You was right about that Chico. He's the one who got the cops on you." I'm almost growling so that boy would take me serious.

But all that fire he had for Chico was gone now that he was outside. A gangster wouldn't ever listen to no sheep like me back then. They'd snap their heads shut tight any time a woman tries to tell them what to do. The only thing on Manny's mind right then is good hard fucking and he just put his soft hands all over me, and I couldn't get out another word.

"You talk too much, girl," he said, rubbing his hand up my thigh and under my pretty pink skirt. "There's other things we're doing now."

The reason why men don't got brains is because they think it's all spread out in front of them like a picture book. Women know different. I know what you're thinking about a loca like me, that I'm just some little dirty-kneed girl who can't get nothing done. But I got a smart head. I look under people, under their skin and eyes and the way that they move to see what they're really trying to say. Men got rocks for brains. They think things are black and white, right and left. They think they got friends and they got enemies, but they don't know a damn thing about it. These fools will trust their homeboys with their sorry lives.

Sometimes we'd all get together and have a barbecue at the park. There's me and the other girlfriends running around making sure the food's good, the tacos and chicken all steamy and spicy just perfect. And then the men standing around swigging beer and talking business, jawboning and backslapping and sometimes taking out their guns and jerking them around to make a point. I didn't always wanna be doing food, though, all that stirring and wrapping and putting out the plates. I wanted to be over on the vatos' side of the line and listen to them talk about clika deals. But any time I tried to cross over, when I walked up to Manny and his homeboys and listened in to what they're saying, Manny would slam me. "Hey, chavala. This is man business now, go on over there." He'd put his hand up and then look at me, giving me his stop sign, and I didn't press it.

They'd all hang around in a bunch getting drunker and drunker, eating our food with their big mouths chewing open and sloppy, and pretty soon they're grinning and hollering and you couldn't make out half the slurry things they'd say. But I got eyes and ears anyways. And Chico is Manny's favorite. After a six-pack Manny would start play-punching Chico on the arm, laughing too loud at his jokes, and pretty soon they're hugging like *maricónes*.

"*Hermano*!" Manny would say, leaning over Chico like a lover, his face all soft, nothing like he ever was even with me. "Hermano *mío*, you and me gonna take this town! We gonna take this stinking place!" He'd wave his beer in the air, sticking at the sky with it while he talked. In those days Chico didn't show his real colors, his C-4 side. He'd just nod his head and smile with his twisty mouth while Manny's voice boomed up big with all his plans. "Yeah, Manny, man. We're gonna jack out," Chico would say. "We're gonna be *firme*."

So when Manny got out of jail, when he's so busy trying to get under my skirt to what he's been missing, it wasn't no surprise that he don't listen to a sheep like me. Too in love with that boy Chico to think on what I said.

Nothing happened after Chico gave Manny up to la chota for a long time except the Lobos was going places, and I was trying hard to get there too. In 1983 we had forty-four vatos in the Lobos, not counting me or any other sheep. All the boys tried to look just like Manny. They buzzed their heads so that the hair stuck up straight and thick like a brush, and they'd get these crazy black and blue taks, tattoo LOBOS on their necks and chests or EP—for Echo Park—on the thin skin on the back of their hands. And after they took those special Lobo names, it got so that I didn't know who was what. Some day one *loco* does something, says something, and he gets his gangbanging nickname. Muerto, Laffey, Popeye, Memo, Bennie. Yah, ése you Bennie now, they said to this vato Alberto, this boy who's short as a grade-school girl so he like to try and prove he's the baddest vato loco around. He got doped on speedy white pills one night so that seven Lobos had to dogpile his ass, and even with them boys holding him down he still bucked out his arms and legs like a rodeo steer.

It was a big crew doing good business dealing out Manny's guns, and there was so much fire in the Park that I saw police driving down the streets looking different, looking almost nervous. The Lobos were getting tough enough to maddog the cops, howling cusses and sticking out their bony boy chests and making macho faces at the big blue suits. "Qué *RIFA*, homes!" they'd be screaming even then, and throw up that Lobos hand sign.

With all those boys came the women. Hustler girls like me with our sprayed-out hair and our faces painted up glamour shiny, dark red and frosty brown on the eyes and cheeks, mouths like stoplights. The deal we made was to sex the boys hard, any time they wanted, and in return they'd take good care of us on the money end. They called us sheep, "good for fucking," was what they said. The more the money came rolling in, the tougher the vatos got, and you had to make like you love begging or else you wouldn't get a dime. "Hey, Manny, buy me a new dress, eh?" I'd say with this doll-baby voice then touch him light on the hand. I knew how to play that sheepy game better than anybody else back then, giving him sugar kisses and back-seat jobs. I tried to tell myself it don't matter, even when he teases me with dollars. "Gonna cost you, girl," he'd say sometimes, then grab at me too hard. Yah, so what, I'd think after. Better than where I came from, right?

He was acting the same as all the men, thinking women are only good for sex and cleaning and squeezing out kiddies. That you can yell and push on them and it don't matter.

"Get your funky brown ass over here," he'd say some-times when he sees me sitting down not doing nothing. "Make me my food, girl." Or "Chingada, I'm only gonna tell you once, hear? Clean up this fuckin floor, I ain't living like a pig just cause you're lazy." Where I come from that's how the men just *talk*, that's what they say to chicas to keep them in line, and it started getting to me. See, cause I already knew how it felt to have a gun in my hand and hear clika secrets, and I didn't wanna forget it. But every time he'd talk nasty to me, them things would start fading like an old ghost, and I'd have to push hard to keep that strong blood in me alive.

Like I wanted to learn how to drive bad. Got that itch. I was dreaming about a candy-apple lowrider just like I'd seen some of the vatos roll around in. Saw myself in it. Play that bass *hard*, girl. Look around tough at the light, stick your elbow out the window. And I wouldn't have to take no RTD every place I go if I got my own ride. So I brought it up to Manny like it's natural even if I knew I was crossing that line again, the same as when I wanted to hear the vatos talking business over barbecue. Sheep don't drive here, it ain't womanish. They walk or bus or wait for their men to get behind the wheel.

"You know, you can teach me," I said to him one night. There'd been candles and red wine, *mariachi* love music on the tape deck. I figured it was the perfect time. I blinked my eyes sexy and tried to smile real wide. But he don't like it when I talk big.

"Girls don't drive, stupid!" He'd been purring and rubbing on me like a tabby cat but now he scooches back and gets all tight-lipped. "Yah, you're stupid. Acting like a chingada." I can smell Sutter Home on his breath but he sounds sober as a stone, and I know I buzzed it.

"I just wanna get around, you know," I say, softer now, but he don't listen.

"God*damn*," he says, and that hand that had just been touching me soft was starting to tight up into a fist. "Why you messing with me? You think you too good, eh? Wanna drive like a big man? Well you can forget it. Why don't you sit your ass down. You don't see no other woman driving round here."

I'm looking at one of the romance candles we've still got burning, and it's orange and gold with blue in the middle. I think that if I keep looking at the blue part I won't lose my nerve. "Manny, hey, now lookit. You don't got to talk to me like that no more cause I'm the woman who told you about Chico, ése. I help you out good, right?"

"You help me out if you learn to shut UP," he says, reaching over and cuffing me on the shoulder, but my eyes stay fixed. "No," I tell him as tough as I could. There's a sick feeling rising up in my throat when I think about what he'd do if I make him too mad. But there's the blue color in the candle, and I figure I'll say it anyways. I turned around to face him before the brave in me backed down.

"I do it," I say. "I help you out good."

But see, that shit cuts you down if you hear it long enough. I was *this close* to being like them sheep. You could of seen me being the same old sprayed-out chavala they got crawling all over the Park, wiggling some screaming kid on my hip, cause pretty soon you start thinking the same as everybody else. That is, unless you've got a hard heart like me. And that's a heart you've got to earn.

Once when I was sixteen, Manny and his homies had some big-head meeting at his house so they could talk about what gun deals they wanna do with Long Beach. I'm in the kitchen, getting them their beer. Manny always tells me to keep his Corona nice and cold and when he wants one, he'll snap his fingers loud in the air like I'm a maid.

"Homes," I hear him tell Chico, "we just ask them for five hundred, and if we don't see it we go POP, right? SLAM them in the head!" They're all laughing at the idea of seeing some cracked-skull gabachos. "Make them bleed a little and we'll be seeing that cash quick."

I can hear them pretty clear from the kitchen and to me they sound like overgrown pickpockets with bad tempers. I can't tell what they want more, to make a man bleed or to get his money. They sure as hell don't know nothing about *business*, though. Cracking gabachos ain't gonna make you rich in the long run. So before I could think twice about what I was doing, I bust in and tell them my mind.

"Manny, you can get more money if you show the gabachos how good the guns are. Give those white boys one gun, they come running for more. Sample." I felt proud like a businessman when I say that last word, roll it around in my mouth before I give him his ice-cold beer.

But he don't smile or say, Hey woman, you've got a good head. You do me proud. Instead Manny just gives me that stop-sign look, and the other boys glare at me wicked too.

"You think you got some brain on you, bitch?"

That stopped me tight for a minute. I open my dumb mouth but don't say nothing. I'm feeling all weird and clumsy cause all these vatos are eyeballing me like I'm some sheep gone off the deep end.

"What's that?" he says, then winks over at his homies. "Lookit. Girl's all fucked up."

When he talks like that in front of his vatos, I forget who I am, Lucía. They're staring at me and I can see how their eyes are laughing, and my cheeks are burning hot red shame color while they squint up and shoot each other funny looks. And all of a sudden I get real scared there. I start wondering if it's true what they say about me, that I'm just some stupid sheep. That

I made up the rest in my head. I stand there weak-gutted in front of Manny and I look down, feeling my lips shaking cause he's the loco big head with all the answers shutting me down ice cold. Even though I told him. I'm the one who told him about Chico, and I'm the one who helped him with the guns. But he forgets all about that, don't he?

"What you doing, girl?" he says to me, this sting coming up in his voice and his mouth a snappy rubber band. "Baby gonna cry? Boo hoo, ésa." My lips are shaking harder but he don't care. "Get on out! Can't have no chavala like you around here."

"I hear that, homes," Chevy chimes in, and he's high-fiving Manny now. "Shoot. Sheep can't be messing with no MEN."

I can't believe it now, but I *was* acting like a sheep there. I scooted away like a beat dog with my tail between my legs. Chicas can't do nothing good, I hear Manny saying, and for a while there I'm believing it.

So you see how it almost was. I was gonna be letting babies suck off me and pretend that having a man's all I want out of life. But I save myself. I just needed to remember something I forgot. All I had to do is go and take a good look at my broken-down mami. That's when I knew I'm not gonna be no dirty sheep my whole life. I couldn't let that happen to me, not ever gonna be like her. Cause that's some bad dead-end road.

I used to tell people lies about her, to help me forget. "She's dead," I'd say, and I wouldn't even blink. "Died when I was a baby." It wasn't true, though. She didn't even used to live that far. Her house was just a mile down from me in Echo Park, but I don't got no shame. I do what I do, it's that simple. I've got my reasons. She's set up in her own place, sits in her chair drunk and dreaming. It ain't my business. She ain't my trouble at all.

When I used to feel bad, there's some times I'd go and visit. Try and say, Hey, Mami, you *pasa* all right there? Usually I'd only get more loca when I see her, but the last time set me straight.

"Eh? Qué? *Quién es?*" I heard her croaking out from her bedroom in that gravel-pit wino voice. I go over to her apartment after Manny slams me down, and it's worse than I remembered. When I open up the door I see this dark hole of a house, a rotten-egg smelling, trash-looking dump. Big Gallo jugs spilled on the floor, Tijuana clothes piling up. Not like me, she ain't nothing like me. I keep all my things clean.

"It's me, Mami. It's your girl," I say to her in Spanish, because that woman don't speak a stitch of English. I walk in to where she is and see her staring out her window at the sky, watching the dark blue night coming.

Some women, they just lay down and die nice and quiet. My mami's taking the hard way out. A red wine *borracha*. She's drunk herself so big she only fits into one chair in the whole damn house, and her hair's everywhere, bushing brown and curly so she looks like a bum. These red wet eyes looking out from milky pale skin, and there's that bad nervous smell she has. I've got to turn my head for a minute, cause it makes my stomach tight up sick when I see what being a sheep can do. She's a damn old whore, my mami. When she was younger, she was the hardest sheep you ever saw.

Not always. Way back when I was a little *niña* and she ran me over the border she held on to me tight, tight so it's hard to breathe but I felt sure with her strong hands around my middle, and when I looked up at her face in that dark night, she looked like the pretty moon, smiling down at me. She's nice then.

Back in Mexico sometimes I'd play *bandido* with her, scooch down in these small places in our house, the closet, under the bed, just so she's got to run around and find me. "*Chula?*" she'd call out. "*Chulita?*" almost laughing and her throat full of music cause we were playing our game. "*Vamos!*" she whispered in that same voice when we was running the border, I could hear how she was full of fire. And she used to sing me songs at night to help me sleep. She'd do them old *Mexicano* lullabies *bien* pretty.

Now her arms are these brown floppy things, fat skin folding over. I see her hands loose hanging down, they can't hold nothing. And her voice rotten from all that drink.

"Mami."

"Qué? *Díme?*" she says.

She don't know who I am yet, so I bend down and pat that weak hand. "It's Lucía, Mami."

"M'hija!" She perks up some, her lips jerking like a smile, but I don't feel good being so close. She wipes her mouth and I see how those lips are dry and bleeding, cracked like a drunk's.

"Mami, I just came by to see how you doing," I say, and it starts slow. I'm getting this good mad feeling burning up low in my chest, a wildfire spreading that makes me wanna hit something, and that makes me strong. She's as good as dead and might as well be. This ain't my mami, I tell myself. This ain't the woman border-running with her fast legs. My face is hot, but I don't feel sick no more. Painless. I see that blue sky getting black through the window, but her face don't look like no moon now, do it? It don't matter none. Bring that black sky on. Look at her, she's trashed out. It makes me wanna break this house up and tear it to pieces. "Wanted to see qué pasa with you," I tell her, standing straight.

I look down and my hands start shaking.

* * *

After that, I don't know. I started moving, racing into the big time. Every dog has its day, right? That was mine. But you've got to do it nice and easy. With a homeboy like Manny, a girl's got to creep up on him like a surprise. I kept my eyes open till I found out how I'm gonna get my say. Then one day it hits him fast but it's too late by then, Mr. Macho.

One morning Manny's in my kitchen working on the business end. He's looking over all these papers, trying to figure out how much is coming in, who owes what. Like a *bodega* woman at the end of the month, figuring out his Echo Park and Long Beach deals, adding up what East L.A. gets. I'm feeding him breakfast but his face is just hanging like a drape. He's drumming his fingers on the table, tapping his pencil. I see there's nothing but scribbles on the page, doodles, cuss words, a couple numbers jumbled together. And I moved like a hungry bird.

"Baby, what you doing?" I said, nice and sweet, putting fat rolls of *pan dulce* on his plate.

"Shut up." He pinches his mouth. "I can't think with all your talk." His head bent down, and I could see how slow he was, his eyes moving lazy over the papers, none of it making any sense.

"Eat your breakfast," I told him like I was his mama, like I didn't hear what he said. I sat down at the table. "Honey, I can do the maths for you. I just do it for a minute, while you eat up."

That was one of my best times, then when I see how his slow eyes can't make sense out of the numbers. But it almost shook me too, cause it showed how he was only good for starters. How he could only get the Lobos off their feet but he couldn't see nothing through.

That didn't stop me, though. "Here," I said. "It won't take but no time, and I got some good foods for you here."

Manny takes his *pan* and chews real quiet while I made my pencil fly. I worked it up real nice. "See?" I said, looking him

straight in the face and showing him what I could do. There's
this mad, proud feeling coming up in me, and I'm remembering
my mami's red-stained eyes. "Long Beach owes us big."

After that Manny started letting me do the books with
no trouble. He just didn't let any of his vatos find out that a
woman's doing Lobos money business. I didn't care, though. Let
him talk big now, I thought. All I knew is that my sheep days
was over after I picked up the numbers, making it all go round
with my little calculator head.

It's strange, almost. When you start looking *hombres* in
the eye, not scraping at the ground and smiling, you feel all different inside. Things don't look the same. You stop moving
around all curled up like you don't want nobody to see you, stop
nodding your head at everything that comes out of a vato's
mouth. After I picked up the business end, I started walking
straight like a man does, taking them long-legged roomy steps
so people start getting out of my way. Watch it, ése, that's the
look I had on my face. And all the time I told myself I was worth
something. You're somebody, chica, I'd think in my head. Don't
listen to nothing else.

I was the first boss woman in this town. After a couple
of months of doing the books, I knew more about the business
than anybody else. I wrote every penny down, kept receipts,
businessman balance sheets. Figured out prices, even, then told
Manny what to charge and how to bargain down suppliers. Told
him nice, of course. Said baby and smiled so my teeth showed.
But I could tell you what we was owed down to the last dime.

Except I didn't just want to be some banker. It's too
clean, too dry. It don't pay good enough, neither. I was still getting my weeklies from Manny and sometimes got to steal a little

skim from off the top, but it wasn't good enough no more. I ain't cut out to be no middleman. So after a while I started looking around to see what there was for me, and what I saw was big-eyed sheep. There was maybe fifteen girls hanging around the Lobos, stuffing their chi-chis into tight dresses and making tamale dinners and keeping their vatos happy in bed, trying to get knocked up. Most of them was worthless lazy-brains. Milkmakers. There's Rafa's girl Monica, who gave him a little Paco, and one of Popeye's sheep gave him another boy. You couldn't walk half a block without seeing some fifteen-year-old *mamacita* dragging a kid by the hand and lugging another one in her belly. That mess ain't for me. I saw them fat baby faces crying and the Lobos all smoking cigars like high-rollers, but it didn't make me feel moony or jealous. When I'm around babies I get cold and skittish like a racehorse who sees a deer mouse. But I guess Manny liked the way it looked. Whenever he'd hear about a new baby, he'd flick me a look like he's getting his own ideas.

"What about you, mama?" he finally says one time in bed, reaching out to squeeze my cheeks and you could see it in his face that he wanted something.

"What about me what?" I said. We was lying down after a good tussle. I'd caught him weak and sleepy but with his dukes up and so I'd got to rough it just the way I like to best, nipping at his soft parts and pinning like a wrestler and talking a blue streak. A round like that'll take all the mean out of you for an hour, but I was bone tired now and rolled over.

"You start making me some babies," he goes on, giving me another goose. The messing around woke him, he's up on his elbow and flapping his jaw over me. "I'm looking bad being the only one with a vieja who can't squeeze out no little doggies."

I didn't say nothing, just smiled a little so he'd shut up, fell back asleep. Manny's so worried about how he's looking to his crew it made him blind. He wanted a happy Lobos family, with him sitting on top of the cake like a bridegroom, getting chicas pregnant so he could show all his gangsters what he could do. I'd looked around at those sheep getting big and fat, crying weird and whiny when the boys went out to do a deal, and I saw their bellies stretch out over their feet and their little brats howling like teeny monsters and making everything all sticky. Me, I like to travel light. The next day I went to Family Planning and got on the pill nice and quick and didn't tell a soul.

So I made sure my girls didn't have no babies, but Star Girl and Chique was just two little snot-nosed cholas when I first laid eyes on them, anyways. Star Girl's real name was María, she was this little illegal just like me.

"Where you from, chica?" I said when I first eyed her, cause she reminds me of somebody. "You Tecate?"

"No way! Puerto Peñasco, ésa. I got some Villarreal blood," she said fast, proud of the Spanish red she's got running through her veins. She was Paco's woman, still fresh like a schoolgirl, with light-colored skin and this linda face that sometimes, when you see her in the right light, looks like the full moon. Wide brown eyes. Star Girl looked sheepy pretty, but she had this tight mouth, hard like a rock. I could see she was mean inside, that she could stick through them bad times. And I knew why too. Girl's people was from the gutter. Maybe she was light-skinned Villarreal but all the same, I'd heard Paco'd picked her up off the street three years ago, that she'd been hungry and had her hands out, and she stuck to him faster than glue. She was still stuck on old Paco, too. Like she owes him something. Spoke only soft words about him, treated him respectful when he's around. Spent her Saturday nights playing them backseat romance games. But all that didn't worry me. That mouth told me that she was too tough to be a sheep, too angry to be a mama. She wasn't no candy-heart princess. Girl was a fighter.

The other one wasn't as tough but she had her own game. Chique's name is Consuelo, and she was fatter then than I am even now. Fat and ugly like a sow, her big nose and teeth sticking out of her head, ass stretching out from those pink jeans. She wasn't anybody's girl exactly, but she wanted in so bad she'd take any homie any time he wanted it. The boys would pass her around when they'd break up with their woman or get bored, and she never would say no. Old Chique was just waiting lonely in the corners before I found her. But I saw that she had these tricky eyes and that she'd hang on boys like she was lonely and empty. I knew she'd do anything I said.

I get them both over to my apartment one afternoon and sat them down in my dumpy kitchenette. White plastic card table to eat on, curls of linoleum kicking up from the floor, no view but my foam-mattress bed and a Goodwill lamp the color of a roach. But you wasn't gonna see me acting shamed. I stalked around them, taking my new long-leg steps. Eyed them up and down like heifers put up for sale, cupped my chin like I'm figuring on a price. They didn't know what was going on, what Manny's old chica could want with them, but Chique was so pumped to just be in the same room with me that she was breathing hard, and her lips jumped up in a fast shit-eater grin so I know she's nervous.

I sat down in my chair and put my big black boots up on the table and slit my eyes down at them nasty so they can see I mean business. "You just wanna be sheep your whole stinking lives?"

Star Girl looks at me all careful, giving me that gutter mouth so I almost smiled. "Hey, I ain't no sheep," she said, curling a rope of hair around her finger.

"You sure are!" I told her. "You're a sheep sure as the sky is blue." And I start laughing so hard at her little *pendejita* head that I can't stop myself, watching her sit there all wound up, getting tight and mad at me and trying to hold her tongue.

Chique wants to laugh too but don't, keeping that hippo face of hers calm. She knows something's up. "Nothing wrong being a sheep but if you got something better I'm listening," she said.

I looked at those little locas on the other side of my kitchen table and told them my piece. "I've been watching you two. Begging and whoring and whatever. But I saw something." I turned to Chique. "You look like a fighter, ésa." "And you," I say, giving Star Girl the up and down. "Honey, you're a bitch on wheels, anybody with two eyes can see that clear enough." I shined up my nails on my shirt for a second and let that sink in. "And I don't think neither of you like grubbing around here for your dinner. Or putting on them cotton-candy dresses. I say you got a little fire in you. You wanna take a hit at something, make your own money. Get yourselves some respect. So you girls are gonna start running with me now. Eh? What you say? But it's got to be our secret."

That's when I knew they'd work out. It took them a minute to figure out what I meant, both of them looking down at their feet so I can tell they never heard a woman talking like that before.

I knew Chique would take it, that it would be the first good thing that girl ever heard, coming from poor nothing and spreading for Lobos just to feel like she had some kind of stinking sheep life. She didn't have no questions, she was ready to jump in right away. "Our own clika? Sounds good to me, Lucía," she said. "I'm anywhere you tell me to be."

I was wondering what Star Girl would do, sitting there all pretty next to ugly Chique and maybe thinking that Manny's girl went off *la* deep end. But the light came up in her face and she just smiled, nothing mad in her anymore. "What about it?" I asked.

"I'm with you, loca," she said, her face like a flashlight.

A gang's got to get the moves down right or else it's not a clika, it'd be nothing but just a bunch of ragtag big mouths making trouble. But I knew how to do it. Kicking with Manny had taught me a thing or two about grouping. Even though he didn't let me listen in on his plans, giving me his stop-sign hand at the park and shoving me out the room if he's gonna have some big secret meeting with his homies, I'd picked up enough about what it takes to get a clika going.

The Lobos were homeboys Manny'd scraped together off the street, the scruffy-headed badasses he'd picked up from liquor stores, from the park, and then jumped in so they could be real loco gangbangers. Getting gangsters to join him was easy as pie cause he'd already made a name for himself by jacking Gato, the specials dude, way back when we was all still babies. By the time Manny was seventeen he'd been moving in on that vato's business for months, getting nickel guns from his suppliers and moving them out on his corners, and when Gato tried to get his action back Manny took his time and showed the neighborhood who was the new jefe.

It was the middle of a Tuesday, the day after a good rain. The street's still slick, storefronts streaked with dirty runoff water. Manny's doing his business out on Alvarado in front of the mamacitas doing their shoppings and the out-of-work local boys kicking it in front of a liquor store. I'd been sitting on the curb for an hour, on my jacket so I don't get wet, and I'm bored stiff cause he don't want me to do nothing but look pretty while he gets to handle all the money and guns. He'd already sold off two of them firecrackers, and when Gato finally came around, he was making a sale to some veterano who was having trouble with his brother.

"Come on," the veterano was saying, all hush-hush cause he's scared a black-and-white's gonna cruise by in the middle of their deal. "I don't got a hundred, man!"

"There ain't no gun if you don't got the cash, homes," Manny says, real loud so everybody can hear. There was these three stringy-headed tagger vatitos down the street throwing their spray-paint sets up on a wall, and when they heard Manny's macho talking they stopped tagging and watched him. "What you looking at, girls?" Manny yells out to them, with this little grin on his face, and then starts wrapping the gun up in his shirt. He shakes his head at the veterano. "I don't got time to do business with no welfare bitch, Juanito, so why don't you get off my street and get your ass shot off by your hermano?"

"Come on, Manny, it ain't like that," the veterano's saying, when Gato shows, trying to take back his corner.

"You steal from me? You try and take from me, ése?" Gato screams at Manny, standing out on the street and waving his arms like a windmill, giving him his perfect shot. Gato was this older dude, a junkie who made his smack money from dealing guns, and he was too weak to put up a good fight but he looked rough enough banging on his chest with his fist then sticking his hand down his shirt like he's gonna pull something out.

"Órale, Gato. You wanna piece?" Manny's saying out this wicked smile, slinking up to Gato smooth and balanced like a tightrope walker, and the veterano scrams on down the street. Not me and the tagger babies, though. None of us was even breathing. They stayed gripping their spray cans. I don't do so much as blink.

When Gato sees Manny moving up strong, he pulls out his switch fast and slices him a little on the face, leaving this thin red rip on his cheek, but Manny's blood is already too hot to feel it. "I've been waiting for this, baby," Manny says, then slams him right there where he stands. Gato was still waving his switch around when Manny starts boxing him under the clear window-pane sky, clipping him on the chin, smashing up his face, till the old cat boy couldn't see out his eyes no more, couldn't do nothing but drop his blade and put his hands up to cover. Didn't stop my old man, though, even when Gato does a two-step on a rain puddle and takes a fall. "Yah!" Manny's yelling every time he throws a punch down to the ground, his lips curling up and the war sounds coming out his mouth, and old Gato got redder and weaker there with every slam, losing in front of me and the taggers and the other Parkers watching from far down the street.

After that Manny was the word. *El Patrón*. The tagger babies told every little fool in town that he'd taken out the biggest pirate in the Park with his bare hands, and everybody wanted to be his gangster then. "Hey, patrón!" the little Parkers would call out to him when he's walking down the street. "How you doing, ése?" They all wanted him to give them a good look. But Manny didn't just take any old boy. He was looking for the mean-faced ones, the homies that knew how to talk bad and steal dirty. The ones who wasn't afraid to fight.

You knew who Manny's gangbangers were when you saw them. In them good old days I'd see the whole street go quiet when they showed, the Parkers giving them careful sideways looks, the mamacitas scooting their babies out of the way. Those vatos was the buffalo-walking motherfuckers that looked like they could stick you without blinking an eye. They wore these red bandannas poking out one pocket and a bump in the other so you knew they was packing, and the best ones had razor-buzzed heads on and slasher taks up their arms. Big or little, though, they all thought they was kings. As soon as a vato got jumped in he started swinging down the road and high-fiving his homies, badassing ladies on the sidewalk. "Hey, make room for this loco, son," I'd hear them saying to some border brother or regular joe who didn't cross the street when they see them coming. Pretty soon, everyone in the neighborhood got out of their way. Nobody wanted to make waves with a Lobo.

But the Lobo boys wasn't so smart, no matter what they thought. If you looked under their hot-shit show-off you'd see that all those vatos had just one job. Right hands, taggers, even the third-raters, all of them was just delivery boys. Manny was the only real king in town and his new house over on Ross Street was the soul, man. The beating heart of the Lobos. That's where the vatos would go for the meetings and to get their jobs, you'd see them running out his door then coming back later with a handful of cash. Later the money would come from coke deals, but back then it was the skim from throw downs, weed, or guns, and guns was the best. Specials, Glocks, Smiths, you name it. Manny always had himself a bag full of fire, and he didn't want for no buyers, neither. He'd get his contacts out in the Park or in El Sereno, Boyle Heights, Long Beach, to give him a score and when I got lucky I'd hear him doing deals over the phone. "Four to a brother out in Boyle?" he'd say, usually to some business vato he'd met on the inside. "That's gonna be a grand and change, ése." He never gave in on no price. Then he'd call up one of his right hands and tell them where to go, and even the hardest Lobo would do his job superquick then hand over the money just like Manny told him to.

Any time Manny wanted to sell a gun or a big load of weed he'd hand the deal over to one of his main boys. Manny called Chico, Beto, and Paco, then Chevy and Rafa, his right hands cause they was ready to slice open an enemy or blood up a buyer that didn't pay up, and so they got the juiciest sheep and the most money. Got the most room on the street. The rest of the Lobos was just taggers or third-raters. Tagger babies are the locos who sprayed our sets all over town so people know we own it. They'd dog around here with their spray paint cans and their fake-tough faces, bragging how they did a job up on the freeway signs or almost got busted by the police for messing up a mural. "Hey, homes!" they'd laugh out to each other. "You see the job I did? Got up twenty feet that time!" Taggers could go either way, be a right hand or a third-rater. Just depended on how they did. We have some taggers around here that made out real good. Dreamer and Tiko got themselves famous from cross-ing out C-4 tags and fighting strong over streets so they're war-riors now, doing big-time jobs and stuffing their mattresses full of money. But if a tag boy don't show his colors hard enough, or if he breaks a rule or don't end up bringing home some cash, he's gonna be looking like a third-rater real soon, selling a couple a reefers on the corner or throwing down viejos for their booze money.

Top of the world, homes. That's where they all wanted to be. Manny, right hands, taggers, third-raters, then sheep on the low bottom. It gave them a fever, trying to scratch their way on up there. It made them blind. Manny was a good jefe in his day but he didn't have his head on tight enough. I was the only one out of all of them who saw clear. You just need two things. Money and a cool head. And I got both now. That's why I'm the one who wound up sitting on top, looking down on all these vatos and sheep who can't see tomorrow till it reaches out and sinks its teeth in like a snake.

After I'd been watching Manny close I grouped my girls like mini-Lobos. All I had was my two right hand cholas, but I treated them right. We had a good old-fashioned jumping in, just like the boys do. A jumping in's where you fight all your homies at once. It gets you into the gang life, official like. We did it in a parking lot. After dark. I got those cholas out on the asphalt, under the bright yellow lamp lights, and stared them down like a charging bull.

"You bitches still not good enough to be in my clika!" I screamed at them, and they started and jerked in surprise, eyes and mouths big circles. But after a beat they settled and snarled back so they could prove that they wasn't really sheep deep down.

"I'll jump you in, baby," Chique said, sticking out her round flat face, twisting up her ham-colored lips, and spitting out nasty talk just like I wanted.

"I'll beat the fuck out of you first," I said. Star Girl and me went after her, our hands reaching out like spiders, gripping her head and her hair and her throat. Chique's fat ass moved up like a pillow and we slammed it down, then chopped and slugged and scratched. I laughed wild and high, all my strong feelings going into her, and Star Girl yelled out too, loud and long like she was singing some old war song.

We took our turns. Next was Star Girl, and her jumping in was a little harder since she'd showed me that garbage-pail mouth of hers that tugged on me somehow. Even though she had that pretty little moon face, I was gonna take that girl on wicked to make sure I had her number right. Me and Chique slapped her around the face, and pulled on her hair, sliced into her with our rings, our nails, ripping her dress, shredding at what was under there, not so much that she needs the doctor, but hard so some blood's spilling on the ground. "Take it TAKE IT!" I'm screaming while I'm rabbit-punching her in the side and rolling her down and she's trying not to cry, getting all bruised and red looking, her skirt flipping up and her mouth tight the whole time while we shoved her back, and her face curved and twisted into a knot.

They did me last, and like good locas didn't hold nothing back. I didn't think those weaklings could do much, that I'd have to teach them everything, but they slammed on my head like it was a rock. I knew that cause I'm *la chola primera* I was gonna have to be stronger than any old girl, but I've had enough practice in this life, I wasn't Manny's woman for nothing. I stood there like a mountain even when they tried to break me down into dust, a fist hooking the side of my head, elbows in my cheek, uppercuts in my gut, whipsaws in my legs, I see Girl's rust mouth and a flash of white eyeball and the pain stitches up all through my chest, up into my head. They gave it to me nice and traditional.

That night was my favorite. I felt slamming. After we did the jumping in we went over to the park and sat on the cold, wet grass, letting the cool air smooth us out, holding on to each other soft as kittens. You couldn't hear nothing but how we breathed hard and fast, like racers, and our breath making soft clouds. I brought out my knife and flicked it open, and they didn't look weak at the switchblade, just to show me how they would be worth it. We took that knife and split the thick part of our hands so that the blood ran down our arms in a long line. Pressed our hands together so the skin's close and hot and tight, and I felt it all mix in like we was sisters. It's a kid trick but I learned it from the locos, and sharing blood's saying you're family.

"There, you mine now," I told them, and smiled wide.

They got their new names that night too. We sat there on that grass, all bloody and bruised and loving each other, my chest sore with that feeling. The sky was black and big above our heads, little pin-point stars thrown up there, and there was no sound in the park, it was just us three feeling brand new.

"OK, homiegirls," I told them. "We've gotta come up with your clika names because we're a new family now."

They thought there for a while, quiet like in church.

"When I was little I used to love looking at a sky like this," Star Girl said after a spell. She was bending her head up and I could see how her eyes was big and round, how her moon-shaped face was dreaming up at them silver lights in the sky. "Now I feel like it's *mine*, know what I'm saying? Like that whole big sky is mine. I own them stars."

"Well, you get to be my Star Girl then, ésa," I told her, and my mouth hurt cause I felt like crying but I wouldn't show it.

"All right. I'm gonna be Chique," Chique piped, all of a sudden. "Ain't gonna go by Consuelo no more."

"How come Chique?" I ask her.

"Cause I'm a tough little chola like you, right? A hard little chica, nothing soft about that name."

"That's right. There ain't nothing soft about it."

"What about you?" Girl asked me. "What you gonna be?"

I sat there thinking for a long time, while they're rolling on their backs and trying things on for size. But they all sounded stupid. Nothing fit. We couldn't stick a nickname on me cause I was always gonna be the same as the day I was born. I was too much Lucía to be anybody else.

We started out with these little hits, just like Manny's boys did. Got to walk before you can run, right? I made my girls practice before we tried out any big time. At first we was doing mamas, them poor-ass Salvadoran and Oaxaca mamas who dig around here, doing their little shopping and carrying all them babies on the hips. Them women are as weak as lambs but they always got a couple dollars on them. They save up their pennies like squirrels. We'd run up to a lady, circle her like Indian fighters, and I'd poke at her some and laugh. What you say, girlfriend? You gotta dime? I'd say, making my face big and smiley mean. Poke her again. They was caught fish squiggling around shiny on hooks and they had these flat open eyes. We'd push down and get us the bitty cash they had, sweep it up and run down the street smoking like a train.

I loved seeing them mamas squirm and watching their faces getting wrinkled and red, but that's just a little *peso* action. You've got to go to the whitefolks for the real money. Before I got my hands on drug deals, the best jobs was stealing them sweet credit cards. Pickpocket baby, that's the easy cash. Órale, all them richie folks, you can spot them from a mile away. They wear clean-pressed suits and fancy shoes, silk ties, and you know they've got a square of pretty VISA plastic in their wallets. For a while there, me and my girls was riding the RTD to downtown. Chique was good, but Star, she knew how to smooth cash out of any businessman's pockets with her quick fingers. We'd sneak up catburglar quiet behind them, then BOOM! "Hey, watch it, motherfucker!" Me and Chique'd be bumping into some gabacho banker and Star would slip her silky hand into his pocket nice and soft. Gabachos don't ever do nothing, cause they can't trust their own selves. They're too polite and not sure and get too freezed up with their fine manners to act fast enough, and we'd just run faster, heart jumping up like it's gonna come breaking out of my chest.

After is the best. My locas would be breathing hard with a red flame in their cheeks, I wanna hug them. It knocked me back, eh? Girl looking over at me with her star-bright smile and I never felt better. You *mine*, I told them. Gonna take care of you because you done good for me. We familia. And I meant that solid, there wasn't nothing that could break us up. I chose them cholas.

So we was secret little girl gangbangers, but it didn't matter to the boys none. I didn't tell Manny nothing. I didn't have to. Knowing I had my very own chicas was enough for right then.

Manny was getting big and strong in the Lobos, leading all those boys around like puppydogs so that you couldn't see nothing bringing him down. Looked like he'd always be on top.

But I kept saving up for winter, putting the pickpocket money in jelly jars, getting my girls together, making my little plans. Doing those books and learning how to be a businessman. Because I know there ain't no forever.

Cecilia

It's not like I don't remember the good times. But now I know that the things my brother was doing were bad and that I was bad too because I loved him for it, because I was proud of him, my heart so full and big every time I looked over his way. The church taught me that was wrong. It showed me how gang-banging ain't nothing but the devil's mess.

But in the 1980s the Lobos just took off like a bird. That white powder brings in so much, you feel like you could buy and sell any man you see walking down the street. Like you *own* the street and everybody on it. And no one you ever knew had ever felt like that before. We were drunk with money. We loved the way it looked, the thick green piles of twenties and fifties stacking up. Even the way it smelled, dusty and plain. How it felt in your hand. I knew things were different in the Park after

Manny got a handle on cocaine dealing. There was an excitement, electricity, it was like sex, this wild roller-coaster ride. The boys talked faster, smiled more, they laughed louder. That is, except when Manny came in to the room, when they'd hush down and wait on his every word. And since I'm his sister I was like the princess of this town. I was the fanciest girl on this side of the freeway.

I know I'm no beauty. They call me Muñeca because I'm short but that doesn't make me dainty. I got these square hips and shoulders, like a little fat box, and I'm Aztec looking with a flat brown face, too dark to be any real good. Thick hands. You can be that way if you're a man, but a girl has to be light and thin and small all over. She has to make men wonder. But me, I show myself too much. My thoughts flare out of my eyes, there's a hard smile on my mouth. And my body moves so hard and clunky, bobbing from side to side. My feet land heavy on the floor. Nothing's a secret. I don't got special things to say, no sweet whispers. I'm not the chica making my eyes look down with that flirting, squeezing out those dimples like the sheep do. I don't move my hand toward a boy's shirt when he says something. I never met a man smarter than me, and even if I don't say nothing it still shows up on my face. I look all the Lobos straight in the eyes. Not like a woman *should*.

But the bigger Manny got, the more Lobos he brought in and the richer he made them, the prettier I looked.

Manny got a dealer out in downtown, a fancy superdude he met in jail who'd done business with the 4th Streeters. A Colombian, and Colombians know they're better than us. This one was smooth and slick with his fine-boned face and his suitcase full of money. I saw him a few times, in his shiny red car, his copperpot skin and silk shirts, the thin gold chains he wore around his neck, a small black plastic beeper on his belt, like a doctor. Mario.

I was over at Manny's new place after school one day, sitting in a corner watching his new color TV. He'd got so tired of me and Mama that he moved out and into a house a few miles away, but he couldn't get too far since Echo Park's no big city. The guns had brought in good money, and it showed. He had fancy striped wallpaper up and this black leather couch, a new beige plushy carpet, piles of take-out enchiladas and stacks of beer in the refrigerator. Just being there made me feel rich.

I'd overheard some gossip about the big changes that were coming in the Lobos. These men have big mouths on them. They stand around planning in their loud voices on the street corners at night while they flick their bright red cigarette ends, and so nothing much is a secret around here. But Manny doesn't talk business much to me, and it's no place for a woman to do any asking unless you're like Lucía, so I just waited to see. That afternoon Mario came gliding in, graceful like an ice-skater, the silk of his clothes making brushing sounds, the smell of his musky cologne mixing in with his sun-colored skin. All the church in the world ain't going to make you blind to that. I could sit with my eyes shut and my legs crossed up tight, but I was still going to see how that boy had his glamour.

He didn't see me though, did he? Didn't look my way even once and I tried to shrink up there in the corner, tried to hide my ugly self. Manny walked out to see him in the living room and they shook hands in a strong, macho sweep, I could hear the clap of their palms, like two little *toros* doing business. In his other hand Mario carried a metal case, the shiny, silver kind that keeps things nice and safe. My brother was dressed up so he doesn't look so much like a gangbanger. Usually he wears his bandannas and his t-shirts rolled up so that people can see his Echo Park taks, the blue color running up and down his arms, skinny letters spelling out LOBOS on his left arm and a tough-looking switchblade on the other. That day he was in fancier clothes, dressing more like Mario in soft slacks and a button-down shirt, open so that his smooth chest showed.

"I got what you want here," Mario told my brother, and I just sat there quiet like a rock, not looking up from the television, like I don't hear nothing. Sometimes the men will just forget about us and if we act right, quiet and blending in, they'll let us stay in the same room when they're doing the important things. I'm drinking up every word.

"Let's see it then, *'chuco*," Manny answered, sounding like his old self even when he's dandied out.

Mario placed his pretty case on the living-room table and popped it open. I was so wound up and waiting in my chair that I almost jumped when I heard that loud snapping sound, but I stayed real still while I rolled my eyes hard over to Manny, so that I could see what that boy was up to.

Mario looked down proud at what he brought us, like he brought some present special for a *cumpleaños*. "My boys say this is the finest Colombian," he said, his accent coming out like soft music, not like us with our chopping talk. "A little talcum in the cut, maybe too good for you people."

Here they were, bags of the Big Time for Manny. Fancy Mario had plastic bags of white powder in his suitcase, all lined up like bags of sugar in a store.

"I got the money to show you how good," Manny told him, but he was too happy to get too much macho in his voice, and a smile came over his face, toothy and wide. "Hermano," he said, slapping Mario light on the shoulder like he was any other homeboy, "you gonna help me make this town into *something*."

After that we knew, guns are something you *use*, not something you sell. The money's all in the high. And for the

Mexican people, the best high is cocaine. Not no nasty little rock like you're seeing today. Coke makes you feel rich, that shiny powder, cutting lines on mirrors, rubbing your lips numb with it, sniffing it in rolled-up money. Manny brought the Lobos up the ladder with that cocaine cash. The vatos sold it on the corner to Echo Parkers, out in the open, from the back seats of their *ranflas*—those cherry lowrider pickups—that they parked by the curb. There'd be the radio playing out the window and onto the street, and they circled the stash and the buyers like it was a party. All the homies from down the street would come down to see. The *barrio* people don't got much money, but they would pull out their crumpled-up bills from their pockets, shy looking, and buy as much as they could. Maybe the better customers were the students. USC, UCLA boys in their letter jackets and blue jeans, their clean snipped hair and clear eyes, driving down to us in their Jeeps, their Celicas, looking nervous and excited. We gave out a couple of addresses and phone numbers and they'd call and come by, giving us their new dollars, ATM money, stacks of crisp bills for those little powdery bags. It went right into Manny's pockets, into Lucía's little calculator, and the Lobos got more cash than they ever saw before in their lives.

I have more experience now. I see the world as a bigger place, I read magazines and books that tell me about all the different kinds of people there are. So I know that money we had's not so big to some Rockefeller, we weren't turning into any real mafia, with jets and vacation houses. We just had enough to spend, enough to buy the things that we saw and liked. Fancy clothes, hopped-up ranflas, speaker systems that'll blow your mind, gold necklaces and watches and earrings. Maybe Lucía there was real smart and secret about some of it, hiding skim in her mattress, but me and Manny weren't going to worry about nothing. There was no trouble yet, the locos and the women were getting along, and all those big bills just tumbled down into the stores, through our fingers and onto our bodies and up our noses.

Yah, you won't believe it but I got real pretty then. No one was going to turn me down. Fifteen years old and I wasn't my mama's anymore. I belonged to my brother. Hanging out at his place, forgetting about school, turning my back on Mama, who got smaller and sadder in our apartment, not talking to me, hating Manny a little, knowing she'd lost out on ever having a good family. "I used to have a son," she'd say, the lines dragging down in her vieja face, but she'd look over at me, wondering if there was still some hija left over. I didn't care. I'd do anything to be a part of my brother, a part of all his fast action.

Even though I wasn't ever going to be the main chola. I was second, always. Lucía was still his favorite. I knew she was doing the books for the Lobos even though none of the boys were supposed to find out. They were too stupid to figure it anyway, that Lucía's got her little girl locas and was holding on to the money, counting out all their dollars. I knew that it wouldn't even dawn on their dumb heads that a woman can do some thinking for herself, that she could know some things they don't, but I didn't say nothing. I knew it was their little secret, Lucía's and Manny's.

I got my piece of the Lobos in other ways. The vatos needed girls as lookouts, as decoys, so they left me out in the street to watch out for police and East L.A. gangsters. The Lobos would do their deals on the corners with the Echo Parkers or in the houses with the college people and I was all eyes for them, making sure everything stayed safe. I spent whole nights sitting quiet in the dark, my eyes glued fast to the road, to the houses all around, listening to the evening barrio sounds and seeing the street lamp wash the neighborhood in yellow light. I could hear people talking or fighting, their voices stretching out of their windows into the street, the sounds of babies crying and of crickets, and I kept my eyes wide open and sharp as a hawk's, watching and waiting for any sign of trouble.

So I had my use, but the best part was still getting all that attention from Manny's boys even though I never had the feel for sex much. When I look over at the men nothing comes over me, I don't feel that hot covering my skin like I do other times. Down there, in my stomach, in my secret parts their sweet words and Mr. Latin Lover touches didn't do it for me, but my head wanted it bad. I loved being Manny's princess. All those gangsters came calling on me even though I look like a ditch-digging *bracero*. But that's the kind of power a woman has. Not like Lucía thinks, her head ticking with all her money thoughts, thinking she's the real driver. No, a woman can only make men do what she wants with the sex. Even if she doesn't like that little price so much. Even if, like me, she might like some of the other things instead.

Beto used to tell me, "Girl, you got skin like velvet." He was the vato I chose, out of all the others. He's a small dark square like me, blocky. Tough scarred mouth. But watch out for those fists of his. He's even meaner than he looks.

His words fell flat on my ears. I couldn't feel sweet and juicy when he told me how hot I was, when he put his hands on my face or curled them around my waist. I was just giving him a blank smile, like I love it. But I was so strong with the idea that a boy almost as good as Manny would want me, that someone would be looking at me that way, after all that time thinking I was dog food, that I was ugly and trash, that I never even stopped to think about who this girl could really love. Now that Manny was making them all rich, the locos circled around me, giving me my choice.

I picked Beto because he looked like he would be going somewhere. He had that fast hard way about him, reminded me of my brother, and he made a lot of deals go down for the Lobos. Manny loved Chico more but he'd call Beto his right hand man and treat him special, patting him on the shoulder like they were *compañeros*.

What I wanted the whole time was to be looked at that way, to have someone get real still and quiet when they saw me, like I was the most beautiful thing. And Beto would do that, he would see in me what he wanted, a girl wearing a skirt with her hair down, hands folded and modest, patient and willing just like any other girl, and he'd reach over to me soft and serious.

I wanted that and to have myself a baby. A woman's got to have a baby. "I'll juice you up real good, Muñeca," Beto said in his thick voice, and he had that macho thing about him, cool and hot at the same time like my brother, that I didn't mind it so much.

Girls in the clika had babies like they were buying dollies. Most sheep don't know the difference until the kids pop out of their bodies with all of that blood and the tearing, the crying and drooling and feeding and nights and nights of no sleep, and their man out playing with some other girl who's not spread out in the hips and tired all the time. It's nothing like what you see in the movies, but I knew that even before Beto got me knocked up. Didn't matter to me. Having a baby's the only thing that would get me a better life.

In this town a woman doesn't have a hundred choices. Can't make yourself into a man, right? Can't even pick up and cruise on out of here just because you get some itch. And even though people talk all about doing college, that's just some dream they got from watching too much afternoon TV. No. A woman's got her place if she's a mama. That makes her a real person, where before she was just some skinny or fat little girl with skin like brown dirt, not worth a dime, not anybody to tip your hat to. But even if the government checks start coming in because you had little José or little Blanca, having a baby's no free ride.

One right hand named Ernesto, everyone called him Chevy because he loved his cars, he had this girlfriend named Laurita. She must have been eighteen, and was trying hard to make him a kid by giving him crazy sex any which way so that she could get a belly full, and she was getting scared because in Echo Park eighteen's old to just start making hijos. She was nothing special to look at, not as bad as me but nothing like skinny Lucía (back then), and that Laurita would do anything just to have herself a son.

There was this one time at Manny's, the Lobos were having some meeting and us girls were in the kitchen, standing around and talking. I was with Beto then so I could be there with them. I fit in, just another lady in the kitchen making gossip with all the chicas. Us doing our business while they did theirs.

Laurita nudged up to me, edging past the other girls so that we stood there shoulder to shoulder in that hot little room full of chattering women.

"I finally caught!" she said, her face red rosy, the kitchen light around her like a halo, she was hugging herself with her own arms, proud with what she could do.

"Congratulations, chica!" I said. "You been trying, how long?"

"I've been jumping Chevy like a wild woman for a year. I started to think I was dry!" she answered, laughing at herself, and I imagined her and Chevy having sex in their little bed, Laurita doing things with him that would make her own mother loca. She patted her stomach, it was still flat against her dress. "But it's been worth it." She looked down at herself. "Hasn't it, chico?" she asked the little ball inside of her.

Some people think they can be a mama when they really can't cut it. The next nine months I watched Laurita get bigger, her belly stretching out over her feet, her face getting all pale and green, she had to throw up half the things that she ate, and she didn't know about the health things, what you can eat and drink and how you can't smoke, those rules they even show you on the TV, in stupid commercials between shows.

Laurita started to get old-lady wrinkles by her mouth that she didn't have before and her eyes were dimming down from bright stars. You could see clear as day that she wasn't feeling right and was starting to change her mind. After three months her body bloated up hard and sore and her feelings roared out in big crying spells where she'd scream at Chevy so loud you could hear her clear down the block. He'd brush her off with cusses, maybe even give her a clip on her head or shoulder, like it'll cool her down. But it didn't.

Right before she had her baby I went out to the park for a walk, anything to get away from my praying-mantis mama, and I saw Laurita there in the middle of the grass and the benches, rolled up under a tree like a ball, like the baby inside her. Alone. She's huddled up and shaking, and I could hear how she was crying hard and jagged like a little girl.

"Chale, *Dios*, I don't want this no more," I heard her say to herself, and her voice sounded like it was coming from the bottom of a well.

The baby came out nice and fat anyway, even though Laurita had been smoking Camel Lights and drinking beer with dinner, and drinking wine and whiskey any time she got any excuse. A boy, just like what everyone would want. Chevy was so proud of himself and his new little Cisco, who had a nice set of lungs on him. That baby would cry every minute of the day.

After the labor Chevy came to Manny's to tell him his good news. "I got me a *son*, man," he told my brother, tears in his eyes, and I saw more soft feeling in him then than he ever showed to Laurita.

I heard that when Laurita went into labor she was so sad that she didn't move a muscle, just stayed there and rocked her head back and forth like she was saying no, tears coming out of her eyes too. People say she didn't say a word the whole time, and when they pulled the baby out of her, red and pinched look-ing and already filling up the air with his *gritos*, the nurse put him on Laurita's chest, so that they could look at each other eye to eye for the first time. Maybe she gave him a little smile, but nothing else, you could tell that girl was going wrong in the head. After a few days we saw that she wasn't holding him close, and she didn't care about looking into his face and counting his teeny baby toes. We gossiped like old chicken hens about old Laurita around our kitchen tables. And after a month, the poor thing didn't have even a name yet.

It turns out Laurita didn't care about all that. She told us she was just going to call him Baby, like he was a cat or a doll and not her own blood son. That is, he was Baby until Chevy took over. Vato put her in line, maybe slapping her around a little and giving her a piece of his mind. About how this was his *niño*, his little *man*, and she damn well better get her act together and take care of him like a real woman would. Chevy was the one who decided to call the baby Cisco, because that's what his brother's called. But to Laurita it didn't matter. She looked at Cisco and just saw a screaming pink thing, a howling red mouth wanting to take her milk from her sore, broken breasts, a ten-pound demon demanding her love and all her thoughts every minute of the day.

Poor old girl. Got to pay that piper, doesn't she? Yah, you got to pay up and big if you want to be a woman around here. Laurita saw her pudgy baby with the red spots on his face and thought, This ain't it. Chevy playing around with skinny cholas in the night time. Doesn't that hurt some. She's sitting there all fat and rocking her son so that Chevy doesn't get mad again, wondering if there was something else she could've done, some other way that she could have gotten out of being nothing but a poor nothing brown girl.

Well that's her and not me. I love babies, love them because they'll give you a real good life even with all that mess. My body's all wide, my hips stretch out like a doorway so that I can have the little niños easy, I know they'd just slip out and say hello. And I can be nice and patient. Soft-hearted.

I didn't have those cozy feelings for Beto. He was just a way to get where I was going. But I threw my body over his like I loved him anyway, like I thought he was the smartest, most beautiful thing I'd ever seen.

"Betito, can I get you some lemonade?" I'd ask him while he watched his cop shows on TV. I'd run my hands through his hair like it was silk even though he kept his eyes stuck fast to the screen. Always making sure he felt good. "Betito *mi cariño*, you hungry?" And I'd fix him his food, enchiladas and tacos and hamburgers, I'd light his cigarettes and massage his small, tough back if he felt tired, jump up to get his beer.

"There," he'd tell me, when I rubbed his shoulders at night. "Lower," he'd say, and smile.

You know the first time with Beto it felt like a knife was ripping me up in my stomach. It wasn't nothing like how the telenovelas show it, with everybody having great sexy times.

I just folded up for him, nice and quiet, bent up my arms and legs and turned my hips this way and that so that he could get what he wanted and so could I. I didn't have the Catholic in me strong enough then, but even now, I'd still want to be a mama. I never said no to that boy, just opened up hollow and friendly, kept my eyes closed and felt him move me up and down, and all that tender feeling down there making me crazy, like I could be doing it better myself.

Beto would roll over afterwards. "Chica linda," he'd say, and pat me on my head before his eyes closed and he fell asleep, his mouth opening up wide like a tunnel, and I'd lay there stiff and still, listening to him snore.

Since I don't like men for sex that much my face didn't glow out shiny like the way I see some chicas get when they catch their first man. I didn't get moony-eyed and giggly, and I didn't stare out the window while people talked to me. I kept my head hard on my shoulders, waiting for my good thing to happen.

But Mama caught on to me anyway, figuring me out because I was always out of the house, and she heard me crawling like a dog into my room late at night, trying to be quiet, but my sheets sounded like cherry bombs going off when I folded them open to get in my small bed. And all those Virgins and pictures of Jesus that she put on my wall, they were watching me and keeping tabs on how bad I was.

She catches me one morning in the kitchen when I was trying to fix my breakfast, *tortillas* and eggs and lots of hot green *chiles*, something to make me stronger, I was so tired from rolling around with Beto all night, from all the work it takes to become a woman.

"I know you been a whore with that boy," she said to me in that voice like a jab of metal and I saw how her hair was pulled back tight and smooth for work, her face ragged and angry and ready to fight. "Having sex with him like some puta. Acting like dirt."

I ain't strong enough then to lie to her. All my nights of not sleeping, of trying to fool her into thinking I was still her m'hija, the same good girl, and trying to trick Beto and Manny into thinking I belonged in the clika, that I fit right in with the rest of them, had made me as weak as thin ice.

I know now that I was nothing but a sinner then. I read the Bible, I memorized all the Commandments, I can quote scripture and the rosary, I know *la Virgen*'s face like it was my own. But that morning I looked over the kitchen table at my mama and saw nothing but a black widow, a dark crawling thing that was trying to eat me up, to kill all my happiness.

My eyes raised up from my food at her while the sun glared through the window into my eyes, hurting my head, and my mama looked like a sharp-toothed monster to me then. I thought how she had no man, how I had no papa, how she had her sex when she was a girl just like me, and this dark red burning flashed all over my skin.

"I'm a whore same as you were, Mama," I said, making my voice as calm as water, making her still like a stone.

People say that it can't happen but I knew when I got pregnant. I sexed Beto one night, in his bedroom all decorated with silky wallpaper and velvet couches and brown crispy plants. I moved on top of him for luck, I'd heard that it's easier to catch a baby that way, and I was trying to think up something fresh so that I could feel sexy. So it could be more than me hoping for a baby and him with that smile on his face afterwards, like he knows some secret that I don't. He's the one who gets the pleasure. Some warm will come up in him and rush out slick and hot. First he looks serious and quiet, but when it's time he'll yelp like a child, so free and loose like I never could be.

In my head I pretended I was a real *princesa*, long and tall, with silver-blond hair and blue eyes, a pink mouth like a tiny rose, dressed up in white silk like I'm at my *quinceañera*. Nothing like my own dark chunk of a body, rocking over another body that I didn't care about much, sexing a vato I didn't really want, all for something else, just like any other job.

It was sex the usual way, with his face twisting up and then his cheeks getting all loose and slack while I'm just staying hushed, feeling let down. Maybe a little sick too, since no matter how hard I was trying to be a princess, I knew I was just the same, same person, chola number two.

But after I left him, after I gave him my kisses and loving eyes, making sure he had food or beer or whatever he wanted and then letting him drive me home, I crawled back into my own clean, empty bed and laid there, silent and still and calming myself down.

I felt her then, that little baby. A hard pinch in my side, a small slingshot pain shooting up in my stomach, moving fast and planting herself in me, and I smiled there in the dark, knowing, and that knowing spread over me like soft fire. My body was telling me my secret. That I was a real woman. Soon I'd be rocking an *hijita* with her sweet-smelling head in my arms. I rubbed myself then. I felt myself all over with my hands, my stomach and breasts and legs, so happy that they could finally do something for me, something for my own self, and I laughed quiet in the dark like a little animal. I brought those hands of mine up to my face and kissed them, kissing myself in congratulations, my palms feeling the shape of my smile.

This is what I thought: Babies are what make you a woman. Better than being a Princess, better than being Manny's. A baby makes you Somebody. And now that's what I was going to be, a mamacita. In Echo Park I see them, all the ladies with their niños, talking to them in those low, happy voices, spending their days feeding, laughing, singing to them, and the men, I thought, would look at them and think: There, I've made it. Brand new daddies' hearts well up like water in the tide. They stick out their chins, their chests, and start looking at their women with new love and new respect. Sure, I saw the ladies raise their low voices sometimes, sitting there on park benches, their eyes growing wider and the veins bulging out in their necks when the babies won't never stop crying, the mamas' tempers welling too like water in the tide, but faster, and more dangerous than any man. Sometimes those mamas would scream at their hijos so hard I never thought they'd stop.

Like I said before, even then I knew that there's a price to a woman having that kind of place here. That being Somebody's going to cost her the hard way. But it all seemed super worth it. Getting a homeboy to make himself soft with you and respectful, and getting the ladies to move over and make room for you on the park benches seemed like it was worth just about anything.

The first few months, they were beautiful. I took to being pregnant the same as a fish loves swimming in the water. I felt her inside me, growing and stretching out like a flower, needing me to keep her safe. I'd sing songs down to her, always kept her covered from the sun with my sweater. That baby girl made me glow all over like a firefly. I was warm on my cheeks, on my skin, on my belly, wide and bright. So I could look at tomorrow then. I could look at *mañana* straight on, knowing I had my prize waiting for me there at the end of my long road.

I'd paid good enough for tomorrow too. I'd got me a man and a baby and that makes you a real fine *señora* here. Once I had them two things I could sit on the park bench and read my magazine or talk about *novelas* with the other ladies, Wanda and Panchita and Frida. They were all Lobo chicas, but they weren't sheep no more. Once a girl has a baby she gets real respectable, even when her man's running all over town she can hold her head up proud and high. Those women had it made. They'd sit all in a row wearing their kick-off shoes, bright red lips and fingernails and big loose clothes if they were still fat, and watch their stroller babies sleep or scream or play out on the grass by the lake. It used to be that I'd pass on by them, before when I was just Manny's number two, and they wouldn't give me one look, wouldn't even flick a lip or eyelid my way. They were a mamacita club, as tight as any clika, and I didn't belong nohow. But that all changed in the months I was pregnant. Once they saw my round belly they made me my room, scooched over and smiled up friendly. "Two months?" Wanda asked, giving me a little pat. "No, she's three," Panchita said, letting me in, and I sat down nice and easy.

That was my best time. I had my place. At night the park belongs to the vatos, they group around in a circle under the dark sky and smoke their red-end *cigarillos*, but during the day it's a different world. It's got this blue-green duck lake in the middle of the trees, and people walk around and feed the snapping birds bread crumbs and then sit down and eat their lunches on the grass. Me and my ladies would kick it there for hours on the brown hard benches, watching the sun shine off the water and hearing the ducks quacking for more bread. I'd gossip with them about who the sheep were hooking and cluck my tongue at their crying hijos. Once in a while I'd rub my poor ankles so that they'd snatch their heads and say, You ain't seen nothing yet, ésa, or I'd say how I was getting so ugly fat so they'd hold their own loose *panzas* and tell me, Just wait, chica, O Girl, it only gets worse. They were like fresh air and springtime to me. Even though the whole time I'd hope Manny would walk on by, so that he'd see me with them ladies and be proud of me, I liked it how we didn't talk about men or clikas or gangbanging out there. We could spend all day only talking about our own selves and our babies.

"You got the morning sick yet?" Panchita would ask me. She looked just like a mama should with her fat face and belly, flip-flops on her chubby feet and her hands too round for rings. Her old man Hoyo was a second-rate Lobo tag boy but from the rough way he acted you'd think he was a right hand. Parties, weed, drunk-driving speedy down the roads late at night. He didn't hit her or nothing, but he didn't keep up his money end regular. She'd have to run on after him at the Lobo meetings sometimes, because that's the only place she'd know he'd be. I'd seen her do it before. "Hoyo? Hoyo? Honey, I need some money for the baby, right?" she'd say, trying not to beg in front of the other vatos while he dug some dollars out of his front pocket. But it's a good thing she got it while she could. That vato wasn't going to last too long with all his bad ways. But like I say, we didn't talk about nothing like that on our benches. Men didn't matter. Not Panchita's low-down Hoyo or Wanda's love-and-leave White Fence East L.A. loco, Lucky, this older dude who ran back to the eastside when he found out she was pregnant and wouldn't give her not even a penny even if she did beg, and not Frida's borracho husband, Popeye, who was only good enough when he wasn't smashed out of his head on malt. And not Beto. They were all background, the same as the lake or the grass or the ducks. We were happy to only sit there and talk about how the babies was doing, and even how we were feeling, which is why Panchita wanted to know how I was, me with my sick greenie face from throwing up my breakfast every morning at ten o'clock sharp.

When I told her how I couldn't hold down nothing, she nodded her head real wise. "*Sal* crackers," she said. "Does the trick supergood."

"No way, ésa," Wanda laughed, low and smoky. She was back skinny already, wearing her sexy tube-top clothes and her touched-up red roots even though her boy wasn't three months old yet. It didn't surprise me how she was dressing up fancy, though. It's cold and lonely to be without a man if you've got a baby, and she was out to catch a fly with a little honey. I'd heard she was giving Chevy some eyes cause he was already sick of his Laurita, who'd got big as a house and was slapping the baby around when it screamed too loud. "Ain't nothing can help that, you gonna puke the same if you eat *carne asada* or bread," she told me.

"Peanut butter," Frida said, leaning back on the bench with her eyes closed and rocking her baby stroller with one foot. "Straight outta the jar." She'd been up all night with her little boy Oscar and had drag-down lines the same as my old mama, and from the dried-out look on her face I could see she knows what she's talking about.

"Oh, Cecilia. Don't you worry none," Panchita said, and touched me light on the shoulder. "You gonna be fine the same as we all was."

They thought I was special just like them. And better than I used to be, when I was that old regular girl kicking it on the street. It was sweet to be so far inside, learning secrets and making gossip on the bench. Nobody looking at me like I'm some freaky chica that doesn't belong no place. I was a Somebody then. Even the other sheep started asking me, How you doing, girl? and giving me their jealous eyes, and the vatos steered clear because for sure now I belonged to a man. And Beto, at first he treated me gentle, smoking his cigar and acting so proud because the other homeboys patted him on the back and told him, Congratulations, man. You gonna have a real fine baby loco.

Everybody was real good to me then. I walked with my head held up and my belly sticking out proud, I wasn't feeling like no number two no more. That is, except with my mama. In Echo Park, it's big happy news when a girl has herself a baby, but my mama, she's Old World style. She went more loca on me than I've ever seen a woman go. She had that Catholic in her good and strong, and seeing me getting round with my baby made her think she was living with the devil himself.

When I started showing I'd wear my big balloon dresses and scoot in and out of the house quiet, thinking that I can hide a whole pregnant belly from her sharp eagle eyes. But my mama, she's got a nose for trouble as sharp as a hungry cat's and she sees sin before it turns around the corner. You can't fool no Catholic woman, they'll bloodhound the bad out of you faster than you can run and hide.

I was four months when she had me figured. I thought I'd been playing my game real good, throwing up quiet in the morning and wearing my fat-lady clothes, but pregnant women, they walk different. High or low, depending on whether you're going to have a boy or girl, and I was stepping girl-low, scraping my heels on the ground, my shoulders and head bent down, my hips already tilting, and Mama could spot that sign the same as a flashing red light.

"O Dios mío," that's what she says one morning when I walk into the kitchen to get some of those sal crackers. I reached up to the cupboard to pull out the box and when I start munching the crisp salty dry things and feeling the sick going down I see her staring at me over her cup. She knew it then for sure, somehow. She sees how I can't stand straight up no more, how I move tender-footed and walk too wide, and I've got these green gills around my eyes. "Dios mío, Dios mío," she starts saying, each time she calls out to God her voice gets bigger but it didn't sound like no church prayer, more like a blackboard scratch. She put her fingers up to her mouth and her own eyes got all pink and wet, little tears squeezing out and down the cheeks. Her coffee cup slammed down on the table with a thunk.

"Mama." I tried to make my face look baby-doll sweet and virgin-stupid, but she'd already sniffed me out.

"*Ay*, help me not kill this girl right here in my own house, right here on the floor, God," she said, loud now so she's almost yelling and I covered up my belly with my hands.

Still, my mama didn't try and kill me. It's the daddies that beat their hijas when they get knocked, sometimes they'll pull pregnant high-schoolers out on the street by the hair or slap them blue across the face, but since I didn't have no papa and Manny didn't care one slice about me being bad, Mama had to try and get me the other way. She started praying over me all the time, getting kitchen sink water blessed on Sundays and buying up more Guadalupe Mary candles and milagros and porcelain Virgins made in Hong Kong from the bodegas over on Alvarado Street, and she stuck them all over the house so it looks like Mass in our living room.

"I can't have no bastard in my house, Cecilia," she'd say when she reminds me how I have to get married speedy quick so my baby doesn't show too bad under my white wedding dress.

"That boy's got to do you right. God sees what you are, hija," she told me, near every day.

I made like it doesn't matter. I wasn't hungry for wedding cake. I was a mamacita on the bench even if I didn't have no ring on my finger. So when she's making the holy water cross and giving my belly her evil eye I'd think about my mamacita club and how Beto liked me good enough. I'd tell myself how I was going to have my baby niña real soon and how she'd love me with all her heart, just me, and it made me feel strong enough so I could shrug tough and walk away when Mama gave me her trouble. But I can't say she didn't scare me none.

The locos here, they act like they don't believe in God. They laugh at the church-going viejas and the *padres* who sometimes try to walk around and make peace. "Stupids. Fools don't got nothing in the head," Manny would say if he saw Parkers walking to the mission on Sunday mornings, and the other vatos would laugh straight out loud if they saw a padre on the street. "Hey preacher ése," they'd sing over. "Hoo hoo!" The thing is, though, that's mostly clika tough talk. If you break open any Mexican, it's red Catholic blood that's going to come spilling out. Even the baddest gangster makes the cross when his homeboy dies and then says his little prayer, and when his lady has his baby he'll be there wearing a collar shirt when it gets baptized. I wasn't any different. All my mama's talk about God and devils and hot hell fire gave me some itchy skin.

Mama, she'd got Jesus strong way back before I was born, back in Oaxaca when my papa left her high and dry. I've never even seen a picture of him, and most days she won't say one word about what he looks like, neither. "That don't make no difference now," she'd tell me, and make this dry-prune face so I can see how she doesn't like remembering. But there used to be times that she'd feel soft and warm and let me tug things out. Once she gave me a gold ring he'd bought her, and there were other days she'd give me other little pieces if I'd beg her hard enough. "He had dark skin, just like you do," she'd say, and I'd stretch out my hand and look at it real close to see what color my papa was, but then she'd shrink up again, crunch her mouth up like she tastes something bitter. "That's all gone," she'd remind me. "He died, hija, got real sick from *bolas*." Other times, when she'd had a bad hard day cleaning too many houses or some rubia she works for treated her nasty, she'd tell me different things. "He was trash," she said once, and her eyes shot out sparks. "I left *him*!" I figured it out soon enough anyways. It doesn't take a genius to see it clear, you've just got to wait around and listen and soon enough you get your story.

Manny was the same as my mama, he didn't like talking about our old days. Even when I was little he didn't have patience for me asking about our papa. "Shut up," he'd tell me, waving me back with his hand. "You worry about them old things enough, you're gonna get like that old lady real fast." There was only this one day he ever showed me something. "You wanna know bad enough, I'll let you see what it was," he told me, when I was only ten and I'd asked him too many times. "Here, you like that?" he'd said, looking at me with them slit eyes he could get and then lifting up his shirt so I could see a dark red strap mark on his pretty brown skin, an old scar he'd got when he was a boy. So I know the story good enough. She was young, just like me, and my papa had that wild horse blood in him the same as Manny but he didn't use it good. Maybe they were married, maybe they weren't. Sometimes I'd wonder if she'd sexed him secret just like I did Beto, crawling into her bed late at night. But it all ends the same. I knew he must have made her hurt hard, beating her or leaving her alone with two babies. Either way, my papa'd made her sad and early-old, and so she prayed rosaries and bought up milagros and talked about Jesus like He was full of sunshine and holy thunder and angry fire. She'd talk about Him day and night like saying His name made her strong enough to save us both.

I wasn't ready for saving right then, though, even when I started getting my own piece of hurt. I stayed as far away from my mama as I could, because all I wanted to do was be with my people. That's what mattered. The Lobos and my niña. By that time Manny'd grouped himself more than a hundred vatos together and they were running a mean stream of cocaine all the way from Echo Park to the far end of Long Beach. We had ourselves some boom times, Manny fixing himself up all handsome with these fedora hats and leather jackets, and he was buying up ranflas for his boys like they were penny candy. Before we started having trouble with the police, he made sure that they were all living like little kings.

Like Beto, he was flying high. He'd drive to downtown or Long Beach with a trunk full of stash and come back with a bag of money. He had his style. Drove a gold-leaf Mercury with suicide doors and had a little beeper in his pocket. Wore a thick gold watch lifted off some gabacho on his wrist. But seemed like he didn't have much time for me no more. He'd been smoking the cigars after I'd caught my niña, acting all proud in front of his homeboys, but those days ended quick enough. Even though I just wanted to kick it on the bench with the mamacitas I still felt bad when he wouldn't answer my phone calls or smile when I came walking up to him on the street, because he was my man and I knew I needed him to keep my place here.

"What's wrong there, baby?" I asked him, trying not to sound scared or sad when he started getting colded up. "You all right?" I rubbed him soft on the shoulder and gave him his little kisses, the same as I always did. But I could see how things were changing, like I'd figured they would. Everybody knows it's hard to hang on to a man around here. When I started spreading out, getting wider in the hips and fatter in the face, I could see him watching the other chicas, them pretty bird-legged things flirting with him in their little skirts. When they'd walk past him, sexy with their hips wiggling and you could see their flat bellies under their skirts, it made him get shiny in the eyes and he'd get this little smile on like he wants to take a bite. "Hey, girl," he'd say, to Norma, Brenda, Monica, whichever one's close by, like I'm not even there. "What you doing?" I'd reach over then, touch him on the hand or the cheek, or whisper something soft about how we got to go so that he'd remember me, and he'd get this sour-lemon face on and I could tell. I knew it, and he didn't even try to hide nothing. He showed me clear as day how he wished so hard he hadn't got stuck with me.

See, men don't like no ugly women. Nobody loves no ugly woman. Fat ladies, ladies with brown blotches on their skin and pouches under their eyes, they're the ones sitting alone at the bus stop. They're the ones that don't have somebody to talk to when they're lonely. I never felt more good *and* bad when I was pregnant with my baby, because I had my love wrapped up tight inside me, just waiting till the day she could pop out and say hi and let me kiss her all over. But I never felt more lonely before either, since things with my man weren't the same no more.

With Beto, it started with these little things. He won't call me for a week or he gets a flash of bad temper and slams a door. Or worse, there were those days when he'd say something hurtful. He could shame me pretty fast with his nasty mouth.

"Lookit you. Ugly. Don't you care? Put a dress on!" he'd say, them bullet words slipping through his lips easy and hitting me straight on, while I smooth down my hair with my hands then run off to change out my stretch pants and t-shirt.

Baby's in a bad mood, I'd tell myself. He'll be sweet in the morning. He'll tell me he's sorry.

But he never said sorry, and I just let it go.

Then he drinks too much beer some night and when I say something, Honey, maybe you slow it down, in my soft voice, he doesn't answer, just grabs me tight by the wrist so that it hurts from twisting the wrong way, and I get all scared there for a second, my throat clenched up so I can't breathe till he lets loose and tells me to Get out. "Go on," he says, thin-wire sounding. "Go on, get out my face, bitch." Or he gets angry for nothing, he doesn't like the way I cook him his eggs, I don't clean the house nice enough, or he thinks I look at him funny, and he pushes me. Light in the beginning, a little pat on the shoulder or the arm, telling me to Shut up, or Do that over, and I've got to take a step so I don't fall. It didn't hurt, only push. Pushed me back with his hand like the boys on the playground, it doesn't give you pain but then you feel hot flash on your skin and your heart speeding up. "There, you hear what I said?"

And it didn't stop at that. Men, they get that taste for beating on their lady. It's like whiskey, worse maybe, they take a drink then they get more thirsty so it doesn't ever stop. It only gets harder, a little bit more each time till finally you feel it, SLAM, there on the shoulder, on the back, and I hear his breath come out and my head snaps over, and there's no hot flash then, all I feel is scared dumb.

Listen. If you've got a baby inside you, you have to keep your hands down low. So if you bump into something, like a chair or a table, or if you take a fall you can reach out and keep her safe. Make sure she doesn't get hurt. If I ever have another baby I'm going to walk more careful, stretch those hands down like a shield, and nobody's going to touch her.

I was four months when I could tell it was going to get bad. At four months you feel your baby night and day, you even feel her in your heart and it makes your ears prick up to danger. It was at his place where I'd always go three, four nights a week to make him dinner, clean his room up, water his dead ferns, then maybe we make some sex although it was getting tougher for me then, I was sore and full and didn't feel good, still sick in the morning and weak-kneed all day long, but I was sharp as a razor and could hear them bad winds blowing before they hit me.

He didn't even want sex that night, after I cooked him his *frijoles* and a little corn tortilla that he eats quiet with his hands and then pulls his beer down too fast. I'm standing there in the kitchen but he doesn't get up to smooth me with his rough hands like usual, he won't come over and tug on my skirt or give me his sexy tiger smile. He only looks up at me with small eyes, and I know he doesn't like what he sees.

"What you looking at?" he says, and that scar was carving up his lip. "Eh? What you want?"

I could hear what he's got under his voice and so I smiled friendly, like a puppy rolling over so the big dog can see her belly. "I don't want nothing, Beto, I don't want nothing but to make you happy, baby."

"Órale. Cause you can't be giving me that face."

"No, honey. Hey. You like your dinner? You want it hotter?" I smiled wider so it hurts my mouth.

"Get over here."

"Baby, I can warm it up real good, I'll put it in the micro and it'll taste better."

"Get over here," he says again. "Now."

But he was the one who came to me.

He walked over in big long steps and all of a sudden he's standing right by me, too close and I'm scared deer dumb. My mouth's open but no sounds come out when he raises his hand and brings it down like a rock. "Yah, I don't want you giving me that face," he said in my ear, but after that all I heard was a thin, fast noise.

It ain't like you can get ready for these things. The first time you get it hard you don't even know what it is. All you think is What? and then the rock-sharp slam and your head jerking, and them breathing noises he makes, like he's running. He didn't beat me till there was blood then, he only gave me some hurt there on my cheek, on my shoulder and arm, on my side, and that time I kept my hands down low because I still had a mind that could think quick. I didn't cover up my face, I didn't try and grab him by the thumb and make him stop. I just kept my hands down low and flat open, so they could catch the floor when it came flying on up to me. So I could keep her good and safe.

You can tell when a woman's carrying a girl baby because she walks low, and you can tell when a woman gets beat by her man because she walks away. Keeps far from her own people. A woman that gets beat doesn't want a soul to find out. She thinks they'll judge her wrong. That they'll say it's her fault. That she doesn't deserve a man and that's why she gets hit.

You couldn't see much of my bruises. They were deep purple and blue. With dark green on the edge. Some were quarter sized and some stripe shaped, down under my shirt, under my arm, over my back. Beto was careful with me and wouldn't let nothing show. He hit me smart so nobody sees. But I started keeping far off from my people anyways. Stopped kicking it with my mamacitas, stopped talking to my mama, didn't even go by Manny's any more even though I missed him so much it made my eyes burn. I thought they'd see my face hanging, or see some pink come up over my collar, and they'd figure it out right away.

You don't deserve no man, that's what they might say. You don't deserve no baby, neither.

And see, I was right. Lucía, she must have smelled the fear on me, the sour coming off my skin or on my breath. And that woman knows just what to do with scared. Twists it around into a hook and then sinks it right in.

"What's doing, Muñeca?" That's what she started asking me, innocent-like at first. But she didn't blink when she looked my way. Those big eyes took it all in, my slumping shoulders, my crunched-up mouth. "Tell me what you up to, girl." Lucía, she was grouping already. Even though my brother treated her so nice she still didn't love him, not like I did. Being his number one wasn't good enough for her, she wanted more. So she'd got those cholas together, the fat one and the skinny one. They were bad seeds, you could tell from the way they hung out staring at people beady-eyed, stealing things pickpocket-style, selling a little coke on the side. I heard the stories. And when she looked at me she saw another gangster. Manny's sister has good blood, she's thinking to herself. Muñeca'll bang if I make her. Lucía would catch me on the sidewalk, on my porch. "Hey, chica!" she'd say, giving me some sunny smile I hadn't seen in years. But I knew what she wanted. And I didn't want nothing to do with that. Me and my hija, we were going to live right. Like the mamacitas on the bench. After Beto slowed down I was going to sit right back down in the park with my stroller baby and gossip like an old hen. I wasn't going to do no more clika banging. I'm not crazy.

I knew when she'd made up her mind about me. That she wants to check me out. I was walking home slow from Beto's on Sunday afternoon after he'd been messing with me some more. Punching me down on the leg and the hip, banging me up on the wall. "I can't have you making that face, Cecilia," he'd said again, and his hands moved *fuerte* fast. I still had my heart clipping and didn't want to look at no one in the eye, but Lucía and her two bad-news cholas come driving right up to me in this junkyard car.

"Hey you, ésa," Lucía says, opening up her door and getting out. She starts staring right into my face so I can't look away, and I know she's sniffing up that fresh scared smell I've got all over. "What you say you take a ride with us, eh?"

"Yah, get in girl!" the fat one called out from the back seat so I turn my head her way. "We're gonna have us some *fun.*" Sounded like she wants to laugh. The skinny one in the front smiled over at me rat nasty.

I looked back at Lucía and took in how she's dressing different. Harder, not like an old timer, but not like a Catholic girl neither. Pants on, the same as a gangster wears. Dark colors. These days you walk in the Park, you see cholas with their baggies and their plaid wool shirts everywhere you look. But in them days, she looked like a witch to me in all them manly-black clothes.

"No, I can't, all right? I got to get back home to my mama."

"Hey now, little chavala chickenshit. Your mama ain't home, she's begging in that church."

"I got to go home."

"Don't, ésa. Cause you don't want me pissed at you," she said, pulling my arm, and I knew I had to do it. Loca sounded just like Beto when he's mad.

In L.A. not all the Mexicans live together like people say. Our little towns are spread out all over the city. There's Silver Lake, Echo Park, Lincoln Heights, Boyle Heights, El Sereno, Cypress Park, East L.A. proper. To the gabachos maybe we look alike. They can't tell the difference between Echo Park and Silver Lake vatos with their taks and baggies or Lincoln and Sereno homegirls with their dyed red hairdos. And then you've got your Cypress mamacitas walking their babies on the sidewalk who look a lot like the Boyle Heights maids coming home on the RTD after their long days. But it ain't all the same. We feel different from each other, especially the rebels. You cross over on some streets and gangsters will kill you in the name of their neighborhoods.

So you've got to learn the rules. The locos have more rules than any whitefolks. Stick to your own. Fight man to man. Don't mess with the babies or the women. Respect your neighborhood. One of the biggest rules is that you do your bad jobs outside. Drug store, car jack, throw down. "Not here, homes," that's what Manny would tell his boys. "Save it for somebody else." That's why when Lucía starts driving over to Lincoln Heights I got that full hot feeling in me worse than before. Being from Echo Park means we wouldn't be caught dead in Lincoln unless we wanted to make some trouble.

"So, how's it being knocked, ésa? How's your little Beto man treating you?" she asks me, in a voice like she thinks it's funny. I'm sitting in the back seat with the fat chola, who's looking out the window. The skinny one's chewing gum like a cow. Making me sick. I won't say a thing.

"Poor little Muñeca," Lucía goes on, and I see how she's driving with one hand on the wheel like Manny does. "I might as well forget about you, sheep. I don't like my chicas with no babies. But I figure I give you a shot, eh? Maybe you got that Silvas in you somewheres."

"I ain't banging no more," I tell her then.

"No. You're the one getting banged, girl," she says, and smiles at me in the rearview. "That's right, Muñeca. We'll see what you do." She sounds real sure of herself.

I shut my mouth again. Lucía's twisting on me because she knows, and I could tell that talking wouldn't do me any good anyways. From the sheetrock face she had on I knew that no matter what I tell her she's still going to try me on.

We get to Lincoln Heights and the fat chola throws her set up when she sees a street she likes. "Here, girl! Come on Lucía, this is *perrrrrfect*."

"I'm gonna check you out," Lucía said to me when we all pile out of the car, me pressing one hand on my side because I still felt sore. We walked a couple blocks to a bodega, but it didn't look like there was anything to steal. There's burglar bars on the windows but when I take a peek inside all I see is beef jerky, plastic-wrap bread, breath mints, Thunderbird, a rack of girlie magazines, and there's some hard-luck viejo watching black-and-white baseball behind the counter. We didn't go in. We were standing in a circle out on the sidewalk by the door and they started looking up and down the street with twitchy eyes.

"All right!" Lucía barks. She's got one hand in her pocket like an easy rider but I could tell she's pumped up. "All right now, you got it?"

She didn't say more but I knew plenty good what was up. We were going to do a throw down. Throwing down, it's like this. If you want to steal something, you don't steal from somebody bigger than you. You pick the weak ones, the short or sick ones, ladies, anything small you can get your hands on. I knew that score. Manny used to do it with Chico when they were just kids. They'd gang up on ladies and boys walking home alone, circle around them and then bang down till they got every penny they could squeeze out. And that's what we were doing there, watching and waiting for some little bird that we could hit.

Them things ain't for me. I didn't want to throw down for nothing. But it ain't like I'm dead. Even though I had a baby in my belly I still had that gangbanging blood running out my heart, somewhere inside I have that old wild horse in me the same as my brother. And I felt my blood quick up like a hot boiling loca's even if I didn't want it to. They were standing around and acting so tough, wearing their man-looking clothes, and I remembered Beto beating on me and my mama yelling and all of a sudden I wanted to break off loose the same as Lucía and her cholas. I wanted to scream and sing and run away and fight dirty, steal money, hit somebody else real hard, even though deep down I knew I had to pack all them wrong thoughts in a box and close the lid up tight.

"Let's do it NOW, woman," the skinny one said, nervous because she knew if any Lincoln gangbangers saw us there'd be some ugly trouble. "Let's rush them inside! We gotta do this fast!"

"No, we gotta take it light for the new pussy," Lucía told her, looking at me cool as water. "You and Chique just kick it. Don't start acting like no chingadas."

Don't got to take it light for me, ésa, I almost said. I'll show you what I can do. But I was trying to fight it. Trying to be good for my baby girl. I kept my mouth shut.

When it finally happened I felt stupid slow from watching them work so mean and fast. We caught a Lincoln mamacita and her little girl when they were walking in the store. The lady, there wasn't nothing special about her. She looked small. Regular. She was as big as me and had this old ninety-nine-cent store purse strapped over her shoulder, these bright red lips and nails, garage-sale sandals. And when I looked down I saw how her daughter was pretty, with big black eyes like a doll's. Lucía grabbed the mama by the waist hard, messing up her clothes and jerking her so she almost falls back, but she wasn't as weak as she looks. That mama fought back, shooting out her fists chola style, trying to scratch out some eyes and yelling cusses at us, and the little girl started screaming sad and wild down the sidewalk. I stood there dizzy for a second, confused.

"Get it, BITCH! GRAB IT!" Lucía yelled at me, her lips a sharp cut across her face. Chique starts laughing behind me.

"Ooooh, yah. This chavala is sorry," I heard her say. "Cherry can't bang worth a damn."

It was hot there on the sidewalk, I remember. Red hot on my cheeks and chest, red hot from my belly, but funny thing, I didn't feel so sick no more. I hear the mama screaming Fuck something and you could see how her eyes were running, but throwing down was better for me than them sal crackers, I felt as sharp as a steel blade. Wanna bang? I'm thinking. Girl, you wanna bang like them bad cholas? I felt those two things, banging and my baby. Clear as air. I watched the mama's one-dollar purse swinging around one of her wavy arms, and she was screaming herself raspy with a wide bright red mouth and her hair flying, but Lucía was holding on tight to her middle and teasing me with her alley-cat face. Wanna bang? Yah, that'll feel good, girl, you snag it home free. But then when I looked again at the niña I see how her face ain't so pretty now, all thick with tears and snot, and it made me flip on over. Made me feel sick of my own self. No, I can't do that, I tell myself then. I already made up my mind I ain't doing none of that.

Maybe I was standing there for three seconds, it felt more like an hour, but Lucía can't wait for nobody. That snake makes up her mind for the whole world if they let her.

"You take it, Muñeca, or I'll split that stupid head of yours in two," she says, and I believe her. Even though I know she's making me eat her trash I don't got to hear it twice.

I ripped the bag hard off of the mama's shoulder while she keeps screaming at me, and it was easy, like flicking on a light. I felt it like a feather in my hands. We all ran blind down the street, rush rush, trying to find that car, breeze on my hot face and my belly bumping funny and I could hear the sounds of our shoes like drums on the sidewalk while we raced on out of there before a hothead local or sharp-eyed cop could catch up to us.

* * *

On the way home I tried to make my mind a clean white blank, to not have even one word in my head, and I closed my eyes and leaned into the back seat, breathing. Lucía's cholas checked out the mama's bag, digging through then dumping things out all over in a poor pile. A fake leather wallet with twelve dollars in it, the daughter's picture, a folded-up list of phone numbers, no plastic. One fancy cherry red lipstick, the kind that costs. Red nail polish, blush, black eyeliner. A hairbrush. Virginia Slims, Doublemint gum.

"Man, I knew that bitch wouldn't have nothing," the fat one said, flicking her hair back. I cracked my eyes back open and saw how she tried the lipstick on without a mirror, painting herself some red messy mouth.

The skinny one chewed a stick of the gum. "Lucía, hey you knew she didn't have no money, eh? Why we come all the way down to the stinking Heights and do nothing but a shit job?"

Lucía didn't say nothing for a minute. You could tell she was getting wicked feeling at me, and I saw in that rearview how her face was folded up into corners.

"I was checking out this sheep," she says. Makes a mouth like she wants to spit. "But I didn't do nothing but waste my time, did I, sheep?" I knew she was talking to me then. "You're some fuckup you know that? Can't you do nothing?"

"Either she can't or she *won't*," the skinny one said.

Lucía let the car roll around a corner and I gripped on tight to my seat. "You gonna be around here you can't just sit on your fat ass," she tells me, her voice steady calm so you know she's ready to slice me up. "Looking at us like we're some dirt you gonna wash off at the end of the day. Well, I'll show you dirt, Mrs. la Princesa bullshit. The next time I say something, sheep, you don't get no second shot. You're gonna *move*."

I looked out the window, at all the houses and people and trees flying by while Lucía's speeding on back home. Out there in front of the bodega I wanted it, wanted to bang bad. Didn't make no sense. But now that we were in the car things were different. Cooled off. I felt that gangster fever turn back on me and the hot rush get cold and clammy, like I'd been washed in dirty water. I'd stole from mamas and babies the same as these no-good putas, just because Lucía says so. It made me throw-up sick again thinking how I took that mama's purse while her niña was crying, and I felt killer mad too because Lucía'd yelled at me like I'm just the same as her two trash cholas. Like I'm not who I am. It made me scared almost. Sick and mad and scared for me and my baby girl. And when I put my hands over my belly, she still didn't feel safe.

"I don't got nothing to do with this," I said to no one, to what was outside of the window. "I got my *baby* now."

Lucía hissed at me through her teeth and so I shut my eyes again and listened to the sounds the tires made over the road, rough and fast. I could see it all even with my eyes locked tight while we drove back to Echo Park. I knew it by heart. There was the wind outside and the black cold street, the autumn trees sleeping and the sky getting darker blue. Even blind I could see how that sky was only waiting to close up over me into the ink-colored night.

Lucía

The Lobos had a few ugly busts in the mid-80s. That's what sent Manny my boy down later on. Cecilia getting beat by Beto and homies getting busted cause cops got wind of our little blow scene made him lose face with the locos. And once you lose respect around here, there ain't no turning back.

At first, though, we didn't have no big problems. Get busted, homes? Manny usually got his boys out on bail in twenty-four. Or else they take a little vacation, right? Mr. Public Defender, no big quantities, nice short stay, boys learning something inside. We wait for them. The Lobos always stayed loyal to their own. When they get out we set them up real nice. But it wasn't like that forever. The chota started getting madder at the Lobos, and we had a war on our hands then. I don't think none of us really saw it coming.

Once we did a deal with an Anglo who says he's Mr.
USC. He had this shiny white Jeep and college clothes, and when
he asked for a deal the money was good, so hey. These cops
getting younger or what? It was Paco that landed. That boy's not
tough enough to pocket money or do nasty deals behind Manny's
back but he's still the one that gets busted. The weak ones get
it, that's how it always is. We'd had cops bad on us before but
this time they worked him over till he was raw. You loving
fucking LAPD or what, man? Because they love fucking Mexicans around and hard.

Manny introduced a white boy to Paco, then said
"*Pachuco*, you get homes nice and set up, hear? Get rich boy on
his nice skis, work up gabacho a snowstorm." So Paco loads up
for the USC cop with this big bag of blow in his pocket and meets
him at his apartment, just like the blondie asked him to. He
stands there for a minute in the middle of the living room with
his stash and a dumb-cow look on his face, not thinking a thing.
USC cop's looking like a virgin deal in his fancy haircut and
letterman's jacket, but he was really ready to come down like
thunder on our boy.

"I got what you want, man," Paco says, but his eyes stay
looking on the ground. He never could make no eye contact with
an Anglo.

"What's that? What's that?" says the cop.

"I got the coke you wanted, you ask Manny for."

To make sure he gets Paco nailed down for sure, blue-
eyed cop says, "How much?"

And because I told Paco how much, because I'd weighed
the little bags out and made up the price with my calculator and
said, You make that gabacho pay two hundred for a little hit bag,
four for a bigger one, Paco says, "Four hundred, homes."

All those chotas come out of the closets like horses at
the devil's racetrack, pointing their pieces at Paco and scream-

ing at him so it seems to the poor little man that the roof's gonna fall down right over his head. "GET THE FUCK DOWN, SPIC! GET YOUR ASS DOWN!" Those cops got some lungs on them, I've heard their gritos loud like banshees, calling us brown beaners, spic shit, wetback motherfuckers, every name in the damn book.

I'm asking you, who's better, them or us? I know all the people, they're down on us rebels. They talk about how we're killing with our business here, feeding it to babies and shit. And OK, you ain't gonna find no angels down here in the Echo Park Lobos. But the truth is, lots of grown-up men with plenty of money were coming to us and getting some goods for a party or to sweet up their ladies, and nobody ever got hurt.

Them or us? The LAPD ripped up little Paco bad. Pushed him down on his stomach with fists hard like stones, twisting those skinny arms across his back, slapping on the shiny sharp cuffs hard, squeezing them tight. No big thing, he thinks. I've been here before.

But then. One meaty cop, a paper-white no-neck with thick beefsteak arms, bends down and looks at him with those blue blue eyes. Our man's keeping his eyes staring at the floor. "How you like this, hey Mexican?" The heavyweight starts kicking Paco there in the side, in the ribs, his big black boot toe swinging up and digging into the bones, hard, so things start cracking. "Fucking wetback." Another cop hits him hard with those black batons, on his shoulders, his arms, his cheeks, making deep black and blue and red marks the same colors as his Echo Park tattoos streaking up his arms, down his face, splitting his lips in half, but the blue suits keep slamming on him like he's a dog, like he ain't nothing but a dog.

And our boy don't think nothing there. Just turns into an animal, a man does when he gets beat like that, down on the floor and cops are kicking and screaming at him Spic motherfucker. Vato's not gonna feel like a man no more, there's only gonna be a little dark place where his brain used to be wondering, Am I going to get out of here? Will they let me out of here?

Thing is, nothing happened about old Paquito. Manny just let him get all broke up, his face never the same, looking like a dead man after that, all pale and ghostly and wandering around looking sad. The patrón there didn't make a move.

Manny's saying to himself, Hey. Nobody's gonna stop a Lobo when things start going his way, and they're going mine, baby. The business is jamming, the money keeps coming in, and a few bad kicks in the ass ain't gonna change that. Manny was all rich by then and he'd already started rotting from the inside. All he wanted to do was sit up on top thinking, Who's gonna pop out my little doggies? You could see how his eyes was getting milky, how he don't have his old razor-sharp walk. He's just a fat-brained old dude now, not taking enough care of his boys when we get into this trouble.

"Paco'll be OK," Manny says to me the next morning in the kitchen, his mouth full of all that good food I'm cooking him. "Just a few days, he'll patch right up."

I went right on serving him like a maid. His breakfast, his coffee. Still playing like a woman. Me never saying too damn much, but ticking in my little head. Gotta make your move. I look over at him with my smart shifty eyes knowing Manny boy's only good for starters, not gonna make it through. All the time I'm getting sharper, he'd got like some lazy sonofabitch. His face thicks up, getting fat and stupid, wearing his clown fedoras and his eyes not so keen no more with all that money he thinks he had. He's not looking out like he should, cause there's always somebody around the corner looking to stick you in the back.

The Lobos started watching Manny hard after our old boy Paco got broken up. They were wondering, What's the jefe gonna do now? Show them cops, bring down the big guns? Manny's sitting on top of the hill all comfortable eating his enchiladas, not gonna do a damn thing. "Paco'll be fine," he keeps saying, hoping the trouble will fade away.

But it wasn't the last time we had bad blood with the police. The LAPD started drawing lines, calling us out. They'd stop brothers on the street for no good reason, patting us down nice and hard, looking into our faces. "You like trouble, beaner? Give me some trouble," they'd say, smacking us around a little. Then other times, they didn't go for no soft stuff. They'd beat on a gangster every once in a while, trying to send us a message. Manny don't listen to that none, though. He only keeps stuffing them dollars I'm making him in his pockets.

Our locos was just waiting for something to happen. Men wanna see some *action*, when they see nothing's coming they smell weakness just like shit stink, and after that it's just a matter of time till the king gets killed. That's when a woman's gotta make her decision. One way or the other.

The first move I make is to look like I want. No more girlie dresses just cause Manny wants a Venus. I wasn't gonna be a whorehouse sheep wearing them spiky heels and sticking my melons out of slut dresses the rest of my life. At first I'd do it when he wasn't around. When Manny wasn't looking I'd dress chola with my girls, button up my Pendleton, wear them black jeans, tough jacket, put on a dark mean mouth. Check it out, my own tattoo even, a straight black "E.P." tak on my shoulder. I had Chique do it to me, poking her pins down into my skin, bleeding me all up, putting in that ink just like the vatos do. "Hurt some?" she asked, little smile on her pork-belly face, and I just laughed. I knew that no sheep could look like I did right then.

I even got myself driving. You can't be a real grouper if you ain't behind your own wheel. I scraped up my dollars and bought a banged-out old Ford Maverick from a border brother working down at a body shop. It was shit-brown scrap metal riding over these squeaky wheels, with ripped-up vinyl seats inside, a busted lock, and the girl would go flat dead on a right-hand turn at the light. But hell, it didn't matter none. I got whatever *bombas* I want now. These days I ride in a candy-flake cherry-gloss Impala with velvet seats, but that first baby was my best. I learned how to drive out in empty parking lots after dark, squealing around and pumping up the gas like some crazy-ass. Park, Neutral, Drive, Reverse. But once I got out on that road, *wacha* out! The wind coming through the rolled-down window playing my hair and the AM radio blasting some good song, my wheels driving me wherever I wanna go. I'd take my cholas out for rides too, just to see them stick their scrubby heads out the window and taste the sweet night air. Star Girl wasn't doing too swift right then cause of Paco's bloody kicked-in face, but when she got in the car she perked right up, closed her eyes and felt the breeze cool on her skin. And Chique, that girl was made for driving. She'd turn up the radio loud and hoot at the locals as we passed by, laugh when they stopped to take a look. I laughed too. It made my heart jump, being in the driver's seat. I never felt so free.

Can't stop me now, that's what I was saying once I made myself my own boss. I had my keys jingling in my pocket and my homiegirls by my side, and nothing was gonna be bringing me down then. We was busy picking them gabacho pockets down the street and throwing down mamacitas. I even tried to group that chump-change Cecilia down in Lincoln Heights, but she couldn't do nothing but stand there with her mouth hanging open. I was gonna bang her myself but she moved for that mama just in time.

Still, I got to give her credit. I was getting ready to make my move on the Lobos, and after Paco got stung by the cops I knew my day was coming. But it was Cecilia that opened my door. She's a chavala that ain't got no backbone but just the same, it was her.

Sometime after Cecilia snatched that Lincoln mama's bag she got cracked ugly worse, red and blue on her mouth and eyes, you couldn't even see the right shape of that chica's face. Beto shot his wad and hit her outside the lines, and this time it wasn't no weak slap. A woman can't take the kind of blow that he'd gave. Breaks her up. But it didn't come as no surprise to me. I knew she'd been getting cracked, she had that scared shaky face on and she was moving around sore the same as my mami used to after she got boxed by my papi. All beat ladies get the same look, that drag-down puppydog look that makes you wanna kick them harder.

That Muñeca girl didn't want nobody to know, and I'd kept her secret safe cause I wanted a wild card to pull out if I ever had the need. But Manny got the word anyways. Maybe two weeks after Lincoln I'm making beef and bean *empanadas* for his lunch and his mama calls him up crying and screaming loca cause Cecilia'd come home all blooded by Beto.

"Mama, don't worry, eh? I'll take care of it," he said into the phone and I'm keeping real quiet, trying to hear what's up. I squeezed over close to him, but I still couldn't make out nothing. I could only see how his face was clouding up stormy like it always does when he's looking for a fight.

"How bad he get her?" he said then, and I knew. Cecilia got beat rough and now Manny's getting called on to do her right. When he hung up he didn't say nothing and wouldn't look me in the eye. He only ran out the door flash-fast, taking off quicker than I'd seen him go in a long time.

And right then, it didn't mean nothing to me. So what I don't got the secret on Muñeca no more? I sat down and ate my empanada nice and slow. I just lost an ace, that's all, I think to myself. Got plenty more up my sleeve. When he was racing off to find Beto and make him pay, I didn't give it more than a minute. But life, it works out funny. Cecilia getting beat was like setting fire to a bomb.

If a vato's got to save his face by banging on some other homeboy he does it clean, where everybody can see. *Mano-a-mano.* Manny don't care much for his sister, but he wanted to make sure everybody knows that Beto gets what's coming to him fair. So a few minutes after his mama called him you could hear him yelling cusses and come-ons down the block. We all lived so close together back then, in this little square of streets. Manny on Ross, me on Burlington, Beto on Westlake, Cecilia on Mountainview. If you lose your temper, the whole place hears you. And that's what Manny was doing there, putting out his crazy call so all the homeboys and his sister and me knows he's gonna make Beto pay for what he did with blood.

"You fuck with her YOU FUCK WITH ME, ÉSE!" I could hear him bullhorn loud and clear through my window. "YOU FUCK WITH ME!"

They was down on Mountainview. I couldn't tell at first and had to follow all that noise, the sounds of yelling and feet stomping on the ground, but I finally found the right street. There wasn't nobody out but Lobos. Lobos and crows. All the houses was shut up tight, no open screen doors with mamas sticking their heads out to see what's up, and overhead on the powerlines there was some bad-luck crow birds waiting in a row, them caw-caw blue-black shits picking under their feathers and looking down over Manny doing his business. He was in the middle of the road standing tall over Beto, and my old man didn't look like no soft boy then. His arms was jabbing boxer-quick and strong, giving Beto some one-two bangs in the face, punching him up in the jaw and the cheek, the same as where Cecilia took it. The others just stood back and watched. Paco and Chevy and five new Lobo vatitos I didn't know good was hanging close by in case Manny needs some help. Chico was off to the side with his favorite homies, Marco and little Eddie, and his rubia hair was coming down over his eyes but you could see how he was watching careful. Cecilia was there too, standing all alone up on the sidewalk, and under her red skin that was pulled-out looking from all them hits she'd took, you could see her weak jelly mouth, the bottom lip hanging open like she's gonna cry.

"I gotta show you, right?" Manny's saying, his voice icy calm while he's slamming Beto down in the gut, then upper-cutting on the chin. That boy was always strongest in a fight. He did it vicious, put his head down and wouldn't look up again till he thought the job was done. "Can't have nobody fucking with what's mine, chingado, you know that by now," I heard him tell Beto, and then his hands moved wicked fast again.

I walked over to Cecilia, stood real close to her on the curb, and she moved back like I'm gonna take a big bite.

"Girl, why you got that face on, eh?" I ask her, put a little rattlesnake hiss in my voice so she knows to be careful. "Ain't you happy how your brother takes care a you?"

She don't wanna look at me, either kept her black eyes shut or looked up to see Manny doing his work. Manny's trying to get Beto down on the ground, punching on his head then pulling him by the neck, but it wasn't easy. Even back then Beto had tough in him and he was trying to stand straight, legs shaking and his hands coming flat up to cover. Even though he was getting his ass whipped he still tried to look as strong as Samson in front of the homeboys who stood by watching.

"Don't you hear me talking to you?" I say, and Cecilia closes up that jelly mouth, eyes straight ahead. She was making me see red again, and I start remembering how she didn't jump fast for me down in Lincoln cause she figures she's too good to group with a stinking illegal, that she's too good for my clika, her with them pretty clean hands she thinks she's got.

"I said I'd split you, bitch, and I meant it," I tell her.

She looks at me then. You could hear them high loud sounds of Manny fighting dirty on the street.

"This ain't for me," she says, meeting my eyes, and even though maybe she's scared a little I could see the proud in them too. "For you, maybe. But ain't none of this for me."

The girl was right about that one. Manny wasn't roughing up Beto cause he's all sorry she's got some black eye. But that don't matter. A sheep like Cecilia still can't step out of line like that. "You're asking for it," I say, closing my fingers tight. I'm itching to swipe her one but I knew it wasn't the right time, there when she's already beat and Manny's doing his show. He'd finally got Beto down on his knees and started kicking heavy, his face getting purple-black color, and Beto was crunching up on the ground so the rest of the vatos rushed over and broke them up before it was too late.

All the vatos, that is, except for Chico. I was busy with Cecilia, thinking how I got to remind her that I'm still the number-one woman here, but I can see two things at once. While I'm maddogging her, at the same time I'm checking Chico out, him with that hair over his face so I can't tell what he's thinking. And what I see is how all the other boys are helping Manny out, but not the Chico man. He wasn't doing right. In the clika when the boss man fights, all the homies better be standing guard. It's one of them rules, you got to pay your dues. But Chico and his locos from Edgeware wasn't acting like good soldiers, helping out with Beto or patting Manny on the arm. Instead they kept standing to the side with their stringy heads together, talking soft so I can't make their words out.

"Got him, ése, that's cool," I hear one of the new vatitos saying, this tagger named Dreamer. I looked over and see how he's gripping stone-faced Beto under the arms, and then how he pulls off this watch from Beto's wrist and hands it to Manny. "You got him good, jefe," Dreamer says, looking down at Beto's smashed-in face, but I heard some weak in his voice. Him and Chevy and Paco had these worried eyes cause they didn't like seeing their homeboy getting messed, even if it was by the patrón.

Manny was too pumped to notice any of them things. He was dripping sweat and breathing fast and he had that bad-cat smile on his face, but he should of been looking at his people harder instead. "No, ain't none of this for me," Cecilia says again, and I didn't dog her that time. I was too busy watching Chico. While him and his boys was talking, he nods his head Yah and they all turned on their heels and took off with a badass buffalo walk. They didn't even tip their heads at Manny and I knew that spelled trouble, cause a right hand always shows his respects to the boss.

"You like that?" Manny calls out to us, and I see how his teeth look bright white out that dark fighting face he's got on. I didn't know how bad it was gonna get, but I felt this chill on me, ice up my neck. Later on I'd know why, cause Manny'd just made himself some two ugly enemies.

"How you like that, Ceci?" he says, looking right at me. But me and Cecilia just stood there, her staring at her feet and me trying to make a smile. Manny was looking straight in my eyes and waiting, but neither of us say nothing. Quiet out there. Only Beto coughing weak.

"Fuck you then," he says, but he sounds tired. He winds his arm and throws Beto's watch up like a Dodger, trying to hit the birds. He didn't clip nothing but they got spooked anyways, and I got colded there watching them crows fly off, dirt black against the sky and getting smaller.

It used to be that Echo Park was one big neighborhood. You got the park in the middle, with the trees and the grass and that big lake, and then all the streets on either side. East streets and west streets. Time was, we'd say there wasn't nothing different about east or west. Alvarado, Mountainview, and Ross on the west, Edgeware, Bellvue and Laveta on the east, it wasn't a problem. Maybe west's better, but it don't really matter. Everybody was in the same crew. They was all one hundred percent Lobo.

But Chico, he was always *off*. He's a halfie, a half-gabacho coconut. Got born cause some white dude knocked his mama up and then ran off, and that's why he had that girl-looking blond hair, his peach-colored skin. Me, see I'm light but that ain't cause I got white in me. Anybody can see the difference. You got your light Mexican, and you got your halfies. Look at Chico from a mile away and first thing you think is Hey, coconut boy. And it ain't good to be half. Everybody knew he always had that soft in him cause he wasn't all brown, and that made Chico boy there a mean hungry piece. He had these itchy fingers, always being the first to throw, the first to pull out his blade. You could see how he wanted things. How he wants to call the shots. "Right hand, I gotta job for you, son," Manny'd say, and Chico'd get this squinty face. Chico was the meanest vato this side of Manny but he couldn't be the boss, and that stung him pretty bad.

He was a schemer. A cheat. Maybe it was that gabacho blood of his that made him give Manny to the cops way back when. Manny couldn't see it like I can. Him and Manny, they'd been running since forever, but Chico, I could tell how he's too hungry for a fight and he liked too much to kick it with his own crew. Had him his mama and a dark-skinned hermano named Mauricio, and he had his eastside dudes sticking close since I can remember. Sticking too close, like he's planning something. I always saw how something wasn't right about that homeboy.

So after Manny banged Beto and I see Chico walking off with his homies, I knew that's some bad sign. There was some tricky days there, when I'm waiting for something, some word of what's doing. Manny, he couldn't see none of it.

"Why you wound up, linda?" he asked me one night when I'm too nervous to give him a lap dance.

"I don't feel good," I told him, shrugged up my shoulder. "All right?"

"Don't I give you what you want?" he says, rubbing on my arm, making his gimme-sugar lips. "Yah, I do. So don't act bad to me, chica." He rolled over on me then and I figured I'd have to keep my mouth shut tight a while longer. That man was as blind as a mole. All he's got on his mind is sticking it in. But I knew that Chico's gonna make a move, I just didn't know what.

He showed his colors soon enough. First Chico's not coming around no more. Manny can't find him out on Alvarado selling the goodies on the corner like he's supposed. Can't get him on the phone. Nothing. And then we got the word on the street.

Lucía **103**

"He's started his own clika," Chevy tells Manny. He heard that Chico had grouped his eastside crew together, and they're calling themselves the C-4s.

"What kind of stupid shit is that?" Manny said. "That ain't no name for a gang."

Some say Chico called his new gang C-4 after this cell block he was in once. Others go on about how Chico's so hard-assed he's named his clika after bombs, so some vatos called Chico's boys Bombers for short. But we never got a handle on why they're C-4. All them stories whipping around, you couldn't get nothing straight. Like Chevy heard Chico's strung out on black tar and is headed fast for junkie town. "Ain't nothing to worry," he told Manny. "Once he runs out of smack he's gonna be crawling back to you in no time, jefe. He's gonna beg on his knees."

But Chevy had it all wrong. I found out later when I got a different story from Star Girl. She didn't tell me how Chico's bad off, how he's sitting in a corner begging for quarters or getting ready to jump off a high rise. He was doing that black tar *carga*, but it wasn't making him weak. From what Girl told me, it sounded like he was getting stronger and meaner, like a man who gets braver after taking a couple drinks. I figured we'd never see Chico playing right hand again.

"What you know, Girl?" I asked her. She'd met me at my apartment and told me the score she got after paying off some low-end Parkers.

She leans over close, like she's so full of secrets she can't sit straight up. "He's like some bad motherfucker now," she says, and I started feeling so proud how my chola could get better news than Manny's boys. Girl is working out real fine, I thought. But I didn't say nothing. Just let her talk. "Chico's out for number one these days," she goes on. "Says Manny's fucking up, that the jefe don't know how to keep his boys in line. He says that Manny's time is over and it's *his* turn now. He's already grouped himself like twenty, twenty-five rebels from the neighborhood, from east streets. And they all want a piece of the action." Girl starts shaking her head now and pressing her hands together. "Nah, scratch that. From what I'm hearing I think they're hungry for the whole pie."

I saw how Girl was right when I got the feel of the neighborhood. Some days after Chico walked away from us on Mountainview you could see how things was different. Everybody around here knew I was Manny's woman and that used to buy me some respect. Boys nodded when I walked by, sheep gave me them big lipstick smiles the same as if I'm a right hand. They was paying their dues. But now if I started walking down off westside streets I got razor-blade looks from locos, and some eastside sheep was giving me their chins too. Even if I was in the park I could smell it. Ever since I'd got the taste for grouping I'd started running the streets and the park to learn more about clika business, to see how the dealers sold their candy by the corners, how they switched drugs and money with their quick hands under the trees. One time after Chico split off us I was doing my rounds and I passed up the duck lake, till I walked too far over, close to these two bad-eyed locos.

They was sitting up on the far east benches and when they saw me they stared me down bulldog-straight. I didn't know them close and personal but I remembered their faces. I'd seen them kicking it around here and taking orders from my old man before. But that day those gangsters didn't bend their heads to me like they should, like they would if they still belonged to Manny. They was buzzheads, them shaved-head homies with the funky knife taks on their arm and who got the taste for fighting, and they was giving me throw-down eyes. We looked at each other for a minute and they didn't blink, but I didn't do nothing. I just stood there strong till one of them started hoo-hooing me.

"Hey chola! Chollla," one buzzhead sings out, then bangs his legs on the bench. "Come over here, chavala, I'll show you what a real man's like." Buzzboy was throwing them words down nasty to me there on his eastside bench and I felt that cold up on my neck all over again, the same as when I saw Chico buffalo-walk away from Manny.

I tricked it on out of there. I didn't run, didn't get scared on my face, but I tricked out just the same. Don't got to read it on a sign. This chica learns quick enough.

Neighborhood wasn't never the same after that. Like a big white line was drawn down the middle of the Park. You knew quick enough where you could go. Chico, he was keeping hid but you could feel him just the same, over there on Edgeware and Bellvue. All of a sudden them east streets was some dangerous places for a Lobo. We kept hearing stories, how he'd gone gun-crazy and would shoot anybody who looked at him wrong. How he was doing big deals down in Long Beach and drinking up all our dollars. How he was gonna kill the first Lobo he sees on the eastside. But at first he was keeping low and didn't show his face nowhere around here. So all I could do was keep my eyes peeled, my ears open, and wait for his surprise.

Manny didn't like to talk about nothing like that. "Chico?" he'd say. "You just wait on Chico," he'd tell us, make this little laugh like it ain't worth spending a word on. "It's gonna get fixed."

After Paco got beat up by the cops and Chico kicked off from the Lobos, things had took a turn. That's for sure, you'd know it good enough if you wet your finger and stuck it in the wind. Nobody said nothing, but it was there, right there solid in front of your nose if you wanted to take a look. Manny'd hit the skids and he'd take the rest of us down with him if somebody didn't do something about it. There was too much bad water under the bridge by then, anyways, to get all sloppy about it. I knew it was my day. It was my *time*. And I was ready.

I'd kept my own dumpster apartment on Burlington even though he was getting so rich, moving to one of them fancy houses on Ross Street two blocks over. When he asked me to shack with him, I wouldn't do it. My house was still this cockroach dump, no place for a jefa but at least I could keep things secret—my ranfla, my badass pachuco pants and Pendletons. But they wasn't gonna be secret no more. I put on my chola clothes, dressed careful in my mirror, making sure I looked rougher than any woman Echo Park'd seen before. I lined my lips so that they're bruise dark and pulled on my baggies, leather jacket, black boots. Like I'm getting ready for war. "He ain't ready for nothing like you," I said to myself, to what I saw. And then I headed out my door to go and catch me some cash of my own.

"We're gonna talk now, Manny," I told him, walking into that fancy place of his, with his store-bought furniture and his zebra-stripe rug, his brand new TV. "We're gonna talk about me."

"Oye, girl," he says when he checks me out. He's sitting on this big black sofa with his shirt off and I see how he's starting to get all soft looking in the belly and chest, not like the hard vato I first hooked up with. There's red color in his face that wasn't there before, his eyes are heavy like a sleeper's. "Why you looking like that?"

I don't like no soft-assed man. My Manny used to be like a tiger running through the streets and breaking down whatever gets in front of him. I would look at him and get so proud, just

106   Locas

like a woman who's got what she wants. But I didn't feel like that no more. I was just standing there on fire with my own plans.

I took a breath. "You better start liking these clothes," I said. "Cause we're playing something new now, baby. You think I'm gonna let you sit there like a viejo while I'm doing all the work? Who you think's been making this happen? Me, ése, that's who."

He starts laughing like men do when they don't wanna listen to no woman. His smile's cutting into me hard, too, cause I know *I* was the one, not him. Just a matter of time.

"You just a bitch gone wrong in the head, Lucía," he answers me. "Dressing like a man. Something the matter with you, girl. Something's fucked up. And here I am giving you everything you want, it ain't worth it. Go on and pick out any woman here. Any woman. They're *begging* me for some, you know that? You hear me. *Every day* I got some woman after me. 'Manny, I love you, jefe, I can make you happy, baby.' That's what they're saying, but I stick by you. You got the *works* here, see? Got it all. Pretty clothes, plenty money, and here you are dressing like a man. Even got a tak like a vato. You ain't no vato. That's some twisted shit. Think you gotta cock on you?"

He don't even get up yet, just lays there lazy and spitting out his dirty words like I'm not worth the trouble, but he was playing with me. I heard that fire under his voice.

"Yah," I said, standing straight as a board. Getting set. "I gotta cock on me now, Manny. I'm the one making the money go round and round. I'm the one making sure we're not getting fucked by these lowlifes and mama's boys you got hanging all over you. You think they love you, but they don't. Especially after you're tripping on Beto. And ain't nobody gonna help you like I can. So think about it hard, honey, cause I'll walk right out of here and leave you all alone."

No real man's gonna let a woman talk to him like that. I knew it was either he slams me on the floor and gives me my due or he bends over. But not even burned-out Manny's gonna let it all slide by.

He gets up, walks over real slow, and looks at me for a minute. We're just standing there, breathing. And he picks up his hand, looking to hit me hard on my face, like any old Mexican man would who's got his balls. I just got harder balls, woman or not.

"Careful, Manny," I say. "You don't know how to get this business moving. Need me for it."

"Don't need nothing."

"Who you got deals with, chingado? Who owes you money? Don't even know, do you? Baby, you need me more than any man you got around here."

He slammed me in the face anyway. An open hand on my mouth, knocking me back and I'm feeling wet there on my lip that's red and split. "You better learn to shut up, Lucía. Who you think you talking to?" He'd never hit me like that before but I don't show how it shakes me up. Cause I can still tell he's got that weak spot in him.

Looked him right in his eye like I was a man. "I'll be gone, ése. Out the door. You see that? I'll leave you here with Chico and the other junkies that steal from you. And nobody's gonna be doing your numbers, what you gonna do then?"

He knows what it is. I got me a fast brain.

A man don't do or say nothing when a woman wins around here. He won't let her see him break. So Manny just maddogs me instead. He's sticking out his chest and making like King Kong, bringing his fist up like he's gonna let me have it again and I stand my ground, toughing up my face so he sees I can take it. "You're nothing but a cold bitch!" he yells at me, spit coming out of his mouth and his eyes bugged out and bloodshot but then that hand of his goes down, don't it? Like a flag for surrender.

"That's it, baby," I tell him, my chest feeling like it's gonna crack open when I can't show how I'm scared. "You doing real good. Now we gonna talk about what we're gonna do."

Me and Manny never said another word about what happened that day. He went back to acting usual, like it ain't never happened. But there wasn't no going back for me. I only got stronger. I started asking for things, making trouble, getting my own big time started. It wasn't a stretch at all. I was made to be a man, strong and tall and looking out for number one. Got stuck with pussy, and ain't nothing you can do about it. But you see I'm tougher and meaner than any of these sorry boys. Once I got going, there wasn't nothing that could stand in my way.

My Star Girl and Chique know that better than anybody, maybe better than Manny. They stood right by me while I was climbing on top and when I got there I treated them right. I made sure they was taken care of. And Manny didn't give me no lip about it, neither.

"I want a slice for my chicas, eh?" I said a few weeks after I told him I'd walk if he didn't start giving me my cut. We was sitting at his kitchen table, and I knew in the next room there was a whole pile of stash with my name on it. "And not the bad shit, Manny. I want the sugar."

He squeezes up his face like he was making up his mind, but I didn't rush him. Either way I was gonna get what I wanted. "Yah, OK, Lucía, you been a good girl," he says after a minute, sounding like he's doing me some big favor, but he could see how he didn't have no choice. He goes into the bedroom then comes right back out, holding a plastic bag full of powder. It was some of the new Colombian he'd just got from Mario, and I knew handing it over must of hurt. "This here's the best sugar I got," he tells me, proud sounding.

And it was. Like taking candy from a baby. Them snow-whites was the prettiest things I ever did see. Coke's white like cane sugar, like new snow, and that lady puts out even better than she looks. I've seen Parkers sniffing up coke like it's fresh, clean air, and when they come back up all they want is more. "Give me a hit?" I'd heard these red-nosed vatos say to Manny's boys before, digging down in their pockets. Well, my girls got your hit now, homes, and you're gonna pay for your little high, see what I'm saying? Top dollar on my street. After I moved Girl and Chique in on that action I got them tricking sweet deals to the veteranos over on Alvarado, and pretty soon that block was all mine.

"Hey superman, come on, baby, I'll give you a taste."

"What, ésa?"

"Get on over here, I'll show you something special and you're gonna like it, honey. You'll like it *good*."

Girl'd be out there snapping her fingers and whistling out to the veteranos driving down the road, sweet-talking them into buying a bag. Chique'd stand there too, rolling her hands up in her sweater and smiling at the locals swinging by, but she wasn't nothing like my Star Girl. That chica was a natural. Girl had that pretty full-moon face and skinny legs so they'd stop and give her the eye, and she was quick at telling which boys was the high-life veteranos. The ones driving them cherried lowriders or badassing down the sidewalk showing off their new black leather jackets, those are the finest Parkers for us cause they got big bills burning in their pockets. High-life veteranos make the most money. They usually got themselves a lady and a baby and a nine-to-five working body shop or construction. High-lifers don't bang or nothing, maybe even let their women drag them to church on Sundays, but they ain't no different than the rest of the locos out here. They remember their old days. Getting high, money dice, alley-fighting over a *ruca*. Even if they're acting like granddaddies they still got some fire in their bellies. All you have to do is give them a chance and they'll be easy money. "Yah, that's good," I'd tell my chicas when they came home with my cash. "Keep selling to them *ricos* and we're gonna be styling."

Star Girl liked gangbanging. Maybe liked it too good. Since I'd jumped her in she'd bloomed like a Valentine's Day rose, tall and pink and winking out at you. Girl was my *best*. Still tough from the gutter, she would of been one of the finest bangers this town ever saw if she'd lasted. She could pick pockets like a ghost, knew how to rough up mamacitas like a wrestler, and had a gift for selling snow to them veteranos, charged them triple and they'd pay up with a smile. Something about her, see? She was special. Just looking at her made my heart get fulled up. Hey, little sister, I'd think sometimes when I'd see her in action. You're doing real good. Girl looked so proud and tough out there she reminded me of myself. Wouldn't bend to nobody, I thought. She's made of steel just like me.

But ain't nobody perfect. Even Girl needs a kick in the ass from her jefa once in a while. When I'd first handed her a bag I told her how to do it.

"You can sweet-talk them, but they ain't your friends, see? And you ain't their whore. You ain't even a woman out there. So don't let nobody touch you, Girl, cause this is money business."

"I got it covered," she'd said, and nodded real serious. Girl kept her side up too, bringing home more money than four of Manny's boys, shoving it in my hands with her shiny smile. But slanging ain't no easy life. It'll fool you. After a while, I saw how she stopped being careful, laughing too loud when she's dealing, throwing her head back like some showgirl. "Come on, coochie!" she'd started yelling down the street, jiggling her ass so even the coldest vato'd stop and give her the time. "I got it right here for you, lover man!" She was swinging too high, too loose and fast, cause she forgot what she's doing. Dealing looks like a party, you got your white magic and the money's flying, all the homies acting like you're the bomb. But my rule number one around here is stay tight. Never dip in the stash, and never fuck a customer. Ain't no parties where I'm from, see what I'm saying? Maybe the men can be Mr. Supercool loco when they're dealing, laughing and high-fiving the Parkers that come sniffing by, but a woman can't be loose out here. You got to watch your back. And Girl'd stopped watching hers.

I got her back in line, though. Cause I always look after my own. One day I kicked it by Alvarado to see how they was doing, and what I saw was Chique moping by the corner and Girl smoothing down this yellow-toothed veterano named Chavez. I knew he was a high-lifer. He worked pretty steady on downtown high-rise jobs and he'd done good business with us before, but by the way he was bending over my chola it didn't look to me like he had business in mind right then.

"You want some?" Girl was asking him, purring like a kitty cat and touching him on his chest just like a sheep would, and Chavez was standing there smiling back with them yellow teeth, had his hand in his pocket but he wasn't giving over any cash yet. He wanted to make her sheep as long as he could. They was turned away and couldn't see me checking them out, but Chique did, she saw me walking up to them and when our eyes met she just shook her head. Look at that, boss, she was saying to me with her sorry-looking face. This here's a shame.

"You want a taste of honey, honey?" Girl asked him again. She was laughing in this husky voice, a hooker voice, and her little fingers was teasing his shirt collar, moving down to his belt, and poking into his pocket, and Chavez there thought he'd found heaven.

"I'll buy some if I get a taste a you, Girl," he says, moving his hand up and giving her a little pinch on the ass. You could see how he wanted to make my chola beg him like she's some whore.

"Get the fuck outta here, Chavez!" I yelled, walked up straight to them two and pushed him rough so he ain't touching my Girl no more. I felt this hot fighting blood rushing up in me, and right then I would of called out all my dogs on him if he touched her again.

"What's that? Bitch, don't be messing with me!" he starts up, getting his badass face on cause he don't recognize me.

"You know me, ése? Take a look." I was hissing right in his face. "I'm Manny's, see that? This is the patrón's woman talking to you. So you don't wanna be playing with me. And you don't wanna be playing around with my girl."

"Hey now, all right. I'm just joking with this chica, real friendly like." Chavez was smiling now, he'd dropped his tough act but still wasn't running off like I want. "Real friendly, see?" he says again, and Star Girl's stepping back, looking at me quiet cause she sees I'm so spitfired I was ready to pull some out and cut him.

"Yah, get lost, Chavez. I'll see you later," she tells him, then sides up by me and puts her hand on my shoulder, trying to cool me out. "Go on."

He scuffed off, giving me some sideways nasty look. "Bitch is a *freak*," I could hear him saying about me soft under his breath but just loud enough so I hear him.

I turned to my Girl, almost as mad at her as I was at that trash boy, and she was giving me her worried eyes cause she knew I was gonna give her some heat.

"What you think you doing, Girl? I didn't group you so you could be whoring down here on Alvarado!"

"Hey baby, there ain't no problem, I'm just dealing some vato his hand. These homies like a little game, that's all," she tells me, real sweet sounding so I feel my heart tug, but then I see how her eyes are too wide and shiny and her mouth's jerking nervous over her face.

"You strung? Shit, you better be clean. I don't know what I'm gonna do to you if you're dipping." Oh, I was blind-loca then. Surprised even myself. I grabbed her too hard by the arms, squeezing her Indian-burn tight, and she was trying to pull out from me. I knew she thought I'd gone crazy but I couldn't have my chola dipping and whoring the same as them strawberries you see around here trying to sell their ass for a dollar. Cause I'd already left that shit behind. And I wasn't gonna let it happen to my best girl who I'd jumped in and gave a name to and called my familia.

"Come on, no, come on, Lucía," she's saying, twisting out a little and starting to cry, but the more she pulls the hotter I get.

"—I didn't make you so you could be acting cheap like that, hear me? I'll fucking break you, Girl, if you wrong me, cause I ain't gonna have no junk whores here! I saved you, see? I saved you from being a piece-of-shit sheep, you owe me—"

"All right, Lucía," Chique pipes in, and she's giving me some half bear hug so I chill. "All right, that's cool, we're cool, she ain't gonna do that no more," she starts whispering in my ear, nice and calm and light so I loose up a little.

"I don't got time for no junk *whore*," I say, and threw Star Girl back. Both of my girls was looking at me like they ain't never seen me before, Chique careful and quiet and Girl shaking and bawling like a baby. Her red eyes was tugging at me some more, but I'd beat my Girl bloody before she started slanging her ass, and I'd rip any man in two that tried to make her into one of them cheap whores you see here on the street every day. I know them whores. I know too good how they got weak blood, how they'd be better off dead. And that ain't my Girl. She's like me, good and proud and strong just like me. So when I'm looking at her wet face and hearing her sad voice cracking and twisting around, I had to stand there ice cold. I couldn't tell her, Things are better now, Girl, cause I wouldn't be loving her right. And I couldn't put my hand soft where I'd grabbed her hard, cause something told me if I showed her my weak spot, that tug in my heart would break me clean in half.

After I slammed Girl that day on Alvarado she never sheeped a customer again, and I never saw her with glassy eyes neither. Good thing, too, cause I was just getting warmed up. I'd took on Manny, I'd even yelled down my favorite chica, and after that facing up to the Lobos got to be as easy as breathing.

Like I got it so that we're not doing the dead-end deals no more. You think we're gonna make money just selling to a few college boys that snitch on you? No. You got to sell hard. You got to sell careful. The truth is, the chota leave us alone if we stick to Mexican. They get mad if we dirty up their clean college kids. So you take it to the brown locals. They sniff up as much as they can with their pennies, and it adds up if you move enough. There's good business down here in the eastside with them veteranos but especially with the young chicos. If you deal to the Mexican kids, the cops don't come down on you so hard. Take it to the schools, where those little ones want their toys. Seventh grade, eighth grade. Dark baby faces eat it up and it's easy as pie.

"Send the locos down to junior high," I told Manny. "I know we'll be seeing some pretty money if we start doing business with them babies."

He was looking at me again like he don't know who I am. "I ain't gonna be messing with no kiddies," he says, then puts his hands over his eyes like he ain't slept in a week. "Not gonna be selling to no babies," he tries again, but he wasn't giving me real trouble like in our old days. By then I could see that soft in his face.

After I bitched Manny long enough he sent his boys to Garfield Junior High, where Cecilia used to go. The Lobos started hanging around the chain-link fence, sticking their fingers through the holes, whispering to the little ones with bags of talcum-cut in their back pockets. Hey baby, you want some candy? You wanna play some good fun? The kiddies come running like Easter rabbits cause they're just dying to dress up like a cholo and get high the same as grownups. Hey little chico, wanna see something? You know them babies was saying yes. They ran up with their milk money and big smiles, and if they didn't have enough to buy a toke sometimes we'd just let it ride. It was just a matter of time before we had all their money locked up tight, anyways. Those kids were the long term. Get them young, and you're doing good business for years.

I even got Manny to make pregnant Cecilia do the selling down there in Garfield cause she wasn't showing her respect to me like she should. She didn't throw down fast on that mamacita when I told her to out there on Lincoln, and on Mountainview I saw her giving me some attitude. But it ain't nothing I can't handle. I know where your soft is, ésa, I was thinking. I know how to make you move. Big brother, right? Maybe she was swinging around here making like the Virgin cause she gets her ass kicked by her man, but that ain't her soft spot. Her weak shows up in her mouth and her little hands, how her lips tug up loose and smiling when Manny walks into the room, how she touches her fingers together light like she wants to say something but won't. Old Muñeca loves her loser brother something strange. So I know good enough where to stick it in. Even if she won't call me jefa, I know how to make that sheep walk and talk just like I want.

I give Manny a beer one night and sit him down in front of me. "Baby, you gotta get your girl Cecilia back in line," I told him, smiling pretty so he listens.

"What you mean?" he asks, gritting his teeth cause he's sick of me telling him what to do.

I made it sound like it's his idea. "You see how she ain't coming around here no more since you beat Beto out on Mountainview. And that girl ain't gonna stick with us till you get her back inside, honey. Like you say, everybody's family here. One hundred percent or nothing at all."

So Manny told her to go down to Garfield with some stash and made her do some dirty business so she remembers where she comes from. I hear she sat there and cried, putting her hands over her fat belly and hanging her head. "Don't make me, Manny. Ain't cut out for it, I ain't cut out for selling," she blubbered but he was as hard as a rock for me cause he knows where his good thing is. He told Cecilia to sit there outside of the school in a big black coat with some coke in her pockets and sell a couple of bags to the chicos for their little dollar bills. "Hey baby, want some fun?" she asked, same as a Lobo would, knowing I'm gonna put her in the gutter if she turns her back on me.

Poor little Cecilia didn't look so proud after that. La Cecilia *bonita* learned a thing or two about what it takes to be a woman in these parts. More than just big talk. More than the big papers you get from being born over the border. I saw her after, flat bellied then but do I give a shit? You can't fuck with me and not pay the price. I sleep like a baby knowing I put that sheep in her place, down in the street where she belongs. Don't give me them nasty eyes like I ain't worth a dime, girl, cause you're the one's gonna be tasting dirt when I'm done with you.

* * *

I knew when I took up *la vida* it wasn't gonna be no easy ride. I knew I'd have to make the hard decisions. And that's just fine with me. You can look this woman in the eye any day and I'll tell you what it is. Not like my old blind-bat Manny. He was making like I'm Judas cause I want the babies to be buying from us and I make his sister sell a little. "You happy now?" he yelled at me when he came home from telling Cecilia to do the job at Garfield. "You and Ceci, man. All you stupid chavalas gone crazy! You forget who I am? I'm the jefe here, woman. I'm the BOSS!" I had to smooth him out and play that old girl game like he likes, make him think he's got the wheel again. "That's right, baby, I ain't gonna give you no more trouble," I told him, tried to touch him soft on his face so he cools down, but he wasn't giving me no love eyes no more. He'd seen what I can do.

Manny yells at me loud enough, but deep down he knows I can play payback, not only with Cecilia or the gabachos, but I'll slam hard on my very own homeboys who do wrong by the Lobos. Stealing or sucking down our white, that's against the rules, son. Them drugs are the devil, and I don't got no use for junkies. Star Girl saw that quick enough. And the rest of the Lobos found it out rough and fast once I got my say.

Like with that Bennie. That boy Alberto who got his name cause he liked how his little speedy white pills made him go zoom. "Hey chica, word up? You doin' fine girl, fine baby fine, that's right," he used to say to me, his mouth running a mile a minute cause he's so jacked up on goodies. I knew he was stealing skim when he got all skinny like a stick and couldn't shut up. "That's right, that's right, you slammin'." Then he'd crash all down, sleep three days in a row, even piss himself right there in bed.

He's not the only thief. I've seen enough high-wire boys scooting around here like their heads are going to spin right off

their necks to know that we've got a few burglars. No angels
down here in Echo Park, right? And it's nothing personal, like
with Star Girl. Let those pendejos dig themselves their own
grave, you know? What do I care. But still, those junkies just crash
and burn and take you right along with them. And that's *my*
money they're fucking with.

So I sent out a message. Just to say, I'm watching your
ass. Don't get like old trashed-out Bennie. Manny and Chevy and
me got Bennie all alone in the park at night. "Gonna hold a
meeting, chico," was what Manny said to him. "We gotta big job
for you." And Bennie smiles as wide as a skull. Later he comes
running up to us in the park at ten o'clock at night, when it's so
dark you have to stand under the moon or a lamp to make out
the shape of your own hand.

We're all there in the misty park under the trees, but to
me it felt as hot as the Mojave.

"So, Bennie," Manny says. "How you doing, boy?"

"I'm slammin', Manny the Man! I'm here for you, 'chuco,
just tell me the word, homes." Bennie's all hopped up, eyes round
like white eggs.

"Looks to me like you fucked up, Bennie," Chevy says.
Chevy was a regular ladykiller with his old-timer buzzcut and
his tiger taks striping up his neck, and under the moonlight he
looked even meaner.

Bennie looks over at Chevy, starts goofball shadow-
boxing to take the edge off. "No, man. Just a little piped, homes.
I'm cool."

I stand over there by a tree in the dark, seeing the thin-
slice moon shine off the lake and feeling so strong and fierce.
Nothing makes me madder than seeing a man who's turned weak.

"You there a fucking junkie, homeboy," I say then, and
poor Bennie can't even see my face. "And that's gonna cost you.
Guess we got to give you a little lesson, eh?"

Manny and Chevy could slam down harder than most any hit man you'll ever see. They chopped up little Bennie like ground beef with their jabs and uppercuts and body punches till he's crying with his fingers over his eyes, over his mouth, bent over like a wire, like a girl. So he's bled dry except for what I learned him, that he's got to pay his dues. I'm leaning up on my tree and feeling sick, cause being la chola primera means that you got to be like these boys' mama and give them their medicine even when it hurts. But I've got a rush as strong as a river running through me too. The moon's only a thin rip in the sky where the sun's shining through and I feel powerful enough to stamp it out. I could reach up and crush it in my fist, and there wouldn't be nothing left but dust.

Yah, Manny's looking at me like I'm the *bruja* now. Like I'm some wicked witch he don't wanna cross. Cecilia, Bennie stay on his mind, even when he shuts his eyes he still sees how they look sad and broken down. "That's real love, baby," I tell him in my soft voice. He nods but don't say nothing.

I know la vida's a hard one here down in Echo Park. And being a mama to all these locos is a heavy load. But I'm not gonna let them suck all my milk dry and steal from me like little rats. I've got to show them what I can do. Keep them safe.

Cecilia

Maybe my baby died that day I forgot to keep my hands down, when I didn't cover up my belly like a good mamacita would. If I'd just kept my head everything would be different now.

Beto had got that taste for hitting women the same as a *borracho* loves his drink and it wasn't too long before he was banging on me every night, back and forth then down to the floor, my mouth on the linoleum, tasting red inside my mouth. I'd been real careful, always keeping my hands ready so my face hits and not my belly, but then there was that one time he slammed me and I didn't do what I should. It was a night like any other. He doesn't like something I do and gets his mean eyes, then I hear him make that quick breath and he says, "Oh, Cecilia girl, you done it now," so if I'd been fast things would be different. But then his fist came and I wasn't *thinking*, I raised up my hand in front of my face. I had too much on my mind with Lucía and Lincoln Heights and all the trouble Manny's having with the police. That's why I didn't have time to catch myself before I fell. And I knew she was hurt bad then. It felt like sharp hot sticks were running me through, like she was reaching on up to tell me something's wrong.

You could almost laugh. I tried so hard to make them love me, Manny because he was my prince, and Beto for a baby, but they take it from you anyways. I think Beto beat on me because he knew. He'd go on how I'm so fat and ugly but I think he could tell about me, how I feel inside, and it made him loco. What I think is this. You can take these men, with their dark skin and rough square hands that don't have one soft spot on them. Their spiky skin, his things hanging all outside and ugly. His smell like a wild animal when he's over you and his eyes are closed. You can take that, I don't care. Only good thing about a man is what he can put right inside my belly. So I tried and tried and there I was, a mamacita. All my work paid off. My *preciosa* deep inside me waiting. But it didn't work out like I planned. After all that carrying on, in the end I was poorer than a dead man.

Or maybe my baby died when Manny made me go out there to sell the coke to the junior high schoolers. Maybe she just broke right up in there, broke to pieces in my big belly when I'm standing outside the school fence, waving to the sixth graders. They had faces just like flowers.

"You gotta do for me, Cecilia," Manny said. He was dressed all fine and his handsome face looked down at me serious. He knew I'd get all dirty for him like that. "You got to show me, *hermana*. Show me *de dónde eres*." He wants my Echo Park out there where he can see it. To make sure.

You know I'm just like any other girl in my heart. I was sexing Beto to make me a baby, loving Manny better than my own self. I loved him even if he didn't love me back the same. Like when he roughed up Beto. I knew Manny was only making his show for his Lobos and his Lucía. Manny with the dark devil-looking face beating on my baby's papa wasn't doing me any favors because I couldn't be Somebody with a shamed kicked-down man. But me being Somebody wasn't the point anyways. Out there on Mountainview Manny didn't even give me his eye to show me he's doing me right because of how much he cares. He only had smiles for Lucía and his homeboys, and so I knew he didn't do it for me.

I told myself that didn't matter none, though. I reminded myself he's still my prince. That he's still my big brother. I was waiting for my good thing, but a girl can't have nothing for her very own. It's got to be for la familia, or else you're all alone in this world. And you can't be alone cause that means you're as good as dead.

But I don't want to be selling those drugs to no one.

"Manny, I do for you, hermano!" I started crying when he gave me that bag of nasty white coke and told me to go and feed it to them baby kids in the school only because puta Lucía says her piece. "But don't make me do that bad thing, OK? I ain't cut for selling. I ain't made for it. I'll be your message girl, right? I can send them messages real good."

He looked clean and rich and I knew I was ugly from begging him till I was blue in the face, but I didn't care. I never had a heart for hurting people. My belly heated and stung and my chest twisted, and my hands grabbed hold of his arm and his collar with both of my hands before he shook me off and then they pressed together like I'm praying to the pope.

"No, hermana," he said anyway. "You do for me."

And so I did.

"Hey little ésa, you want to play?"

Garfield's one of the schools they send us all to. What a low-down place that is, nothing but a concrete square all falling apart, the bricks rotted and a few windows smashed and patched up again with tape or thin wood board. It's circled in rusty chain-link that's supposed to keep bad people like me away, but the building's still covered with dark blue spiky spray-paint letters that scream at you when you walk by. "L-O-B-O-S" looking down at me from that dirty brown wall. I can't even look. And if you go inside, shoot. I remember it good enough. The rooms are stuffed full of kids and the teachers get so tired they're half crazy, the books have broken spines and there's fights in the halls. Garfield Junior High. I never learned a thing in there.

I'm right outside my old school in a big black coat, an old man's coat, thick wool from Salvation Army for the hard whiskey winter. Wino overcoat. It's got these deep pockets where I can hide my hands, my stash, wiggling my fingers in the space where a man's hands are supposed to go, not no little chica's like mine. I've got my small bag of white powder hidden there, and I'm whistling and walking back and forth down the sidewalk so no one can tell I'm up to no good. I'm waiting for my sister, I could say if anybody asks. I'm waiting for my baby cousin. But nobody does, and I just wait.

At three o'clock, there she is. A little sixth grader. She's going on home to her mami, papi, dinner in front of the TV set with the funny shows. Her face is darker than mine, *morena*, coffee-colored and bright at the same time, shiny in the cheeks and the black eyes, thin small hands like shells.

"Hey o yes, little *machita*, you want to have some fun with me?"

Bait the fish. That Manny's nothing but my big brother, and I got to love him with all my heart. Wiggle my fingers deep in my pocket. And she looks over, doesn't she? But her eyes ain't dark stones, like Manny's. Soft flower face.

"What fun?" she asks. She doesn't have no street tough sound in that voice, only soft and sweet.

I've got that burning in my belly with my baby telling me STOP but I showed the tiny cat sixth grader my toys, bringing out my little bag and opening it. I pretend I've got something nice and soft and sweet inside there like a pretty white rose. Smell that rose, chiquita.

She puts her head down and sniffs just to be like a big girl.

Girl, little girl. Something went bad. Went bad right there inside me, deep inside and there wasn't nothing I could do. Seems like God looked down and saw how I didn't deserve her. So I couldn't keep her. I'd told myself I was doing them things because of love, but love like that doesn't make you right. It doesn't make you clean. Sometimes I think I got what was coming to me fair and square. But I don't got all the answers. All I know is that after Beto slammed on me and Manny made me sell that coke to the teeny sixth grader with the shiny face my beautiful baby twisted up and died.

My baby girl. I know she's a girl, because when she came out all early, the white hospital walls and some *gringo* doctor looking down at me with his empty face and my belly jamming up and my big breasts all full of her milk hurting, I saw her little red self. Too soon for this world, chiquita. Saw her tiny red toes and fingers, I would have counted them too and given her a beautiful name. I saw her little red mound with no penis so I know she would have loved me good. Shut eyes never opened up to say hello.

Come back come back.

Part Two

1985-1990

Lucía

Growing pains. That's what the Lobos started having, cause there ain't no easy way to the big time. Maybe banging was like a game when we was all little locos, but before too long we started hurting something awful. And I was ready for it, baby. You're looking at a gangster who can roll with them tough punches.

I was hearing things, nasty, dirty little things about Chico from Star Girl, who was still keeping her ear to the ground and giving me the news. "Word is that the rubia's planning something, Lucía," Girl told me, squeezing her hands together cause she loved having a good secret to tell. "He's gonna try and move in on Long Beach, or strong-arm our stash. Something. Can't be sure what. All I know is that he's laughing at the Lobos these days. Says he's the one who's gonna be doing deals for the Parkers soon."

Manny, he didn't wanna hear none of that. He still was fooling himself, thinking his Chico's gonna come back. Sometimes after he'd drunk too much he'd look up at me with foggy eyes and smile. "He ain't gonna be gone too long," he'd say, gripping hold of his glass. "Órale, no way, I tell you. That boy and me been through too much." And every time somebody dissed on Chico in front of Manny, he'd get this crazy bad look on cause one of Manny's rules is that you can't talk bad about a vato. "Gotta have respect for the veteranos, homes!" he'd say. "Else we got nothing here, see? Gotta keep our family strong." I knew how all that was bullshit, though. I never had no familia except for my girls and didn't have no strong except for the green in my pocket. So I listened up good to what Star Girl was saying. It never hurt me one little bit to hear the truth.

But even old soft Manny couldn't look the other way forever. There's this one Saturday night when we was all hanging in the park with the homies but it didn't feel like the old times. The boys was standing around nervous looking, kicking the grass and trading cusses in low voices, and the chicas kept together in this little circle, twirling their red hair in their fingers. Manny was making like things was the same as always. "Come on, fools!" he laughed at us, sticking his beer in the air just like he used to, but there wasn't no Chico man by his side now. "This a party or what?"

When we got back to Manny's though, there wasn't no more pretending. Couldn't be. His house on Ross was still the finest crash in town but when we walked inside the first thing we saw was how the living room window's smashed open, and there's broke glass on the floor, some chairs are turned over. I looked at him then and saw how that happy-boy grin he'd put on at the park was off his face.

"What the fuck?" he's standing there for a second in the door like he don't know what he sees, but then makes straight

for the bedroom. He'd kept all the shit there. Every bag of goodies waiting to get sold and every piece of money from the selling
was packed in a pirate chest strapped with locks and shoved
under his bed, and to get the treasure you either had to be
Houdini or use an axe if you didn't have a key. Well, Chico ain't
no Houdini. I walked after Manny slow and stiff cause I already
knew what had happened, and when I get into his room I see
him crouched in the corner, staring blind at a pile of kindling
and busted metal. Everything is gone.

"Only one vato's gonna do this to you, Manny," I say
down to him. I knew I was breaking his rule but then I didn't
care when I saw how Chico had stole all my money. "You hear
me? Wake up, ése! There ain't nobody else who's gonna take
you on like this."

He don't say nothing, won't even look up at me.

"You stupid?" I go on, heating up cause he's squatting
there like a dummy, so I forget how even though he's soft you've
got to keep careful with weak old dogs that still got their bite.
"Goddamn. Lookit this. If you listened to me, *none* of this would
have happened. You should of slammed Chico a long time ago.
You old piece, how much you lose? How much I got to pay out
cause you're too much a fool—"

Manny looks at me then, harder than I'd seen in a long
time, and that stopped me short.

"I see who did this, bitch, so shut up."

I knew then that I'd crossed the wrong line, cause this
wasn't about business. This was about his boy. I cooled down
fast and started purring like a kitty cat so he don't get wild on
me. "Ooooh, all right, honey. All right. There ain't nothing to
get all mad about."

"And keep it shut," he says, stretching up then standing
right close to me so I can feel the old heat coming off him. "All
you crazies who don't know when to *quit*, see? Making me *loco*,

with your little chicken talk, scratching at me, always wanting something or other. I mean, shut the *fuck UP*."

I shifted my eyes away, then scooted out to the hall so we're not so close. "Yah, okay, I hear you, Manny," I was saying, real hushed and shy sounding, but he just followed me out to the living room.

"How much you think I can take, eh? It ain't too much more. Not *too much*, cause this old vato's gonna blow some day! Gonna blow, then you better watch out!"

I'm bending over and picking the glass off the carpet, turning the chairs back up, cleaning just like a sheep would, but he just keeps yelling.

"I'm the jefe round here, see? Don't you forget it. Not *one minute*. You putos don't got nothing but for me, I was the one building the Lobos up from the dirt. I deserve *respect*. You people should be kissing my ass, but all I want is THIS." He makes a fist so his arm toughs up for a second, and I see them old muscles coming out. "But not my boy, right? Not my man, no, that ése's got his head against me. After what I do for HIM."

The more Manny was talking the crazier he got, his voice getting louder and tighter, and he was walking around the living room, smashing over the glass and punching his hands up in the air like he wants to hit somebody. "Chico, eh?" he's yelling out in the middle of the room, to nobody, to Chico, to me. "Yah, I gave him things too good. I can see it. Thief, that's what you call these vatos. Stealer. Snitch. Crying like a baby to the cops and say where I live, sicked those pigs on me. Little rubia fuck! That's my money, homes. MY MONEY. I show you. I show him!"

Manny's by the broke window and he smashes one fist right through the hole, breaking off more glass and cutting up a piece of his hand, and I stood there watching him careful cause he looked just like a drowning man reaching up for air. "Fuck you. Fuck *you*, man," he says, pulling his arm back, but he ain't yelling now. When he saw how the blood was running down his arm he gets this sad old-man face on like he remembers something.

"Hey, Manny," I said, trying to be nice, but I still wouldn't get close to him.

He wasn't thinking about me then anyways. All of a sudden he wasn't a vato loco no more, now he had this far-off look on, standing by the broke window, the red coming down his arm, and when his mouth curled down soft I could see he was missing his boy bad.

"Can't have too much heart, right?" he says. "See, so I don't care." Manny touched his face real soft with his good hand, like it hurts, and when he started talking he kept getting softer and weaker, right in front of my own eyes. "Chico, but not no more, man. He was like my brother. Hermanos. You know what that means?" Manny looked at me then, his eyes slitting down, then shakes his head. "No, you don't cause you got some hard heart in you. Bitches don't know anyways. Don't know about vatos. *Compadres*. That means like blood. Better than blood. You *die* for your homeboys." His arm was one big red mess now and he was dripping on his new carpet, but he didn't make a move.

"Yah, right, Lucía? Coldest thing I ever seen." He was almost looking like he wants to laugh. "I tell you anyways. When I came here from Oaxaca with my mama I was like *nothing*. You wouldn't a given me one look. I wasn't nothing but some poor Mexican nobody. But not Chico. He was my man from the start. My right hand man. Cause we was the same. Both our families from *pobrecita* Oaxaca, nothing but hungry bellies and no work there, digging in the dirt for food and my papa beating down on me with that belt before he split. I was some wetback scooting down here over the border and running like a rabbit. Chico's the same story. That vato was like the blood from my own skin, and I never thought old Chico's gonna be the one doing me bad. I knew his *people*. His old mama down there on Edgeware living in that poor chicken shack. His brother Mauricio, little brown grade-school *vatito* that tagged behind since he could walk. But I took care. Took care of all of them. I said, They all get a piece, son. Your mama. Little brother. I look after your people. They get a piece of the Lobos. Cause he was like my own blood."

I stood there on the far wall, still keeping my mouth shut, only looking at him break down like an old car. Maybe a long time ago Manny's being weak like that would of made me feel something, like when he took me out by the beach and told me he loved me, opened up the ribbon on my dress like I was a birthday present. Not no more, though. I'd already learned my lesson about looking out for number one. So when I saw him there, touching his face and crying about how he lost his best boy, I only thought one thing. Almost over, homes. Almost over. You ain't gonna last too long.

But all I said was, "Come on, baby. Let me take a look at what you done." And when I walked over and picked up his hand, some dark red color spilled on my skin like a stain.

Manny wasn't looking too pretty after that night. He didn't want nobody to know, but anybody could see how old Chico there'd cut him bad. Right to the bone. So I knew that Manny wasn't gonna let this one go without a fight. No matter how soft a man gets, he don't smile at no slap in the face easy, and he don't take no broke heart easy neither. But that don't mean he thinks straight, does he? That's why when Manny finally got his balls up to give Chico his word, I made sure I was gonna be along for the ride.

About a week later, I headed out for Manny's to see how he was doing, and he was pulling out his driveway in one of his cherry cruisers. From the street I could see how he's all dressed up in tough-ass cholo clothes, black baggies, red shirt, like he wants you to know where he's from.

I waved my arm up so he sees me and stops. "Where you going, baby? Can I come?"

"No, I got things to do. *Business.*"

"You're gonna go see Chico, ain't you? Well, you know I better be there to help you out, honey." While I was talking I scooted over to the other side of the car and got in.

Manny was looking tired, like he hadn't been sleeping or eating, even though he's tricked out in them fancy clothes. "Get out," he says. "Get your ass out."

But I stayed put. I knew he wasn't strong enough to keep me from coming along. He needed me by then. "I won't say nothing, Manny. I just wanna make sure you're okay. It'll make *me* feel better, baby."

He breathed heavy and then starts driving through the streets over to Chico's house. Chico still lived over there on Edgeware on the other side of the Park, and we were heading down the same roads we used to kick around without even thinking twice.

"I guess we ain't welcome here no more, eh?" I say. I was looking out on the sidewalk and seeing some old neighborhood faces, the ladies walking home with their babies on their hips, the between-jobs veteranos smoking out on the porches, but the eastside Parkers, even the kiddies playing stickball on the street, they wasn't smiling back friendly at me like they did in the old days.

He gave me a razor look and I quieted back down. I knew Manny'd been hearing enough talk lately. After word got out that Chico stole from Manny, the Lobos was on fire to do some payback. Especially Beto. He'd started flapping his big mouth, trying to get back to being a right hand even though he was nothing but a third-rater after Mountainview. "Chico's gotta pay that price, right?" he'd said to Manny in front of the other vatos. Trying to face him. "That boy stole the whole load, not no little piece. We gotta stand tall, jefe. I do it for you." Beto had pulled out his Glock from his pants and starts playing with it like *el* Clint Eastwood. "BAM! BAM!" he yelled. "Like that." But Manny wasn't gonna let Beto have a say in clika business. "Hey, dog pound," Manny said, putting Beto back in his place. "Shut your sorry ass up, eh? There ain't nobody here who cares about what you got to say, so sit down."

Manny was still driving slow down the streets like he wasn't feeling none of that heat, and from the look on his face I can't tell how he's feeling inside. He wasn't saying one word. All I could hear was the sound of the car rolling east and my own heart beating, but I knew how to play that boy. I put my hand down on the seat, close by his thigh, and I stretched out long and easy so he could feel me there like a soft wind, pushing him.

He loosed his grip on the wheel then. "I know what people's saying," he tells me, keeping his eyes on the road. "Hey, you know? Fuck them. A vato's still got to have his *honor*. Cause we've been family. Gotta honor your brother by getting the story face to face like a man, can't bang him just cause you hear things on the street. And I don't wanna hear nothing different about it."

When we got to Chico's house, I walked behind Manny through the door and saw how Chico was set up like any other big head. There's his blaster stereo, a monster TV, some shiny silver weights rolling on the floor, clothes and off-the-truck shit piled everywhere. Chico's sitting in the middle of the room in this big old La-Z-Boy, and when he looks up at us he don't look surprised.

"Hey, ése," he says, staring at Manny. "You come looking for me?"

He wasn't grinning at Manny like he used to, like a right hand man. He looked cold. Like a stranger. His eyes all wide like flat blue glass, pale skin whiter than I remembered, and he's skinny with his bones sticking out of his face. Mouth a thin straight line. He spreads out his arms like wings and laughs. "Well here I am, baby!" You could see how he was spiked higher than a kite.

Manny stood there straight-backed, trying to make like it didn't hurt. He swallows. "Ése, you high?"

Chico bends his head back in his chair and closes his eyes, making some sick stony smile. "I'm flying, boss man."

"Offa what?"

"I got me some good carga. Mellow me out."

"Well you looking strung."

Chico opens up his eyes again, staring straight at Manny. "Yah, well, what you gonna do about it anyways. You gonna sic your bitch on me, Manuel el patrón?" he asks, laughing again.

"Chingado. You can't be stealing from the Lobos. Where you come from ése? You think you're C-4 now? That ain't nothing."

Chico rolls his head around, chest bumping up with his laughs, coughing up some, and it made me feel shamed just to watch.

"You ain't never been no Einstein, man," he says, then flicks his eyes over at me. "Always think you got it all figured out." Chico punches the air BAM, fast like Macho Camacho. "But you ain't figured out a thing, eh? Take a look, stupid. I'm one hundred percent C-4," he says, and boxes with them swifty hands again. I could see how he's got bruises and new C-4 taks on his arms. "I'm a man in my own town," he tells Manny. "Not hanging offa your ass my whole life."

There ain't nothing that hurts a man worse than that ugly truth. Manny hunched over like he just got hit, shrugging up his shoulders and gripping his hands tight, and right then I knew there wasn't gonna be no going back.

The room was too quiet. He wouldn't look at me and wouldn't say nothing more to Chico, but that vato wasn't fooling nobody. I could see how he'd been lying to himself. Manny didn't pay Chico no last visit cause of honor. Cause of that soft heart of his, maybe. But it didn't have nothing to do with pride.

"Let's go," I said, pulling on him, but his head was bent down and his hands felt icy cold, and it took me a couple minutes of tugging and teasing to get him to move.

I knew what was coming after that. Even though Manny looked weak in front of Chico, there ain't a cholo alive that can get shamed without biting back. He's got to show himself tough and bloody to his enemy else he can't call himself a man. But I should of known he'd come raining down on me too. Cause I saw it happen. I knew better than anybody where old Manny's weak is, right there under the ribs.

Days later I'm on Alvarado with my girls yelling out at the daddies driving by, when Manny and Paco pull up in that cruiser, right next to me by the curb. It was getting close to night, when the dark starts creeping up from the street and colors up the sky dusky, that twilight time when people get their meanest, and when I saw Manny glaring wicked at me from his car I knew there wasn't gonna be nothing but trouble.

"*Now* you get in," he says, and smiles.

That drive over to the eastside wasn't nothing like the last time. I sat in the back, watching the shaded houses slip past, and I started shaking cause they'd rolled down all the windows so the cold air comes rushing in and makes them more crazy. They looked crazy enough already. Manny was moving back and forth like a wild man behind the wheel, and when I peeked over the seat I saw how they had them bulges under their shirts and how Paco was holding thick steel chains in his hands.

"You jacked?" Manny's saying over to Paco, and I couldn't see a bit of sad or soft on him then, he had the black ice eyes of a hit man. "Órale, homes, cause we're gonna have us some fun!"

Paco wasn't looking like no warrior though. He was skinnybones and whitefaced by that time. We was calling him Ghost cause he looked so bad after la chota got him down, and from where I was sitting I could see how his neck looked thin enough to snap. But he still tried to play that game. "Qué Rifa, partner," he says, then pumps up his fist and grins. "I'm jacked way up, man!"

Manny turns his head back to me, and he don't look like no lover. "So, girl. You so hungry, right? Wanna be a player? Well you're gonna love it, baby. Just like you want. Gonna taste the big time tonight."

They wasn't hauling me to no big time, though. There ain't nothing as fucked up as a driveby. Men, they always think that having a gun makes them John Wayne. You ask any vato about his first job and he'll start maddogging you right away. Hey Hey fuck you, ése, they'll say. Vato here's got the FIRE. He'll tell you how he was Mr. Loco Sharpshooter, bringing down all his enemies with his itchy trigger finger. But ain't none of it like the movies.

When we got back to Chico's house I was squeezing up in the back seat, trying to keep out of the way. The moon was hanging over us, bright silver cracking open the black like a clean shot, and Chico's house was lit up warm yellow from the inside. I could make out his rubia head through his window, and I saw his hands smoothing down some fire-engine sheep, the old-timer kind that wears skin tights and lays it down easier than skipping school. Manny and Paco got out of the car and hid there for a minute under the dark, and all you could hear was their fast breathing and the freeway sounds.

"I made you, ése," Manny's saying, in this dry gravel voice, but from where I'm sitting I can't see him. I hear his clothes brushing together like he's twisting around, then the cold sound of metal clicking. "OK, Ghost man!" he barks out. "Let's fuck this boy here UP!"

Manny and Paco walk out to the front of the car and start pulling it all down. Their shots firecracked out in the night, and their arms was shaking like they're trying to hold on to a fucking bronco. Each time their bombs would go off they'd jerk back, but that didn't stop them from trying to slam all that lead into Chico. "BAM BAM!" Manny's yelling. "You the MAN, homes! Coming to get you, brother!" Paco's laughing next to Manny like he thinks he's Scarface, but he was squeezing weak on the trigger and wobbling cause his skinny legs can't hold him. Chico started screaming these high sounds from out his house, or maybe it was his sheep. Then he must of pulled his out too, cause I heard the slugs whizzing by like fast wind.

"Come here, pendejo! I kill you, mano a mano!" Manny yells back, cause a badass ain't supposed to back down no matter what. I bent down, my hands covering up my head, and my mouth and eyes wet and hot while I heard Manny keep reloading until there was nothing left but smoke and the sounds of bells. Chico ain't yelling no more, and his sheep's quiet too. The whole neighborhood's gone dead. Not a dog barking, not a baby crying, just the silver-shot moon overhead and the night air around us.

"Ghost man," I hear Manny say. "Qué rifa, eh? We show them old Bombers."

I didn't wanna see nothing then. I just wanted to keep curled up in that back seat with my eyes closed when Paco didn't say, Yah baby we showed them good, but I knew I couldn't hide out there forever. I peeked up and saw it. Old Ghost was there on the ground, shot messy in the neck and legs, busted out and bleeding from the gut, eyes rolled up white and mouth open. Black-red everywhere on that white shirt.

"Paquito man?" Manny's asking him, like he don't understand.

But I see it. Not breathing, man. Not breathing. I know what a dead man looks like, so what am I gonna do? Take a dead Mexican to Kaiser? I ain't gonna be playing with the chota. Paco'd been a real tight Lobo and I knew he'd saved my Star Girl from the street, but there ain't nothing now. Only meat on the ground where a boy used to be. A woman's got to know when to walk away, and I didn't take a minute to make my move. I took one look then crawled up to the front seat and revved the car, and when I looked straight at Manny through the windshield he ran into the car like he was trying to lose a red-horned devil that was chasing his tail.

Like I said, these men think they're gonna do the big macho driveby, but turns out we didn't get no one. We broke up Chico's house full of holes, but he must of hid under his bed like a girl, his head under his hands. He didn't even get a scratch. He's got them nine lives the same as a kitty cat, not like the Ghost. I only found out later that they didn't kill anybody when Chico and his C-4s start showing on our side of the park, so all the Lobos could see how Manny couldn't even do a little thing like put a bullet in a man's head.

Chico had been hiding out on the eastside, but he took the driveby as an invite. Next thing I knew Chico and his C-4s was trolling by our houses in their lowriders and sticking out their bug-eyed maddogging faces so that the grandmas start shaking in their shoes and the mamacitas tuck their babies into bed early. "Where's your boy?" C-4s would yell out to the Parkers, then laugh wicked when they ran away. Manny got real scarce then. He didn't wanna get killed in a payback, so he was spending his time hiding out in my place or kicking it at Chevy's, looking like a coward while Chico got bigger and stronger, scaring all of us on our own streets. "It'll cool down," Manny said one night after jumping up scared when he hears a car backfire down the road. His chest heaves up and he's shaking his head. "Oh, shit! This'll blow over, Lucía. You just wait." But from how he starts laughing too loud I know he's lying.

Cause of Manny Ghost got beat and then he got dead, and Manny wasn't even taking it like a man. The Lobos, though, they need to see their boss act brave. They needed to save face. I knew they'd cut the string soon enough, and that's when I started nibbling on little Beto's ear there, nice and juicy. Baby, you're gonna be the new patrón, I tell him. You're gonna be better for the Lobos than old tired Manny, he don't got the fire in him no more. We *need* you honey, I say. Beto drank in every word.

You think I'm a whore cause I switched over? Sure, Manny does. But if you wanna be a winner like me, you got to survive. I suck off him or him, no big difference. What are they gonna do for *me*? That's the question you got to ask. What can I make him do for me?

All you people think you know all the answers. But you're just blind. You don't know nothing about it.

I was born in Tecate. It's a poor cow town where you have to eat beans and bread for dinner every single night and we didn't even have no cows, just miles of short gold-brown grass everywhere you looked, four walls and two beds, the toilet's outside and the water's brown and muddy, but we learned to drink it all right. Me and Mami and Papi dreamed about the States all the time. We would do anything to be like *los Americanos*. So we paid all our money to a coyote and he zoomed us over nice and quick. I was just a baby girl then but I still remember, the night was black and Mami held me up in her arms and we ran fast, just like he told us to. It was the getting over part that was easiest, though. You think it's gonna be all sunshine when you get to pretty California, right? California's where you got your palm trees and your stucco houses, your flowers and white fences. But after a while you have to look around and see the shit. Just cause you're standing in sunny California it don't mean a thing. Run away from Mexico? You can't. Mexico's right here.

My mami and papi wasn't like no *Happy Days*. We rented this one room and washed the gabacho houses and pulled the weeds, all the time dreaming of that green card. Well, there ain't no green cards I ever saw, right? The only good green is cash. Those border brothers promised that we'd become fancy Americans but they just lie and lie. Nothing's easier than stealing from some stupid illegal.

And one day there's no more money. The end of the month starts speeding up to you on greased wheels but a body's got to pay the rent just the same. Around here, that's the man's job.

My papi used to be a proud macho. He was tall and light-skinned and had the jade green eyes like me. A straight-backed man. But when a father can't bring in enough for his family, it's like a curse. It shames him, and any time a man feels a pinch it'll be the woman who pays the price.

You've seen women get beat by their men. A girl gets out of line and the boy slaps her one. But it was different when my papi started coming home full of piss and fire like a monster cause he can't get work as a janitor, cause he can't be no house-painter. "Hey, Mexican," the gabachos said then, "Gotta speak some ENGLISH." And when he can find some job, scrubbing shit from gas station toilets or picking dates down in Palm Springs, he's only making pennies. I remember feeling hungry in that shack we was living in, seeing the scared and sour look on his face. We all knew it was earthquake weather. And finally it hit.

Mami never was no beauty queen, no Rita Moreno. She got fat fast after having me, wearing her big dresses and her polyester pants, garage-sale shoes. And she got soft inside, too. She kept loving her man like he was God, even when he cuts up her face with his fists. "*Fea!*" he screamed at her, and she's crying. "Vieja! What do I need with an ugly bitch like you? You killing me!" he's yelling, his pretty face red colored and the veins coming out of his neck, his eyes bloodshot from drinking tequila, and the strong smell of some puta coming off him so that even I know what's up.

See, take a hard look at me. You see any bruises? You see any shitty diamond ring? No. I don't need no one. This chica knows qué pasa. No man touches me like that now. My papi drank himself blind and then he'd come home, open up the door and stare us down. We knew it would hurt. Every Friday night, after he spends his sorry-ass week begging the gabachos to scrub out their toilets and trying to learn the language by watching *Columbo* and the *Mary Tyler Moore Show*, he'd show up from the bar with his belly full and his fists ready for a fight. "How you doing, baby?" Mami asked him, but she can tell what it was. She goes into the kitchen and tries to fix him up some food to take the edge off the booze, but it ain't no use.

He goes over to the radio, turns it on and plays some ranchera loud so that those stinking happy voices fill up the whole room, singing Ay Ay Ay! and making me crazy. He leans back his head on the wall and closes his eyes. But you can see his twitchy hands, itchy fingers moving and that's bad news.

A woman can't take no punch like a man. After a while he'd wake up from his little drunkie sleep crackpot mad and let her have it. "Gotta have our talk, chula," I remember him saying. "*Vamos a hablar*." He slammed down on my mami like she was a punching bag and he's Roberto Duran, giving her an uppercut so that she's bleeding from the mouth, and he wouldn't stop for Dios or the devil. She got broke up so that she can't even open up her eyes and I can't breathe there in the corner, where I stayed quiet and learned my lesson. Even then I was thinking, Mami, you're just a loser. Me, I ain't never gonna be like that.

The thing with these men is that you don't win a prize if you just hang on and take it. Mami wasn't winning no lottery with Papi there, you know what I'm saying? An hombre won't stick around for some fat lady and a girl, with no son in sight. No man can put up with that. So they leave. They pick up and go, take some shirts and cigarettes and check their wallet for money and then they're gone. *Adios*, bitch. Papi just packed up and ran off one day, like a sailor who jumps ship and swims back to dry land.

That's fine, eh? Did this girl here a favor.

But I remember back then I thought we was all dead without old Papi. My mami was always a woman who looked to her man. "*Todo lo que tu quieras*," she used to tell him, and then make this sweetie pie face. Whatever he says, OK, that's what we do.

But a dick don't give you no brains, right? It don't give you a heart neither. He knocked her up with me when she was just fourteen years old, when she was only some dirty little bird from Tecate. She couldn't speak no English but she still ran over here with him, with me on her hip. From her I learned that trust is a woman's worst enemy. It keeps her in the dark. After he split she spun around the house, pulled on her hair, sang old Mexican love songs, and some nights she'd grip me tight by the arm and stare into my eyes. The only thing that would cool the woman down was wine.

Even a drunk still needs to make a living. You might say, Hey, Mexicans clean houses. You can make good money there under the table, tax free. But my mami wasn't cut out to be no cleaner lady. She couldn't even wipe up her own floor. Can't write her name, neither. Can't add two and two. She's dumbed down with drink and too scared of immigration to ask a gabacho for work. We was illegals, so what? "Illegal" don't mean nothing but a fucked-up life. Baby gets sick? Don't got no food? Hard to get those food stamps, man. Can't find a job? Who are you gonna talk to? Nobody. They always ask you for the papers and you're scared out of your head Mr. INS will come and get you. Well, check me out, Mr. INS. Get real close. Don't like what you see, eh?

So. Mami started making money the old-fashioned way. When a lady looks around and sees that end-of-the-month train flying up to her, she'll do what it takes. Scratch a hungry woman and you'll find a whore, it's that simple. Mami got set up with her little sugar daddies, these lowdown vatos with pencil mustaches and dirty hands who smelled like grease, like pigs. Every one of them was the same as the rest. I remember their names: Carlos, José, Enrique, Fernando. Some had that slicked-back hair and dressed in these suits that was shiny in the asses and elbows, but they still swaggered around like they were Mr. Suave. "Hey, little chica," they might say to me before, then chuck me under the chin. The others wore these stained white t-shirts, busboy pants. Those ones just tapped their foot when they saw me, and she'd have to rush me out. But either way, them boys don't care about nothing but getting off. Paid her ten dollars for a fast twelve minutes. Mami gave me my little dollies, and I'm waiting out there in the hall, singing some song. Humming Mmmmmm, mmmmmm and looking at the ceiling. Smelling that grease and the whiskey and hearing the bad noises from inside.

Oye, ain't no big thing. If a woman wants to whore, that's her call. But that's history for me. This is today, and you see I'm nothing but a tough Lobo grouper now. I'm the one who's calling the *shots*.

I wasn't never like Mami. I caught the English quick. Went to school up to the seventh grade, I ain't no dummy. And I watched the TV, listened to the white people talking, did my ABCs and read them books. Did my little maths. This chica was always thinking of the good life. I always had my eye on the big time.

So Manny can think I'm that puta. He don't know what it means. I know there ain't no whore in me. I work it hard for la number one.

OK. If a chica round here wants to get her business done, she'd better get a man. It's a cheap little rule but I learned that thing early. If you don't got a mister behind you, no one will listen to a word you've got to say.

When I fished around I saw that the only good man for me was Beto with that baby scar on his mouth. He was thick and tough like a block, and he didn't bend out there on Mountainview. He reminded me of Manny in the old days. Beto was on the outside too. He used to be high up in the Lobos, but after he got slammed out by Manny he was a third-rate gangster. And third-raters are supposed to scrape and jump and keep quiet till they're spoken to, which made an old right hand like Beto burn.

I'd heard how he was pushing things at the Lobo meetings, piping up when he's supposed to keep his mouth shut, laughing too loud when nothing's funny. I could use that. A man who falls from grace gets a little crazy, but he gets stronger too.

I started to dog him, like he's the one I wanna be sexing now. You know he believed I loved him. They all think they're such don juans. I was making doe eyes and whispering in his ear like a honeydripper. "Beto, you're the special man, ése," I said. "That Manny's getting soft, right? He's a loser, honey, and the Lobos need a leader now. They need a tough-guy patrón just like you."

He kept quiet while I pawed him, but he smiled a little under his scar. I knew I could sweet-talk him into anything. There was still Cecilia, but that got cleared up quick enough. She's a fat, wet-eyed weakling who can't even make no baby. Beto didn't have to think too hard about it. He knew I was *la bamba*. So a couple of weeks after Manny blows that hit on Chico I paid old Betito there my visit. I was fancied up in my best pink skirt, the one they like grabbing under, and my hair was teased high, my lips as red and glossy as ripe cherries.

I go over to his house and he don't even act surprised. "Hey Beto," I said when he opens the door. "Wanna feel good, sugar? I can do it." He just smiled, like he knew all the time.

Like I said, men are too easy. I got that boy thinking he's the patrón so fast, he was eating out of my hand like a bird. I saddled up and smoothed him down with feather touches, and then made him get all tight and bursting by pushing him till he got to that edge and teased it with my tongue. But I didn't stop talking the whole time. "You're gonna be that jefe, honey. I see it in you. You've got it in your eyes. You're made to be the boss. So we're gonna get rid of old soft Manny, right?"

"Yah," he answers, moving up. He's grinning like he thinks he's already some king.

* * *

When the Lobos had their next meeting, I start making my move. It was the perfect time, cause all the right hands would be there. Before every meeting they all drive up to Ross Street in their ranflas, revving loud and showing off. Outside the house it looks like a lowrider show. There's blue bombas parked by the curb, red Monte Carlos, tricked out Bel Air cruisers. They've got Echo Parker paint jobs, flames on the hood or the pretty face of the driver's ruca on the door, fuzzy dashes and chrome girls on the bumpers, big shiny stereos in the trunks. The gangsters swagger around each other's cars, whistling, Eh, ése, looking good! That's some candy, vato! like backslapping salesmen before they head inside to Manny's living room.

They bring their sheep too, and the chicas hang out in Manny's kitchen, try to look sexy for the men. They squeeze into their short red dresses and spray out their hair, and walk sway-backed like showgirls. That day all of the rucas was there, shimmying and cooking up tamales so the kitchen got crowded and hot with the air full of spice and girl noise. I could see Cecilia, her bent head back by the oven, and I ducked so that I didn't have to say qué pasa. Then I catch Star Girl and Chique standing around in their short skirts, but I smiled cause I knew they was my locas.

"Hey hey, *reina*!" Chique says, running up to me before the meeting starts. She's laughing and patting me on the shoulder, but then Star Girl comes up, slow and sick looking with this white face that's pale but not moon colored. Girl's as white as chalk now. And her hair's turning black because she wasn't dyeing it no more.

"You sorry cause of Ghost?" I ask her. Seeing her bad off like that pulled my strings some cause she had my soft spot. But I knew I couldn't show it.

Girl did me proud then. She gives me her mean eyes and crunches up her mouth. "I'm OK, ésa. Getting through fine."

Chique shakes her head. "Ain't so, Lucía. Girl here's doing bad."

"Well, stiff up, chica. I'll get you some payback."

Star Girl almost laughs, but I could tell she was hurting. "I know you ain't crying too hard for my Paco. But you got some bad look on, Lucía. You gonna pull some down?"

I just gave her a pinch. "Maybe," I said.

The sheep are supposed to stay put during the meeting. No woman's allowed to go into the Big Room, where all the boys are. "You stay in the kitchen," the homeboys say. "We're having a Talk." But not this chica. Those days were over. I was dressed just like a gangster in my hard-assed jeans and red bandanna, and I walked right into that Big Room like I belong.

The Lobos were sitting down on the floor or the couch, smoking weed and Camels and the air's smoky, like a gambler's hideout. Manny's sitting on his chair wearing his brown fedora with the feather, and from the way he's talking loose and easy I can tell he don't know that his days are numbered.

I sit in the back and Manny's giving his talk, going, "We need some more cuetes, cause C-4's giving us that bad heat. Gotta do a BIG hit, little éses, eh? Show 'em qué rifa!" He punches his hand in the air.

One pipsqueak goes, "Órale, sí!" but most of the other boys stay good and quiet. Manny keeps talking, too dumb to know what's up.

"Who's the vato loco? Let's take us out some Bombers, homies!" Manny's pushing, but there's no volunteers. Everybody's keeping their eyes to the floor.

Beto's sitting by the wall and when I walk in he looks back at me. His skin is pulled tight over his cheeks, his ears are flaming red, but I give him my little smile and he stands up tall. He clears his throat, getting ready for the fight.

"Homes, forget it. You bringing us *down*," he says, mad-dogging Manny by clipping out his jaw, and his voice boomed up like a preacher's. All the Lobos started staring at him beady-eyed. "Only reason we gotta do some hit is cause you FUCKED that Chico thing UP. Right?" He looks around, making a hard mouth. "And what, man? Chavala! You leaving old Ghost on the road like he's garbage, what's that shit?"

You could hear the vatos rumbling, talking low and excited. Some vato says, "Shut up," but then I see some of them nodding their heads.

Manny eyeballs him serious. "Careful, little man. You gonna bleed if you don't quit it."

That's when Chevy checks me out sitting in the back. "Jefe, what's she doing here, man? No bitches in the Big Room, ése!"

Manny sees me there and he gets some cold look on him. He thinks he knows something.

"Fuck you! I ain't no bitch!"

"Manny!" some other boy hollers. "Get that sheep outta here!"

"Shut the FUCK up! Shut up!" Manny starts yelling, jerking up like he's being pulled by wires, and it almost makes me laugh out loud. You can tell he don't know what to do.

Beto goes on. "Lookit. He's no jefe! Manny's gone weak, like a gabacho. What the C-4s saying, eh? You hear it. Say he's gone soft and stupid!" He grabbed his balls, reminds me of a howler monkey in the zoo. "The Lobos need a patrón who's still got his *cajones*, right?" Beto looks at me again but I keep my face careful, wanna see how it turns out.

"Órale," Chevy says, trying to cool things off. "Beto, sit your ass down, man."

Manny didn't need to hear no more, though. He was sore eared and sharp toothed already.

"De dónde eres, ése?" he growls. His eyes thin down to black arrowheads and his fists clench together like claws, cause he still loves being in the ring.

But Beto's so fired up he can't see how old Manny's out for blood. "*De aquí*, homes!" he says, gives his crowd a big grin, tries to eyeball me again. "Not a sorry-assed motherfucker like you, all right?" I can tell he's feeling too strong. He should be careful when he's messing with a fighter, even if he does look like a has-been.

Manny rushes him then, his head down like a bull's, his fists cocked up and swinging like hammers. His first shot's to the gut and then he hooks one up to the face and lands it clean on the nose so the bone breaks, and then you start seeing the blood, the red mess dripping down Beto's mouth and smearing up his cheek like war paint.

The vatos all scattered from the middle and made a circle, some of them cheering for Beto, some for Manny. "Go LOCO!" Chevy's screaming, I don't know for who. "Give it to him hard, homes! You can do it!" The rest of them was hollering that way too, jumping up their hands and moving their heads like they're ducking punches themselves, and the sheep all run out of the kitchen to watch the show. Norma and Brenda, these two dark-skinned ugly-duck cherry-pickers who had their thing for Beto, they start crying but you could see the loca in their mouths, how their lips stretch out so they look like they're grinning. Panchita and Frida, these other sheep who belonged to some taggers, start hooting like old whores, screaming for more blood. "Oye, give it to him good!" Wanda, this gabacha-looking Jalisco redhead yells, her chi-chis coming up in her tight black halter top when she's bouncing like a cheerleader.

And Cecilia, well shit. That girl comes running out of the kitchen fast when she hears the noises, and when she sees what it is she tries to jump her fat self right in it. It looked plain stupid, her wearing some old maternity dress cause she's still so big, trying to fly like Superman or something. A couple vatos caught her instead, held her down while she's crying and flapping her wings so that the men could keep fighting. Ceci didn't call for no one, didn't say no boy's name, but I knew what she was doing. She was trying to keep her lover brother safe.

I held it together, keeping quiet in the back, standing by my chicas Star Girl and Chique with my mouth shut. All I wanted to know was who was gonna win. Maybe it's Beto, and I'd gambled right after all. He was standing straight up just like when he wouldn't bend on the street, but this time he wasn't just taking hits, he was coming out of the blocks like lightning. Even though Manny had the upper hand, bigger like he was and a better fighter, Beto didn't back down an inch. He shoves up his head and chest and growls, "You're finished, chavala!" before going right back into the thick and gripping him in this bear-hug clinch, grabbing Manny by the head, scratching up his face, and then doing this loco thing I ain't never seen before. He bends down and starts biting Manny like a pit bull. Square old Beto there, looking just like a kid next to taller Manny, chomping down on his face and trying to tear it off. It was ugly, those white teeth and Manny's brown skin pulling and the blood coming out. I didn't wanna watch, but I couldn't take away my eyes there, neither. They was fighting cause I wanted it. Made me feel like the boss seeing my work in action, right? Even if they didn't know it, them two was fighting over me.

Manny tears away from Beto and you could hear the sound of things ripping, probably his shirt but to me it sounded like skin, and his eyes were just slits. A woman's scream shoots from his mouth and the blood's coming down his cheek, out the bite mark, and I knew then that he's gonna bring out his blade and one of them boys could die.

"Oh you gonna hurt, ése!" Manny says, and then he pulls his long knife out, the one he always had stashed in his back pocket. He starts switching that knife back and forth in the air and stabbing it at Beto Zorro style. "Gonna have a good time cutting you up, boy," Manny laughs, and I saw him flick his bad eyes my way. I almost smiled there by the wall cause he was my old man again, the kind that don't blink. Chique's fat face bends down to me, "Boy there looks good, eh?" but I didn't say nothing.

Beto had a scared look on now, his lip hanging down and his nose smashed looking, his big eyes puffing already. He knew that he had to pull a pretty fast card trick to get out of this one, but for a minute all that vato could do was stare at that shiny knife snatching around in the air like it was a silver snake. But when Norma there starts crying and Beto hears her choking up like a grandma, he comes around.

Norma's screaming, "No, Manny, *please*!" and everybody's gone as crazy as a shithouse rat with the boys cheering and the sheep bawling and laughing, and Beto slams right for Manny, like he's so macho he don't even care some knife's in his way. Both boys fell over, holding on like they was hugging each other, gonna kiss or something, and they rolled around funny looking on the floor.

Everybody's thinking, Where's the blade, man? Who gets it? But you can't tell. They're just pounding on each other's heads with fists, rolling and making grunts, and I wanted to know who the patrón was so bad that I had to close my eyes for a minute and just listen to them fighting, sounded the same as when a butcher breaks up his meat. But when they don't stop, when one boy don't bend over dead right away, we knew. Manny dropped the knife.

Beto kicks away quick so he can find the switch and stick it in Manny before he's the one that gets dead, and he's almost blind there running his hands down on the floor. Manny's eyes are needle sharp. He scrambles over the carpet and sees the silver, there's one swipe up and then he brings it down so fast you hear his arm rip through the air.

I wondered later, Why didn't Manny there just do him in? A Lobo kills his enemy, right? It's the clika way. I might of changed my mind about him if he'd just shown me he could be strong like I need. But that's why he's a bum. He can't see nothing through. Silvas could beat a vato bloody, but he didn't have the killing thing in him, no matter how tough he looks, how hard his eyes can get.

He stuck old Beto, but he didn't go for the heart or the throat. He brought that knife down right on Beto's right hand, and stuck it in so that it cut right through and split the wood floor. There's blood on his face and on Beto's face, and the bright red coming hard from Beto's broke hand, squirting up around the blade. Then those boys sat back for a minute and stared at Beto's hand, like they don't believe it themselves. It was bleeding ugly like a killed pig. All the vatos in the circle let out a big breath, Whooosh! but some of the sheep got tight lips, disappointed looking. "Fucking punks," I hear Wanda say. "We think we got some tough machos but then lookit this."

So I still didn't know. Even after all that I still couldn't be sure who's gonna be the Lobo boss. Manny was fighting like a devil for a minute but those coward moves made him look weak. And what's worse, there's Beto pinned on the floor looking like a fool.

The meeting was over. Boys was shuffling their feet and shaking their heads, sheep kept making these thin sour faces and curling up their lips. "Weak, eh?" I heard one of them say, and another giggled, and then they all walked out the door. Leaving me to do the dirty work. I moved up slow to my two men with my lips stitched tight, my hair crackling. I wanted them to be more scared of me than any switchblade. I showed them a stony face, blank eyes, and I didn't say a word. I just reached down and pulled that knife out the wood, out his hand, it made this slip sound and a cracking noise. Beto's biting his lips so that he don't cry, but he blubbered like a newborn anyways. He was all broke up, with a red baby face and red mouth and pink eyes. I shouldn't blame him. It had to hurt. But I tell you, I thought those two was the sorriest men I ever laid these eyes on. Manny showed his weak colors by not finishing the job. And seeing Beto pinned down? It made me shamed.

The Lobos had their hard times after that. You couldn't tell who was el jefe with both of them boys looking at me like starved kittens. And we was a weak target for the C-4s. Chico got wind that the Lobos didn't have a *número uno*, and then him and his locos wasn't just maddogging grandmas on our streets no more. No. They started shooting at us right and left. Drivebys got real regular in these parts, Bombers spraying bullets at vatos walking down the street, or plugging into our houses in the middle of the night. Gangsters can't always shoot good, though. They'd hit almost more grandmas and babies than anything else, but they did catch a couple of Lobos. Chevy got tagged in the shoulder, but he was lucky. Other locos got dead. Little Rubén with the lowriding baggies and Hoyo, this tagger who had himself an ugly wife and a fat screaming baby, them boys was mowed down in the middle of the road. And this other vato named Smack got it right in the head. Wicked looking, that thing. Smack's dead face got blue and purple and puffy like a blowfish. So anytime you'd see some Mexican wearing yellow, you knew it was trouble.

The C-4s, they're real different from us Lobos. For one thing, the Lobos wear good colors: midnight black and blood red. Fuerte! Chico had his boys wearing yellow, like they're a bunch of lemons or something. Yellow t-shirts, yellow baggies, those fools looked like girls wearing Sunday school dresses, and we had ourselves a good laugh over that. "Hey, LIMÓN MARICÓN!"

we'd scream if we saw a Bomber driving around the Park in them fruit colors. That is, we'd laugh if we was packing. By then, you could see how everybody'd started carrying some. It didn't matter if you were a right hand or third-rater, all the vatos had a bulge under their shirts. Most of the time the neighborhood was quiet, and the homeboys would swagger up and down the street like guard dogs. But if they saw any flash of yellow they'd reach down and pull out their piece just in case.

I got my girls armed up good. We'd been carrying those tin-can specials that weighed light in your hand. After the battles started, I wanted something heavy and thick, a glossy black killer that would set a man's knees to shaking if he looked down the barrel. And I knew just where to go. We had this gun man, named Ramón. He was an old-style veterano with slicked black greaser hair and kicking knife taks, a dangerous spark in his eye. All the chicas thought he was so fine. He could pick up shiny foreign jobs off the street for cheap from the 4th Streeters, these wicked East L.A. homeboys who'd made their name by knocking over gun shops in Tarzana and Eagle Rock. You know *that's* some tough job, cause them N.R.A. people! Órale Pancho! They're whitefolk ex-cops with mustaches and no money, and they just sit in their little stores and stare at their fancy guns, waiting for a chance to blow off some homie's head.

"Hey, chica," Ramón says when he sees me walking up. Me and Chique and Star Girl drove over to his house this one day, so I could buy us all some presents like Santa Claus. We're in his bedroom and there's some beautiful stock on his bed, these brand-new 17's with double action and a stash of hollow-points. Ramón's shaking his head. "Women with guns. Guess I've seen just about everything now. But money's green, right? And I hear you all got some problems."

Chique's looking at him like he's a mambo king, fluttering her eyelashes and making kissy lips. But Star Girl was more like me these days, after Ghost bought it. She didn't care about men no more, she'd found out quick you can't get paid good that way. Girl kept her eyes on the gun and had a hard stone mouth on.

"Yah. It's gonna blow over soon," I tell him, then look over and start laughing at my homegirl. "SSSht! Chique, you gonna throw down old Ramón right now?" I ask her.

She squirrels up her face and darts out her pink tongue. "Don't play with me, Lucía!" she barks, blushing till she's rose colored.

"Cholas!" Ramón starts flexing a little. "'Nuf of this loco to go around, you know what I'm saying?"

We're all laughing, but then I see Star Girl's not playing. She's eyeing them guns serious. Girl pointed to the bed, picking out her piece. "I want *este*," she tells me. "*That* one."

When I saw her like that, I felt them strings pull again. I wouldn't show nothing, but I was loving her like she was my own sister.

"Give us three, homes," I told him. "These chicas are gonna get us some style!"

When we got outside I put them heavy things in my girls' hands. Our fingers fumbled around their clicks and triggers, our arms weighed down like we carried a block of gold. But they made us feel strong. Muscled. Star Girl was gripping hard on the gun and heaving it up, like she wants to shoot something then and there. I laid my hand on her arm and she felt as hot as a torch. "You're looking fresh, loca," I said. She cracked me her smile.

I bought those guns cause I wanted us to be like Dirty Harry. And feeling a piece solid in my pocket or seeing it peek out black and gleamy from my panty drawer made me feel like

a Pro. I never did without a real gun again. But it wasn't all just
for show off. The war around here got so rough you had to pack
a little protection.

We lost some good men to the C-4s. And first, hey. Let
them vatos get killed, right? Rook and Laffey buy it, but that don't
sting me. Then Chevy loses his arm, after getting tagged it just hung
there loose by his side, so he couldn't be a buzzhead warrior
no more, couldn't be no ladykiller. I'm thinking, So what? And then
some little homies like I said, Rubén, Smack, and Hoyo. But after
a while even I get itchy some. It wasn't like only deadweights
was getting killed. Some of my favorite boys got taken out.

Smoke, he was one fine man. He used to do deals in the
Valley, blowing down there in his bomba, bringing me back some
good money. Usually he did deals with Mexicans, just like I
wanted. "*Quieres, vato? Lo tengo bueno, ése,*" he'd sing to the
Valley homeboys and they bought up all the cheapie bags. But
sometimes he got lucky with the rich Anglos too. "You wanna
little sniff, son?" he'd ask them out on Ventura, and you know
all them gabacho boys was trying to snag them some tasty Colombian. Smoke was so good he never got caught, so I said to
Manny, Go ahead, let him deal white. And he never stole from
me, neither. He showed respect. "Hey, jefa," he used to say to
me, then grin a little. Smoke knew where the shit was at.

Boys like that was getting killed in our war with the
C-4s. Smoke got surprised one day when he's walking in his door
and two dirty Bombers blowed him in the back coward style. Then
this other vato, Largo, a tricky-headed brainiac who could squeeze
top dollar from a bag of low-grade talcum, he died a week later.
The Bombers did him driveby, never showing their chingado faces,
and poor old Largo caught one in the heart while watching the
TV. His old lady found him looking like a mess the next day, I
heard she cried herself crazy. I got the shivers myself. Like I'm
telling you, war don't do nothing but cost me plenty.

The Bombers lost some blood too. The Lobos was heading down to the eastside night and day on missions, but they could get sloppy without a leader. One Sunday afternoon they caught this middleman called Pedrito while he was playing a quick game of craps in the gutter, and a stray zig-zag took out a fifth grader along with him. And I heard we almost got one of Chico's right hands, a homeboy named Marco, but the driveby bullets only plugged up his legs and his left hand and the other birdies wound up killing a regular joe who was standing too close. I know what really was hurting that Chico, though. A couple of Bombers sheep caught it too, and there's nothing worse to a man than knowing he can't keep his women safe. We used to have a rule down here that you leave the girls and babies alone, and keep the war between the men folk. I'm liking that, eh? Let them fools do the dying. But cause Manny can't keep his vatos in line, there's no rules no more. Lobos started shooting down Chico's boys even when the weaklings was around. Or even worse, some Lobos was trying to bust up C-4 sheep on purpose, just cause they was easy marks.

I'll admit this. In the middle of the war I'd started to get scared and fuzzy brained. And it ain't cause I'd grown misty eyed. It's cause the sky was pitched dark and I couldn't tell which way was up or down. And that don't suit me. I'm not a woman who likes the sea, with its shifty tide and secret storms. I like dry land, mountains and rock. Something you can grip on to, something you can hold. But I'll tell you when I knew I was gonna be *la grandota*, the big boss. There was this one day when somebody finally threw me a line.

When you're losing, a *guerra*'s no good. It hurts you worse than most anything. You're not making money with all the rebels running around crazy and getting killed. You can't get no deals done. Chico knows that, me too. He's a red-eyed junkie, slowed down on carga one day, the other you see him with his white speedie face, doing *blancas* trying to keep himself together. He was popped bad. But he knows the same as me that fighting blind only leaves you with two losers.

It was Sunday night, me alone in bed sleeping and it's Chico who's pounding down my door. He must of been watching me, right? There's no other way he's gonna know I'm not with somebody. "Lucía?" I hear him saying out in the hall, knocking hard and making me jump clear out of my bed. "Lucía! Come on, girl, it's Chico. I'm here to have us a *talk*."

I didn't know what that boy was up to at first. "Get out of here, Chico!" I start yelling. "Don't make no trouble for me!"

"No, I'm straight up," he says through the door. "We're gonna talk straight up."

I pulled out my cuete from the panty drawer and gripped it tight, with the safety off. He wants to take out Manny's sheep? He's here to pay some back? But he had his strong voice, and there's that Dirty Harry I got in me. I figured I'd take the chance.

"What?" I'm asking him through the door crack, eyeballing him hard like I think I'm the Man.

Chico's standing tall out there, but he's got empty hands. He opens them up so I can see. "You know you wanna talk to me, chica," he says. Laughs some. "Órale, I hear there ain't no other Lobo who's got it together."

So I let him in cause he was sweet-talking me like that. It's the middle of the night, and I was feeling loca high cause the main C-4 boss man comes looking to *me*.

I point him, Sit down. And I was easing back in my chair nice and slow. I check him out then, Mr. Diablo in my living room, and I'm liking what I see. Chico wasn't speeding hard, but he looked like he'd taken some bad hits. He's got an old thin-skinned face on his gabacho-looking self already, and he was what, twenty? Nothing fresh going on there. Still, he had them tough eyes and dirt voice and I couldn't help but think, Oh, chica, you're hitting the big time now, girl.

"Say what you want, ése," I tell him.

"I know it ain't working good," he says, settling in, and I can see his rubia hair pushed back with that grease. "I want old Manny there dead, right? But all I got is funerals on my hands. So, Manny boy wants to talk? We can talk, OK. Boy there wants to jump down? I see him face to face like a MAN. But this shit, locos coming into my hood, and us shooting down into the Parkers, it ain't getting me ahead. I want it settled, Lucía. One way. We fight, we talk, either. And I know you don't got no primero no more. Silvas can't get his shit on, hiding from me, and I can't find him nowheres. So I'm asking you, linda. What you say?"

Yah, I heard him. Manny was still giving Chico the slip like a yellow belly. Everybody could see he'd lost his heart. So Chico's asking me, and I feel that so good. *Caliente*! *I* was the Lobo they're looking for, *I* was gonna give the go-ahead.

I looked at him straight same as any hombre would, and my heart beat in my chest like a drum roll. I didn't have to think about it for more than a split second. "All right, Chico," I tell him. "I'll settle this."

We had a heat wave that week. The air was thick with it, spun in waves from off the street. Sweat dripped from our faces, our shirts stuck to our backs, and nothing but ice would take off the burn. In weather like that, there ain't no rules. The sun stays stubborn in the middle of the sky, women cheat, men grit their teeth and spit flame at a wrong word. It was the perfect time for a *rumbla*.

I got the Lobos to meet with the C-4s in the park. "You got to stand up to Chico, right?" I tell Manny. "Or else all your vatos are gonna think you're weak." You know he had to say yes, his insides quivering like jelly but his outsides staying cool as winter just to save face. I was calling on Beto, too. "This is your time, baby," I told him. "Don't you wanna prove it to me?" His hand was getting better some, and he still had fire in his belly. "Yah, Lucía," he says, trying to make a fist so I can see.

When I spread the news that the C-4s wanna get it on with us, all the Lobos came running. "Them Bombers are giving us our call, éses, those vatos wanna have it *down*," I tell them, making my way around the neighborhood and chatting up every badass I see on the street. All the Lobos was just burning for their piece of action. They pulled their guns and their chains, knives, and screwdrivers, brave-talking each other into a rage. Chico man says he wants to talk? Lobos are gonna knock that Chico and his boys out the *door*. I just grinned at them and rocked back on my feet.

Check it out. We was like an army there. We picked a hundred-degree Saturday night, and all them Lobos strutted and maddogged through the streets down to the park, punching up their fists and hollering out to each other, "Órale, HOMES!" so they get fired up. "QUÉ RIFA!" The sheep came too, dressed up like it's a party in their little skirts and hooker faces. Those chicas love to see a tough-man brawl. It makes them feel proud, helps them think they're doing their thing for a reason.

It was a fighting hour. Echo Park's covered in this watered grass, you can smell it thick and green in that hot night air, and it's got these trees that look like blue-ink monsters under the moon with them spindly branches reaching out. There's a lake in the middle, and you see the shapes of the trees in the water and the gleam of the moon. It's got a few tall lamps that make this ghosty light in patches. Me and the sheep was sitting on the park benches to the side, just far away enough from the clearing so we feel safe. "Oh, chiquita, this girl's wanting to see them vatos down it sweet!" I'm hearing a sheep bawling behind me. "Oye, that's right on," this other one answers, maybe Wanda with her big mouth. Chique and Star Girl find me then, and we huddled up together on our bench quiet, but twitchy faced too, like some hungry men get when they're wanting their dinner.

I'm watching it. I saw the Lobos scramble their spider selves over there on the grass, walking fast and tough, getting into this circle. In the shadows there, they was looking like a pack of lions getting ready for the kill, with their eyes glinty under the lights, their dark skin shining, the push of their guns showing under their shirts. In that crowd, it looked like Manny and Beto was bumping shoulders and tussling over who was gonna be in front and meet the C-4s first. Beto was swinging his little boxer fists, trying to look strong. Manny was maddogging already by pushing out his big-man chest Beto's way.

Well, they'd better be feeling fuerte. Cause the Lobos was about to fight a wild-eyed pack of yellow dogs.

"Ay, PANCHO! Ven aqui, ÉSE!" Sitting there on my bench my ears picked that up, some boy yelling far away.

You could hear the C-4 locos before you saw any. They was meeting us from the other side of the park, and you couldn't make out any of them yet cause of the trees and all that dark but they was making their war noise so that we'd start shaking. They howled like coyotes who'd just taken down a deer, and the sound makes me clench and twist around like I've got half a mind to turn tail and run. But I wouldn't and my Lobos wouldn't neither. We stayed brave. If you call on a homeboy, he's gotta stick it right up, and a woman like me should do the same. "Boys gonna show them Bombers," Wanda yells over to me, but she wasn't smiling. There was something about them C-4s, the way they was going on, screaming like that. Even though I wouldn't move, it gave me the chills.

They spilled out of the trees then and covered the grass, and even though it was blue dark they looked bright and too many. Chico had done good. He was born to be a boss man, he must of been, cause in a quarter of the time he'd grouped as many vatos as Manny. Maybe more. You should of seen all them eastsiders, they was in that yellow color but it don't look so weak no more. It looked like fire instead, like the sun coming down on you hot and boiling. C-4 locos was piling up behind Chico and he was there in the front, looking tough and wired, his face pushed into sharp corners like he was jacked on powder. And I could see, far over, them C-4 sheep too. In their little crowd on the side. They stayed watching with wide hopeful eyes just like us, thinking their boys was gonna win the day.

Manny and Beto was both standing it down, their arms straight down their sides, their faces that same hard rock. I don't care who it is, I'm thinking. Don't care. Just show me which one, you know? Show me which loco to pick, the strongest one and I'm there. Show me, I whispered. Wanna see.

Chico's got that bennie look. Hey HEY! Wild eyes on him. He walks up to Manny but he was looking over at Beto too cause he don't know who's the número uno.

"OK, Manny. You the message boy?" he says, his mouth crooking up sour. He had them yellow clothes on that matched his rubia head, and he shined under the lamp lights. The Bombers behind him was laughing, making their fun at Manny and I saw them yellow dogs. Hyenas. Chico didn't laugh none, but his mouth kept jerking up in that grin. "Why don't you just lay down, ése? Lay it down, it goes nice and easy."

Manny wasn't as quick and cracked as the baby loco I remembered. He smiles right back. "Chico, we don't gotta be fighting no more. I don't want nothing with you, man. Split sides, eh? It's cheaper that way."

Nobody says nothing for a minute, wondering if maybe we was gonna see some peace after all. They keep staring at each other and making them cold eyes, hoping one will blink. Not a word with them deciding. Sheep are all still and quiet.

But Beto sees how he can get his. Peace won't help him but a battle could make him into a king.

"NO, eh pachuco, that ain't it!" Beto shouts bomba loud, and we all turn our heads sharp to see him stretching up tall and banging his arms around, shooting out them fists some and making like he's gonna pounce on somebody.

"What you say, LOCOS!" he starts calling back to the boys behind him, and you could see them getting pumped and jigging up. "ARE YOU DOWN, HOMES?" he yells, his neck stringing with veins and I think I see dark red washing down over his cheeks. "YOU SOME DOWN VATOS?!" The Lobos heard that call, they was rushing up their voices to answer him YAH! and the C-4 homies started stepping back but I saw Chico's happy cracked-out old face, looking like this is what he wants. Gimme it, baby. Bring it on!

After that ain't nothing old Manny can do, cause they was all burning for it. "You SHUT it, pendejo!" I heard Manny screaming over there, but then the music got so loud I couldn't make him out no more.

And at first it was beautiful. They was far away from me, and I could check it out feeling safe sitting there with all the sheep who kept hugging themselves and cheering. Seeing gangsters fight down like that, any woman's gonna want *that* rush, right? There's yellow- and black-colored boys flashing on that grass, flinging up their arms and hands then bringing out them pretty *plata* switches while the cold lamp light washes down in places. Mexicans know how to throw down old-fashioned, it's like watching somebody dancing. The C-4s and Lobos was skirting around and jabbing and zig-zagging, yelling ÓRALE like it's singing, making them punches like thunder, ése!

So it was dark, but you could still make out who was who. It didn't take Beto long to get some C-4 by the head even with his broke hand. And Manny took Chico right on, they was circling like Apaches, sticking their blades out and trying to sink them in. I could see some of our other vatos doing good too. Rocky and Cinco and Popeye was piling on a couple of heavy-weight buzzheads, and even Chevy was giving it a shot with his one good arm wrapped around a baby C-4 while the other one flapped dead at his side. There was a crowd of quick-fisted Lobos who whipped their bodies on the enemy like kamikazes, I'd see some homie's head come up and a C-4 boy go down, and that thin slice of fear I had breaking me open pinched together tight. But then some Lobo over there's getting the shit kicked out of him, he's flat on the grass and the blood's over his mouth and nose. And now Chevy's screaming and holding his side while the baby C-4 jackrabbits off. I started to smell lead and fire in that close muggy air that keeps getting hotter, and hear the sound of shirts ripping and see all the rough-cut brown skin.

I gripped Chique hard by the hand and felt that hot blood in her too. I look over and see Star Girl's got them white cheeks, she's almost bent double, hands in her coat. And over the noise of the battle I listened to the sheep keep screaming on for the Lobos. Them girls had that loca in them! They could of been good cholas for me if they'd tried. Their big red mouths flared wide open while they're screeching, FUCK 'EM ÉSE! or praying crazy to Jesus with their eyes closed and their hands making the cross. Before it got bad I saw Cecilia standing real quiet by us. Her lips pressed, a floppy dress on, and her big face flat as a drum. Her eyes locked on some-thing, glowing like coals. She was waiting just like me.

In rumblas, sometimes you know when there's gonna be dead. There's a scream that's too high or a face that's too bloody, and things take a turn for the worst. I knew it when I see Beto do a backtrack. He switched away from his C-4 and started chop-ping down on Manny even though they was both on the same side, and Chico was so surprised he eased off to watch. At first it didn't make no sense, but then I see how Beto's gonna have his say here and now while we fought the C-4s. He sticks out his blade and swipes it through Manny's arm and teases back so he tears up a solid wedge of muscle, and all I can see is that red and then I can't see old Manny no more. Star Girl's laughing. Why's she laughing? and there's nothing but vatos all over, all the colors flying mixed up and then we hear that POP! gunfire noise. The rebels start scattering all over the park and some are running up this way, by the women, and I couldn't make out who was yellow or black, there's nothing but cold-steel scared coming up in me and I feel down for my piece for a second but I know I got to spring.

Later people would say it was the heat. That nobody could think straight in weather that burned your skin like fire, and it broke the men's minds. But I say it's cause we don't got religion no more. It used to be no woman's gonna get hit in a rumbla. It's that rule, leaving sheep and babies alone. But we forget it once we hear them firecrackers going off. The Lobos and C-4s was storming down locos and the sheep on both sides, so girls got banged up that night same as the men. Most of us on the benches ran like field mice but I guess Star Girl felt too strong. When the C-4 killers was barreling up to us she wouldn't scoot. Girl pulls down for her old Glock, the one I gave her. Not me. I hear the cannons sounding and what I remember is seeing her messing with her piece before I took off. But she can't shoot it good, can she? I didn't teach her, and that Glock's a hard shot. Heavy, made for man's hands. There was that war noise and the vatos rushing, I look and see Star Girl's weak fingers can't hold the gun down but I'm running like hell, making my fast feet fly me out of danger.

The only thing that matters is how it ends, see. Two dead Lobos and some others got hit bad. In the chest and face. I heard we killed ourselves some C-4s too, so it ain't all a lose. People around here say it's God who chooses the ones that get crossed out. But I know different. There ain't no good reason one way or the other. The only thing to do is keep that brain of yours sharp.

Me and Chique, we're the smart ones. Run girl! You got to run to stay alive. There ain't no shame in that. We ran down them dark streets faster than mercury and back home to safe. Lock up that door. Then there's Cecilia, she's got some of her brother's luck. In the middle of that war she wouldn't move. She kept standing straight and watching out for Manny with her eyes big. Thinking she's some Guadalupe Virgin, right? And maybe there is some milagro there cause she walked out of there without so much as a scratch.

The thing is, my poor old Girl. "I'm OK, Lucía, it don't matter none," she says to me later. Hurts bad. Star Girl, she didn't die on me. But when she was sitting there playing with her cuete and couldn't make a clean shot with it cause I didn't show her how, some C-4 came up from behind and tagged her in the back, making her bone go snap nice and clean. I couldn't help her cause I'm running my ass back home. But there ain't no shame, I got to know that. I can't think it's my doing that she's all broke up. When la chota finally comes around to check us out they saw her down there on the grass all twisted and ran her over to Kaiser. Some C-4 vato broke her so she can't walk, and there wasn't a damn thing the doctors could do to patch her up again.

You know, I was like crazy after that. A tiger in a cage. When Wanda calls me to let me know, "Heard Star got slammed," she says to me, I ran to the hospital like I'm running after death. She's OK, I'm thinking. There's nothing wrong with my Girl. Kaiser's all white walls and nurses raising up their eyebrows at me pointy. Well, fuck you. And there was that gabacha at the front desk, giving me careful eyes and writing things down with her little pen. When I say I'm Star Girl's sister, all she asks me is, "Does she have her papers? Her papers, ma'am?" like it's the only thing. I almost cut that woman right there for her lack of respect. I wanted to make her feel just like me.

But all I did was wait. I stared at the hospital white walls till I thought I'd go blind.

"Hey Girl, you're doing fine," I say when they finally let me see her. "You'll be good as new in no time," I told her and I tried a smile. But I know it's over. Star's looking all small and tiny under them sheets, legs dead and she can't move an inch. "You just tell me who do this to you, ésa," I ask her, my voice cracking up. The LAPD was already snooping around for the C-4 who shot her, but they can't speak our language and they didn't even know how to start looking. The chota can't do a job like I can around here.

"Don't know, and it don't matter," was what she answered, braver than me and damn I couldn't say nothing. Beautiful eyes cloudy, hair tangled and dirty as a dog's. Look at her, she used to be my *linda* homiegirl but not no more. There's still that little star tak by her eye but she's got some different face on her now, all beat down and sad.

So I was going crazy cause she's my chola. You can't be breaking up my chola and not pay hard. This chica's gonna break you back. I had more mama in me than I thought, and there's this black time after Star Girl got shot when I was just a color-blind old bat. I couldn't make out blue or green or even the butter-gold shade of yellow no more. All I could see was a thin trickle of red. A dark rose circle. I dreamed it on him. I saw it tear open his blank face.

Yah Bomber, I'm gonna find you. I'm gonna get you where you live, boy.

Cecilia

She had fire-engine-red hair. And soft brown eyes.
Everybody around here still talks about that rumbla.
They whisper about it in their low voices like they were in church
or confession. Remembering the day my brother got brought
down. I remember it different.

They were all trash, good-for-nothings. Even him, I can
say that now. Even Manny, he didn't really love me. And Beto.
So Lucía takes on Beto, steals him away from me but do I care?
Not after what he'd done, it seemed like he'd beat my heart out
and left me dry and dead-eyed. So I wasn't even mad, you know.
I could see it from the way he was looking at her, his carved face
softing up like a puppy's when she comes by. She walks past
him all smooth. I knew that she's sexing him, I'm not a fool. But
it didn't mean one little thing to me. Let them rot in hell, those

two deserve each other. She's a devil and he's an empty-headed killer. After she'd wrapped her string around him he did whatever she told him to.

The rumbla was the first bad bloody one between us and the C-4s. It was the day Beto proved to Lucía that he could be a Lobo boss and the day he broke from me. But it didn't take me by surprise. I knew by then about them two so I went to the park to be there for Manny. Because I'm a Silvas the same as him and blood always pulls you home. It was a hot-poker night, muggy and close as wet wool, made my knees buckle. But I stood my ground, even when my eyes begged to close down dark on these hot bodies jumping and the faces with red masks, but then over that I saw something special. A pretty girl just caught my eye while the locos started getting shot up.

I can't say bad things about sheep now, because that night I fell in love. Some sheep are good people, not every one's a puta only out for number one.

I saw her right before Manny got thrown down by Beto and the hurly-burly got so bad I couldn't make out who's who. Over on the other side there was this girl with a cotton dress, swirl skirt down to her knees and white high-heel shoes, bronze in her skin like dark sand color. *Hermocita*. She had that Mexican red hair long down to her back and shiny. A C-4 sheep. Taller than me and more pretty, with a little fresh face looking right back my way, she was still and quiet and had her eyes right on me, making this little smile. I couldn't even breathe for a second with my romance feelings that spark and glow like fireflies when our eyes meet like in the movies.

Hello, I think to her. Hello ésa, yah that's me. You see *me*! So she was there and I was staring hard, wanted to wiggle up to her happy. I heard Chique and Wanda screaming, HEY CHOLO, but my heart was beating, Come here, chiquita, come over here, sweet thing. And that's when Beto stabs Manny down into his arm. Cuts him up like meat so the C-4s wild out and start shooting everybody up when they smell blood, there's yellow locos running up to the sheep and I couldn't see my girl after that but I kept my eyes wide open looking out.

Beto's the jefe now. That was the night he did it, because the arrow struck the heart. He couldn't take it, my brother. That knife went in messy, Manny was chopped ground beef in the arm and some on the chest and ribs so he couldn't move his whole self for like a month, and while he waited he got thin-boned and his eyes blanked like vacant lots and his boss-man face paled and peeled off. Manny was out of the Lobos, and he knew it. After we got him back home from the doctors he just sat board stiff, silent in bed with his red bandages and there was that bad sour smell of blood and sick coming off him that curled back and spoiled his insides. Hermano got bitter and grew a poisoned tongue that could snatch out and sting me if I didn't watch him careful.

But that wasn't how it was at first. We were so happy having him home for that little while. Mama and me. She opened up warm and smiling with a man in the house again, it made her straighten up some. A crippled man's the best, because you can do for them but they can't hurt you none. And Manny was as good as crippled.

"*Mi amor*," she'd sing to him, her old eyes brighting up and her hands busy tucking him in or feeding him his steamy soup. Mama was looking like a full-bloom chica even though she's old enough to be a grandma. "Come on, hijo, eat up, it's good for you." There's flowers in his old room, spring daisies in a vase on his table, and she opens up the windows so that the sun comes shining in. A blue and white Virgin praying in the corner for good luck, a bottle of holy water on the bureau. She loved him again like she used to because he'd shrunk back weak as a baby and couldn't do nothing but lie back quiet covered up by blankets. Breathing in that medicine smell. "Oye, m'hijo," she'd say, sitting down by his bed and singing about the day he was born. "*El mas bonito, preciocito!*" she'd laugh, remembering how he was the most pretty boy. But he wasn't hers no more. When she was talking he'd tight up his lips and shut his bad black eyes like he was trying to sleep. He didn't want to see us women and feel like her little goose, but she'd just talk on over his closed eyes.

"You feeling good there, Manny?" I'd ask him when it was my turn to be the nurse. He was needing help getting to the toilet, leaning on my arm heavy down the hall but to me he looked frail as a sparrow. I helped with his soft cotton clothes too, my hands careful with him like he's cracked glass and when I'd take his shirt off I saw that chest blue and red colored, the scars coming up ugly. Not a beautiful cholo like before, he wasn't my wild horse no more. And a broken vato's got his shame.

There were days he'd look at me angry. "Stupid chavala," is all he'd say with his hoarse voice and I'd step back some at first, surprised and my eyes burning. I was trying to love him sweet like I used to because I knew he was the same as a hurt dog, scared and trying to bite. Other times it was more easy. When he had his good days he'd just look at the ground. "Órale, I'm still here, ain't I?" he'd say then, his breath coming up hard, and you almost had to feel sorry. But I was feeling harder against him anyway, good day or bad, because I knew that if he had his chance he'd leave me. He'd race on back to Lucía and beg her sloppy and then try to snap Beto in two with his bare hands.

When I was a girl I used to love that toro in him, sharp horned and lean muscled. I'd moon up at him with big eyes, thinking he's my prince. I'd do anything, be the lookout, message girl, Garfield. But now. It got to be different with him and me. "He got you bad, eh?" I'd say sometimes when I'm changing them bandages, clacking my tongue and shaking my head.

Teasing him because I knew he was too weak to pop me one. "Shut up," he'd answer. "Just shut your mouth." But I wasn't scared any more. I liked taking care of Manny, but not so that he gets strong enough to leave. I can say it. I liked him baby-boy weak. It made me the strong one for once. Sleep tight, hermano, I'd think, watching him lay there with that skinny blue arm peeking out from the blanket. Stay put. Now I wanted to stand over him holding his tea or his milk and whisper, Drink up, Manny, sweet as I could and hide the smile that I kept tucked in the folds of my heart.

It wasn't just me. Everything was different. There was a whole crazy world going on outside our door. We were busy nursing Manny and Mama was doing her cleaning work regular, but Echo Park was busting up. I was trying to keep clean by not talking to any Lobos, my eyes going down to the sidewalk bashful looking when they walked by. Sometimes an old Lobo would see me and say, Hey, Muñeca, but I'd shake my head No. I'm not Muñeca, going to be that good Cecilia now. So I was keeping my nose out of it but you can't help but hear things if you've got itchy ears like me. And what I heard on the street was how Lucía had grown red claws, a mouth full of razors, and she could numb a man cold-stone scared just by flashing him her lightning look. All she wanted on her plate was dead C-4, and it made the woman dangerous.

So you can see. I wasn't supposed to be talking to no C-4. They were the enemy. But after I saw the snow-white flash of that C-4 chica's skirt and saw her valentine face, I didn't care. I had a fever over her. My chest got all tight when I wondered where she's at. I was lying in my bed at night and seeing things, faces coming out on the dark walls, the house all quiet, everybody sleeping and out of them shadows comes her angel smile and it made me hooked and tangled inside so that I'd kiss my soft pillow pretending with my heart thumping up. There wasn't no good reason to go loca over some sheep I'd never even seen before, but I kept remembering them eyes she had. How they looked straight back. I couldn't help myself. And it's a trap, wanting the wrong things. You get all caught up and twisted, but you can't whisper one word. You've got to keep things like that to yourself.

I started looking for her around the Park, thinking I was like this spy, la James Bond. I'd go to the market and see Carla or Josie or Yolanda, these Lobo sheep I used to kick it with in the kitchen when me and Manny were still inside. I'd buy some empanadas and milk and talk about movies or month-old gossip just to see if those cholas could tell me something.

"*Hola chica*! *Qué pasa calabaza*? Some fight, eh? Yah, Manny got it good, you should see him now, he's a sad boy. Hey. You see that eastside chica at the rumbla? The sheep in the swirly dress?" But they'd shake their heads, draw blank faces. "Red dye job," I'd say, raising up my hand. "This tall."

"Why you wanna know?" they'd ask me all scandalous. "That's C-4."

"Well, don't say nothing but Manny likes her, ésa."

I wasn't too worried, though. Finding some C-4 chica wasn't going to be hard in this place because everybody knows everybody. We talk like our town's big but I'll tell you, we've got a small world and we know every little corner by heart. Every street, every alley, all the street signs. I grew up seeing how the lawns look shiny wet on winter mornings and like dry brown straw in the summer. How the tree roots bust out through the sidewalk, making bumps and jags in the concrete that you've got to walk over careful. How the pink sky looks in the afternoon over the power lines. The busted dusty pickups parked in the driveways, the ranflas by the curb, and the pawn-shop bikes on the porch. I don't know much, but I know this neighborhood. We all do. You hear a voice yelling down the block and you can tell just who it is. Mrs. Alvarez, screaming raspy out her screen door at her sons Rudy and Andrés, telling them to get inside for dinner. And the sounds of the vatos playing football out on the road, cussing vicious if they miss a pass or laughing when they're ditching cars.

Sometimes I think that if you know your little place good enough, maybe you don't need to know nothing else. Like I know where I can walk. The Lobos have a few streets locked up tight. Alvarado Street and Mountainview, that's crawling with our locos hanging out and selling powder, showing off their new taks and playing money dice in the road. Ross Street, that's where the Lobo big heads live. Manny used to have his place there, all black furniture and fancy blasters, and now Beto was moving in. If you walked down Ross and saw a rebel, the rule is he'd better throw up that Lobo set real quick or else there'd be trouble. But if you skip on over to the other side of the Park, you've got your different scene. That's C-4 territory, where Chico's Bombers come out of. Edgeware and Crosby streets, if you hang around there you have to watch out for them bumble-bees, they cruise their ranflas down the road hoping to check out some black and red. And take Laveta Street, we get some of the worst drivebys there. The C-4s call it *Avenida de Asesinos* because if a gabacho or an enemy walks in there, it's open season. You've got to keep your eye peeled for the quick-trigger boys if you're on the wrong side of the neighborhood because they love playing high noon with their new guns.

They hate us and we hate them, but we all have the same kinds of streets and houses and trees memorized in our hearts.

So it wasn't going to be too hard to find my girl. And after I sniffed around enough I found out Wanda knows her from the neighborhood, that she's seen her around with Chico and his homies.

I caught Wanda walking home from the store this one morning, she was lugging brown bags on one hip and dragging her baby son Miguel with her other hand. Nobody here knew Miguel's daddy too good. It'd already been two years since she'd hooked with that East L.A. White Fence loco named Lucky, the dude that got her knocked up quick before he ran his tail on back to downtown. Wanda AFDC'd and so she had enough to cover her monthlies, but she was looking wiped out that day, her tube top slipping down and her Miguel crying, puffing out his little tomato face. My belly gave a jump seeing him, because it's Wanda that gets to be a mama and not me.

"You know this tall girl with the long red hair?" I asked her, helping her out with her bags so she slows down and gives me her time.

"Shit. Wait a minute." She breathes heavy like she's doing me some favor, and I get dizzy-headed cause I know she's gonna know. She lets go of Miguel's hand so she could pull out her cigarettes. She takes one out then fiddles with the matches. "Fuck me," she's saying, trying to light up but she can't get a spark. "What'd you say again?"

Wanda's still the same old-timer mamacita I used to jawbone with on them park benches, except she belongs to Chevy now, the right hand who used to go with Laurita. The sheep here act like Wanda's some big winner because she stole Chevy from under Laurita's nose, but it wasn't no contest. Chevy had been looking hard for some new linda anyways, after Laurita ballooned out fat-looking, hollering sailor cusses when she couldn't make her baby son stop crying. "Hey. Get yourself a grip, girl!" I told her, right before Chevy took off with Wanda. I'd seen her in the park rocking the baby and she looked ten years older than I remembered. "I don't get no peace with this one, and nobody's helping me out, neither," Laurita said, and when I saw her watery tide-pool eyes I could tell how she couldn't hold on to nothing by then.

Not Wanda though. She's a cool customer. That woman sheeped herself so big and pretty when Chevy was around that he dumped old Laurita like he was taking out the trash. But I don't look at Wanda like she's so lucky no more. These days I can see how she's a scary chica because she doesn't care about nothing. With sheep, you've got two kinds—old and new. The old-timers make like putas, they have low smoky voices and bad tempers, hit their babies, and scream like *lloronas* at their men. But they dress nice, wearing lots of shiny gold jewelry and high, clacky heels. A sheep has to smooth a lot of dealers to get them pretty chains and maybe a nice apartment, but it doesn't wear nice. They have dark smudge shadows under their eyes, get all tired looking, and some of them like to take hits of powder or carga to keep going. And then there's the new chicas, mostly they're old-time waiting to happen. Catholic schoolers who think the Lobos are so *suave*, they wear little cotton dresses and have those perky hummingbird faces, but even they learn sooner or later.

Wanda, she's been around the road. That sheep is beauty old-style, in these tight tube tops and shiny satin pants, with these scratchy long fingernails and Charo hair poofed up with Hair Net. A real glamour chica. The homies are always checking her goods, when she's walking by you hear those low wolfie whistles, locos smacking their tongues, and there's sex in their lips when they smile out at her. "Hey, chavala," they'd sing out. "Wanna be my woman?"

I'm still standing there on the sidewalk waiting for her to tell me something about the C-4, but she won't talk till she gets in a few drags.

"Yah, I know that girl," she says to me finally, blowing out thin dark smoke. "Name's Chucha."

"Where she from?" I asked her, in a voice as light as the butterflies in my belly, but Wanda's too tired with her son screaming and the heavy bags to even ask me why.

"Eastside, baby. That girl's styling C-4 big time. I used to catch her running here before Chico split off. She's one of his chicas. Think she lives over on Bellvue with her old mama."

Chucha on Bellvue Street, I heard that. She's just a few blocks from me, I knew I could call out her music-box name and maybe she'd even hear. But still, I didn't do nothing about her for a while. Stay away from that bad medicine, I told myself. You don't want to be messing with that, especially a C-4. So in the day I sucked on peppermints to keep my mouth numb and chewed on freezer rock ice to keep my head cool. At night I told myself to dream of bluebirds, cotton-white sheep, Easter bunnies, gold-winged angels.

And when that didn't work I just set myself to taking care of Manny, because busy hands stay out of trouble.

With Manny I was still being good. I was as tough as an iron-bellied fighter, as caring as a mama bear. I was stronger than him even. He'd lay back in his bed, getting better slow in the ribs but worse in the head, rotten thoughts eating him up so that he's like old soft fruit.

"What's doing with the locos?" he'd ask me, looking up with eyes heavy lidded from the doctor medicine and curandera herbs Mama kept shoving down him. *Eucalipto, flor de azahar, aguacate, zapote blanco*. It smelled like a witch's house in there, but he wasn't taking the cure. He'd kept thinning. I could see the trace of his jigsaw ribs and the jut of his wishbone arms, the sharp cut of his glass jaw.

"Hey, shut up," I'd say. "You don't want to be knowing. The Lobos are going to get you dead some day, Manny."

I could talk to him like that then. Like he was the sheep and *I* was the vato. It made me happy because there's nothing he can do to me, nothing he can do but stay still.

"Ceci, watch it," he'd say with his growly voice trying to make like he's Mr. Super Bad. But it was so funny how I didn't feel scared. I felt cool, like this icy chica. And that's not the same Cecilia I used to be.

On his good days he'd scuff and whine like a little boy, and I'd have to break down and throw him a bone. I was careful, though. I tried to tell him about it in pieces so he didn't choke on the news.

Everybody knows that Lucía got evil after the rumbla, sharp as thorns and full of darts, and she'd got smarter too. She'd spread the Lobos out, first stealing all the little ones she can from the neighborhood, smooth-chinned boys for Beto and tadpole girls for herself, the younger the better. Niños were packing snub-noses and Saturday night specials at thirteen years old, fourteen, and babies don't have hearts in them, they'll pull a trigger just to hear it go bang. Then Lucía started sending the older vatos down to *la Avenida* to cross out C-4 tags or to shoot down yellow dogs, and things heated up so vicious that you could see the locals' faces turn rubbed and gray, as well worn as a worry stone.

But the biggest thing she did was start this fight over Garfield Junior High. The Lobos were circling the wagons and planting their toughest hitmen at every corner of the school, but Chico kept sending his boys down there to spy and tease and tag so that our tempers would flare and we'd lose our heads. The spray-paint wars got hot on Garfield's walls, and pretty soon the Bombers were taking out their guns too. Even police had to start pressing it harder, cruising their black-and-whites down the streets more and chasing after anything that wore a bandanna or had a swagger walk.

My brother knew something was up, that's why he keeps asking what's with the Lobos. You could hear the battles loudest at night, the popgun shots ringing back and forth and vatos screaming RIFA or laughing, ladies' voices crying or feet clipping fast down the street. In the morning you'd come out and see new tags, black and yellow C-4 spiderwebs sprayed up on houses, looping over sidewalks, crossing out the stop signs and storefronts.

Sometimes I'd walk past Manny's room and see him staring at the naked trees out his window, his black eyes faded. "So how you feeling, Manny?" I'd ask like always but after a while he even stopped cussing me because I guess he figured I wasn't worth the words.

But Chucha kept on buzzing at me. Thinking about her shifted the ground under my feet. She hung on my elbow and weighed down my hands, I felt her tugging away at my pockets. Her heart-shaped face wouldn't leave me alone, but I didn't try too hard to forget her. There's nothing else to think on then, anyways. Every day's the same with Manny getting sicker in the head and the air's closing around me bitter stuffy so I can't breathe. I had to take my walk. Who's going to stop me, right? A woman's got a right to get some air, that's what I told myself when I stepped out. But really I was all heart moving on down to Bellvue. To check out my girl.

At first I'd just tiptoe into C-4 territory, skip around Patton or Douglas. I kept my head bent so nobody would spot me. And every day I was getting closer to old Bellvue Street. I'd walk down Angelina, Kensington, Calumet streets, staying away from Edgeware but I was still feeling like I was skating on thin ice. C-4 vatos passed on by me some days and my breath stopped short in my throat. But I got lucky. They didn't look too hard at me. They thought I was just some low-rent C-4 sheep who wasn't worth their precious time.

And finally I saw her. Chucha girl was on the corner, smoking her cigarillo and trying to stand sexy. She was dressed a little harder than I remembered, looking more old-timer in these pink jeans, supertight. There's that fake red in her hair and a brick-colored chola mouth. Black sticky lashes, black heart tak by her eye. She was a sheep, the kind I was trying hard not to be, I could see it in her face and how she bangs her hip out, flicks that ash like a movie star. Qué lástima, I'm thinking. A trash sheep, I've been dreaming about one of them trash sheep this whole time. But when she turned her head and looked at me, I saw her eyes light up.

"Hey. That's you, eh?" she says.

This side, that side. The Lobos and the C-4s. The Lobos tell us we have to hate all the black-hearted C-4 people, but I didn't care about all that. Chucha and me got to be good friends. She was this first-generation linda who'd been in Echo Park since the day she was born and never even set foot in Mexico. "One hundred percent Echo, ésa," she'd say, "there ain't no Tijuana here." She lived with her mama too, just like me, in a rat's nest, on the second floor with the brown linoleum and the little potted plants, the space air conditioner's broke so you have to suck down ice all summer.

Other than that we were like night and day. Chucha looked sheepy, running around in her stretchy paint-ons and her strawberry lipstick smile. She'd bark out this loud hee-haw laugh at a knock-knock joke then jingle her plastic garage-sale earrings or grab my hand and start tango dancing. Only seventeen, but she was on her way to being old-timer fast. A wildcat girl. Didn't care nothing about school, didn't even care about tomorrow. "You gotta think about *today*, Cecilia, don't be worrying all the time." No, me and her were different. I can't help my quiet mouth, can't help my old-lady *susto*. But those little things don't matter. Me and Chucha saw some light in each other and *bam*, we're like sisters right away.

I never had anybody like her before, either. The other chicas around here, they have their little girlfriends to play dress-up Barbie with in grade school and to chatterbox with about boys and makeup when they get older. I was always alone or running after Manny, until I saw Chucha smoking like a chimney and looking at me with them brown eyes.

We'd hang out in secret, sitting on the sofa at her house watching the TV and eating *chicharrones* or Hershey bars, laughing and crying at the telenovelas. The novelas, they're Old World stories, only viejas turn on them things, blowing their noses into Kleenex at the sad parts and dreaming about lost love. You feel like a stupid watching them but we couldn't help it because they were so beautiful. I loved *Rosa de Nadie*, *Peligroso*, y *Como tú Ninguna* the best. Those shows had the most glamorous ladies, better than any rubia Charlie's Angel on the English TV. Our morenas wore pretty silk dresses and fluttered their soft brown eyes, and they knew just how to get their man wrapped tight around their finger. "Don't leave me, mi amor!" they'd sob to their boyfriends, crying wet and pretty so that the angry machos have to take them back. My heart would go all soft seeing them cling on to the don juans while the violin music rushes up loud, but then they'd kiss hard on the mouth and you knew they'd be happy ever after. And those men, even I knew they were sexy. More slick and full of romance than any gabacho could be with their handsome faces and greaser hair. Chucha would stare at them too. "Firme, ésa, I want one," she'd say, snatching her head and giggling like a mouse. Little heart tak winking when she laughs.

We had some good times. You couldn't get much better than Chucha. I was never so fresh before, like all of a sudden I've got room to breathe. "You got something wrong with you?" Manny asked me when I started walking with a bounce and smiling too easy. When he hassled me it felt like I had a hot flame right in my eye looking back at him, like I was the fire-cracking chola for once. Because I was the one with the secret. "No, Manny, there ain't nothing wrong," I'd say, looking down then and trying to make my face shy so he won't give me any more trouble. But I was smiling big inside.

See, because I was *flying*. Around here you have to watch what you say or else some hothead gets mad and pops you one or Mama starts screaming and praying her rosary at you. But with Chucha I didn't have to be careful or scared. It felt like I could do anything with that girl. Like I could make some plans, and they didn't have to be no normal plans neither. I could get on the bus and roll on out to Texas if I wanted. Or become a different person, the kind that would yelp and holler a song at the top of her lungs so people would turn around and stare. But most important that rosebud face of hers didn't tell a lie, and I could tell her what I had in my heart.

"One wish, OK?" she asked me once, and I can see her now like she's right here. Eyes shut with her head bent back like she's sleepy, her curry-colored hair draping down over the silky pillows. We were stretched out on her sofa after the novelas, our arm skins touching together light, and I had that warm feeling on my face like I'm out in the sun. "What you want if you get one wish, ésa?"

"I don't know," I say, lying real still just like her. I didn't want to move my arm. "I'm doing fine with the way things are."

"What you mean you don't know?" She sits up, goggling her eyes wide and round at me like I'm crazy, shaking her *cola* around so I almost fall off. "Everybody's got their genie wish, girl. Even a funny thing like you. You can't live in this place and not be dreaming about something else."

"That ain't true, some people are happy with what they got."

"Nuh uh. You tell me. I know there's something in your head."

I laid there thinking blank about it for a minute because I didn't want to tell her I already had my one wish. Got you, girlfriend, I thought to myself. And I don't need nothing else. But then this other thing pops through, something I'd been trying hard to forget. How I looked up at Manny before. Back when he was the jefe of the Lobos, standing over me with his legs planted firm on the floor and his arms crossed like sabers. When he'd tell me what I had to do and I pawed the ground and rolled over just like a little *perra*. You do for me, Cecilia. That's what he told me, and I didn't think I had no other choice.

"All right then," I said, screwing my face up tight to keep my cheeks from turning red. "I'd be a big bomba man strutting myself all over the Park. I wouldn't worry about no babies, or about getting married. See, because men don't worry about nothing. I'd be that."

"Ooooo!" she started laughing at me, bunched up there on the couch and her t-shirt riding up so I can see a bronze slice of her belly. "You think *wild*, *chicana*! Wanna be a man? You got some *ganas*!"

"Chucha. *Cálmate*. What about you?"

"Oh, I know that one." She leaned back again and flipped her hand over her eyes, making like she's Chita Rivera. "I'd be *la rica*! Richer than a queen, me. Buy myself a white Cadillac and a white rabbit coat and a little dog that goes yap yap."

"That's stupid!" I said, but when I looked over I pretended she was a rich lady, wearing floaty silky dresses and marble-sized diamonds like we'd seen on the TV.

Chucha's dreaming gave me this idea. All those novelas were making us dreamy and romantic in the head. See, if you live in Echo Park, you don't see *California*. You don't see the sharp-dressed people who work in offices and shop in stores. Instead all you see are power lines and broken sidewalk, clika tags scrawling up and down the walls and cholos hanging on the corner with their hairnets and cigarettes and thick black shoes. So when she had her birthday, I bought us two RTD tickets, an hour and a half with two transfers heading straight for Beverly Hills, sitting with the cleaning ladies all asleep in a row and their mouths hanging open like baby birds. Me and Chucha walked down *el* Rodeo Drive, peeking in the windows of the stores that sold cream-colored clothes and jewelry like polished bottle glass, oil-shined leather shoes. But we wouldn't go in. We were too full of pins and needles to do anything but wander up and down the sidewalk because I knew we weren't invisible out there. Usually white people look right through you. Gabachos don't have to look cleaning ladies, babysitters, gardeners in the eye, and they won't tip their heads at you if you're the same color of the dirt on the ground, dusky dark like the street, the late-afternoon sky. But out there under the bright rich sun we were sticking out sore, and I could almost hear the gabachos cluck their lips at seeing Chucha's black stretch jeans and wilded-out hair, her dark frosty chola eyes and mouth. There wasn't one good reason for us to be there, so they looked at us straight on. It made us feel shaky because we didn't know nothing about their rules, but after a couple hours we loosened up and got to feeling a little brave, and we wound up making our fun of them Rodeo people anyways.

We eyed a Gucci gabacho and his smooth-haired rubia lady walking toward us on the sidewalk, the same kind of people my mama cleaned for. They were dressed up in white cotton like golfers and looked all proud of themselves, walking so straight like they own the street and when they passed on by they gave us a quick bull's-eye stare. I was trying not to feel shamed next to them, even if they were smooth and smelled like fresh money and I only had this Pic'N'Save polka-dot dress on that was looking raggedy and old there all of a sudden. I knew they didn't know nothing about novelas or neighborhoods, they didn't know where to walk in my part of town, but still, for a second there I wanted to be like them so bad I thought my head would split. Not Chucha. She didn't like gabachos, because she thought they all had cold, hard hearts.

"Hey, ésa, there's Erik Estrada and Rosa de Nadie!" Chucha pipes out loud, making both of them jump high the same as scared rabbits do and the rubia grabbed hold tight on her purse like I'm going to snatch it right there.

"No way, lookit them clothes," I say. "This whitelady's gotta be la Elizabeth Taylor, homie!"

"Wanna bang 'em?"

"They don't look too tough, what you say?"

"Frank," the gabacha says to her man, all nervous looking. "Frank, come on!"

"Oh, don't be scared, little rubia, we ain't gonna hurt you!" Chucha yells out when they scooted off fast, and she starts laughing like a bozo clown, loud and long and holding her stomach like it's going to break in half.

"Come back, baby!" I yelled after them, the same as some old-timer loca would. I wasn't being like myself, like one of them Mexicans whitefolks can't see. I was showing up strong on that street and cackling crazy the same as my girl Chucha. But I didn't feel bad at all then, because I saw how they weren't much better than us, how they're so stupid they think we'd bang them right there in front of all them Rodeo security guards. They don't know what I know, I thought. Even if my mama cleans their house they don't know where to walk in my neighborhood. I didn't care even if they thought we're crazy bending over and laughing till we got dizzy. And not caring? Well, that felt good just like breathing.

I'll say it how it was. She was my only girl. The C-4s were breaking down Echo Park and my house was quiet as a morgue with my sick brother and my mama praying over him by rubbing her hands and whispering all the time. We were on welfare then because Manny wasn't bringing home his money and Mama's cleaning didn't cover the bills. "You're *floja*, no GOOD!" she started screaming at me every time the government check came in because she was shamed that we can't make our ends. But I didn't care, nobody was going to take me away from my linda. When I was with Chucha it was just different. I felt like I could do things. When the two of us were together, I was as brave and steely as a bullfighter.

"We could get out of here," I said to her this one time. "We could go to Vegas, you know. RTD it down to the desert and find some jobs."

"Whoosh! You're talking loca, girlfriend," she says. "You got some *cucaracha* head on you. What kind of job *we* gonna get, eh? I ain't gonna get no job washing houses down there in dirty Vegas."

"No, but lookit!" I waved my hand to hush her up. "There's no cholos or cholas in Vegas, no clikas and tags everywhere. We'd get a nine-to-five, rent a nice place. We could be like regular people."

Chucha wiggles around in her seat, sticks her lip out at me. Her face sets into straight lines all of a sudden, and I couldn't see that wildcat in her then. "That ain't never gonna be us," she says.

"Why not, eh? What do you know?"

She looked at me for a minute and her eyes got soft. She clicked her tongue and tried to grin, but wasn't looking like a girl no more. "Because there ain't no such thing as just regular people, Cecilia," Chucha says, real serious. "People just *is*, you know?"

Chucha had that strong inside her, stronger than me, maybe, because she can see who she is and it doesn't hurt her one bit. Me, I can't see things that clear. My ganas tie me all up in knots, so I can't be happy with what I've got. Can't you be nothing but some square-looking girl? That's what I think in the morning when I catch myself in the mirror. Thinking like that didn't do me one piece of good, though. Nobody's going to love no boxy bracero-brown woman who thinks she deserves better. But Chucha, she's got the kind of tough that sees you through. That girl knows where she belongs even if it hurts.

In C-4, the sheep are bad off. They get cracked worse than Lobo sheep do, but they can't complain. Chucha was Chico's sheep. That meant I had to be careful when I go and see her, and I got good at scooting in and out of the eastside with my head down and my shoulders curled so I didn't catch

the eye of a hero. I should have been afraid, too. Chico had got
to be as big as Manny was in the good old days and was famous
for his cold steady blood. They said he'd pick off anybody who
crossed him or even gave him a crooked look with a quick flick
of his gunslinger hand. Super jefe man, that's what his gangsters called him. They all mooned after their boss. They copied
his walk, his stringy hairdo, how he stuck his chin in his chest.
And they all tried to be as cool and ready as he was with a pistol. I knew they'd scare me or hit me if they saw who I was walking down their street. And maybe, just because of Chico, they'd
do something worse.

But he's no Superman. I've known that boy since he was
a kid so skinny his pants would be hanging too low and dragging on the ground. I remember when he had holes in his shirt
and he looked up at Manny with the same dreamy eyes his own
boys give him now. He's nothing special. Real vatos locos don't
go after girls the way Chico beat Chucha sometimes. Sure, he'd
talk big. Vatos got to protect their women, he'd say when he
tells his boys the reason for fighting this war. But it ain't true.
He's the same as Beto. Any time she does something he doesn't
like he'd whip her right across the face with that steady hand.
When you strip him of his bodyguards Chico ain't nothing but
a stringy-haired bully boy who likes to drive slick cars and wear
hardassed-looking taks and perfect pressed baggies and Pendletons. He thinks he's some ladies' man too and won't ever get
tied down to one baby-making woman. So he had lots of chicas,
locas he threw a little money at and then gets to sex whenever
he wants. He wouldn't call her for days and days. "My man's
busy," she'd say sometimes, but you could see her puffy pink
eyes, how she'd been crying. "Got big clika business." Other times
he'd stone out on carga and get wicked, tell her how ugly she is,
or slap her around some more. And that's why she was dressing
like a peacock, to try and get some of that man's attention.

I could have told her it wasn't no use. He didn't love a single soul except for himself and his hermano Mauricio, this nut-brown fourth grader that liked to tag anything he can lay his hands on. Chucha told me how she'd see Chico give Mauricio pats on the head and hugs when little brother's done a good tag or a good steal, and how she'd heard him tell everybody Mauricio was going to be the next jefe. "Hands off my little ése, right?" he'd say to his homeboys. "Baby brother's gonna be your king someday." No hands off for the chicas, though. It was a prize enough to be one of his girls, so what if you're not his only one? So what if you have to take a hit once in a while?

But I never asked her about it. I left her C-4 alone. Still, I kept watch over her from day to day and so I knew how they wore down their women with shameful words and backhanded slaps. And it was easy to break a girl like Chucha. Chico had caught her when she was too green. She'd been a knobby-kneed sixth grader who liked to pretend she was big by ditching class and smoking cloves out on the curb, and he'd cruised by and put her in his pocket like she was a beach shell. After that, her only job was to make him happy. She learned too early how to bend and fetch and scrape the ground, how to grin when she felt like crying, how to lie. But I guess she loved him.

I knew about her, though, better than Chico ever would. Even though all she talked about was him, I still had this little part of her. I told myself that I knew her better than anybody, and that she loved me in her way. That she had to, because I loved her so hard back.

Too hard, maybe. I didn't have a man to make me Somebody except for old broke Manny. The mamacitas had cut me out, the locals stayed out of my way, and ever since I'd got big with my baby my mama didn't want a thing to do with me because I was a dirty sinner. Chucha was the best thing I had. The only thing.

Chucha, she liked her jewelry. Chico bought her those gold chains to keep her quiet, and sometimes, right in front of me, she'd finger them with this smile on her face. "Lookit what he got me," she'd say, winking and blushing and showing me this sparkly new necklace, one had these tiny diamonds shaped into a heart. "You talk like he's trash but Chico treats me *good*." I'd get green-eyed and hot to the touch when she teased me like that. I wanted her for my own self, and so I set on proving to her that I could string her with bells and tinsel as shiny as any boss man like Chico could pull out of his hat.

I never had but one pretty thing to give, that little Mexican gold ring my papa bought for my mama. He'd given it to her back in Oaxaca when he found out she was pregnant again, right before he'd taken off for good. "See that?" Mama said when she gave it to me, holding it up to the light so I could see the pink and yellow and copper colors glowing out. "It's yours now, hija," she said, and her lips spread and curved soft over her face. I was just ten years old then and I thought I was richer than most anyone with that ring. I didn't know then that things like that don't mean you're rich. They just show you how poor you are. But I take what I can. On Sundays when I'd see all the daddies strolling around the park and holding their hijas proud by the hand, I'd reach down and touch the little round bump. Even after I got big enough to wear it I'd keep it hid in my skirt pocket, and when I'd see all them smiling Sunday faces I'd feel that hard circle through thin cotton and trace it round and round with my finger.

That's what I wanted for Chucha. Some little piece of magic she could hide in her pocket and pull out on bad days, and when she'd look at the rosy gold color it would tell her that I loved her better than any loco could.

"Oye, Ceci, so linda," she said when I put it in her hand, and I curled up my lips as soft as a fawn's just like my mama's when she gave it to me. But then Chucha just sat there for a minute, with a funny look on her face.

"Well, put it on, ésa," I told her, tearing some little strings out of my sweater. I was trying to feel like one of the heroes in *Peligroso* or *Como tú Ninguna* when she keeps her eyes down and won't smile. I tried real hard to make like I'm some tough big-haired gangster who doesn't care about nothing. But when she keeps her mouth hushed up and won't look my way I think, No she doesn't want me, that's it. This girl doesn't want me nohow.

"Hey, it's no big thing if you don't like it. It's just a little cheapie," I tell her.

She looked at me then, straight on like I wanted. "I know what it is," she says, and reached her hand out.

Maybe she just feels sorry for me, so what? It doesn't matter. When she touched my cheek soft I forgot my old *bracero* face and my clunky fat body that can't even make me a baby. I didn't think about Manny or the clikas or how I was living like a loser with my mama. Right then I was warm. I had a soft fire up and down and when she pressed over me there I tasted seawater and breathed in the dizzy musk smell under her hair. I felt pretty like a princess when I saw her rosebud mouth. Better, even. That girl made me feel like a queen.

But just because you love somebody it won't change the world. I know that now. Love can't make you a different person. You wake up the next morning and you've still got the same pair of earthbound feet, the same set of square, boxy hands. And it won't make your heart light, neither. If anything, it gets more heavy, from carrying all that weight.

But I was born with a strong back. Because woman's here to take it, take it even when it hurts so bad you think dead is better than this. That's what la Virgen did, right? She lifted up those soft white hands of hers and just prayed and prayed. Well, I'm not la Virgen, but I can grit my teeth the same as anybody else.

It's all right. There's some nice things here. Wake up in the morning and smell that warm air coming through the window. You can almost taste the sun. Wash the clothes in hot water and bleach them till they're as white as snow caps. Scrub floors and watch them shine. Take a little hot tea before bed and close your eyes. And say that rosary, because that's what's going to keep you moving. See, this is my life now, and I didn't have no choice in it. God chased me down. He saw my bad black heart, my wicked self. He saw me traveling that wrong road and sent me a sign the same as he did with Moses.

Dios gave me them few good months, though. He gave me Chucha for a little while, we played like kittens and I didn't worry about nothing then. We stayed busy watching the novelas, staying out late, taking walks and looking at the trees. I did some odd-jobs washing houses with my mama sometimes to pick up a little cash after we ate up all the food stamps. It's a good life, I was thinking. The best. Chucha was still hanging with Chico but I told myself it didn't matter. The Park was going bust around us that whole time but I was blind and I didn't care. Even Manny left us finally. He got stronger in his arms and his head, and one day we came home and there wasn't a trace except for his tumbled bed and dirty dishes in the sink. No note, no nothing. He left my mama sad and crying, and pretty soon she got them pinched-looking lips again. I saw him later messing around the Park, kicking it on the corner with some old Lobos like Chevy while they did small dealer jobs and picked little rumblas with locals. But every time I tried to walk up to him, he'd cold up and give me his back like he doesn't want to give me so much as a look.

It didn't hurt much, though. Hey, that's his life, I thought. He's got his life now and I got mine. And I didn't have eyes for nobody but Chucha. I didn't want to see no sign from heaven, that's for sure. But God, He's a tough one. I don't care what you want, He says to me. It can't last forever, Cecilia. You're all mine.

I never was much for church going. That's for sad people who need something. Not me. The mission's there for old ladies like my mama. I'd watch her head off to Mass twice a week, clock-regular. She'd put her best dress on, the same one every time. It was dark brown polyester with those little white daisy flowers on the collar, and then she'd slip on white gloves and black shoes with the fancy strap. The last thing was to put the black lace careful over her head before she'd walk out the door. No, that's not for me, I'd think when I see her getting dressed up fancy for her God, and I'd stay put at home most every Sunday, even when she'd give me her sour face. "God knows you, hija," Mama would tell me before she'd go, wrinkling her mouth up mad and it looked like she ate a spoon of vinegar. "He knows them bad things in your heart." But I'd only let her yell me out of bed special times, when I can tell she won't take a no.

You can push a Mexican woman real hard, but not too far. There'd be some days when I know she had it bad, after she'd get yelled at by some richie rubia lady who she cleans for, or when she wakes up Sunday morning after dreaming all night about my papa. I could see it then, black eyes broke glass sharp, even worse than Manny's before a fight. She'd snap you in two like a dry stick if you said one wrong word, and I'd know I have to do whatever she says. Them days started coming real regular after Manny left us.

"You coming this time, m'hija!" she'd say, standing over me while I was sleeping lazybones in my bed but when I looked up I saw them flint-stone eyes and I knew it. She's been dreaming about Papa or she's sorry about Manny's empty bed. Some rubia gave her a hard time. Either way, it didn't matter. I could run around with Chucha and feel like a big shot all I wanted, but those mornings I knew she meant business. It doesn't mean I liked it. I'd wind up sitting stiff and sweaty in that dark old church for an hour, wearing this good-girl white eyelet dress and listening to the padre preach on about Jesus getting nailed for our black-hearted sins.

"We have to open up our *hearts*," padre John would say up there, dressed up in his red robe with the gold collar, and he'd raise up his hands and try to look bigger so we'd think of heaven. The padre's a tiny gabacho, he's got this little-boy body, skinny legs and feet poking out from under his robe. A bald shiny head, his eyes hid behind round glasses like a teacher's. Small hands press together when he talks. All the old Parker ladies love him to pieces. They'd step up quick to get that Communion wine and my mama got a little loca about him too. Around here the viejas fall crazy in love with padres like they're don juans. "That boy talks so *hermoso*," Mama used to say, and her eyes would spark and flutter just because he could do the prayers in Spanish.

The *pequeño* would throw that smoky incense ball around the whole place so it gets that Catholic smell. There's lights from the candles shining soft gold off the silver milagros hanging by a plaster bloody Christ, and all the viejas would get quiet like scared deer and sit up schoolgirl straight. They couldn't take their eyes off the little priest man. Every time I'd go, it was the same old thing. I could make out sad-face Señora Martinez over there to my right, years ago her hombre died from stomach bolas (too much whiskey), and there's Señora Parrales who always rubs her hands together raw, her hijo Kiko was a Lobo and got shot up doing them coca deals. Check out old-maid Sanchez in the front, she's this red-wigged *gorda* with a tongue so forked and sharp she ain't never going to get a man. Mama's next to me holding her breath like she's under water. "Open up our hearts and see the *truth*," the padre sings out then, loud so that you get chills, and the viejas nod their heads yes when he lowers his tiny hands.

I always tried to keep real still and fix my eyes straight on the padre and the plaster Christ and hope Mama can't read my mind. Watch that clock, I'm thinking to myself. Count them crazy slow minutes. *Treinta y uno, treinta y dos, treinta y tres*, órale it's forever till we get on out of here. And when the padre finally closed up his Bible and looked down, when the viejitas would crowd on up to him and try to touch his sash with their brown pruney hands, I'd run out my first chance, breathing in that air and sun and feeling like I could fly.

But I ain't made for flying. I ain't made for nothing but what you see right here, me in this blue dress. I was deaf and blind back then, happy to have my Chucha when she wasn't smoothing Chico all night long. I was thinking that I was as strong as a man, that I could have whatever I want. But I got showed, didn't I? I saw that sign at Garfield and now I know what's what. People ain't made for flying, and a woman can't have no life like a man. I see that real clear now.

Lucía

Loca friend, you're all messed up, Girl. What we gonna do?
When a woman can't walk it's like she ain't the same kind
of woman. You ever seen a girl's legs when they're all broke like
that? Star Girl, she used to be my pretty chola. She was mean
as a shark and she was strong enough to twist and hook a fish
as big as me. But I knew she was mine.

"I'm out of it, I ain't grouping no more," Star Girl kept
saying now, and she had that dead light in her eyes. Almost like
the sheep do after they figure things out. No, I didn't want her
different. I wanted my old Girl back.

But I saw what that C-4 did. She showed me after I brought
her home from the hospital, and she was quiet and dumb the whole
ride home cause of all them pills. I wheeled her into her bedroom
so she can get some rest and I helped drag her up. Before she got

shot we'd got her all set up special in her own place and she had this princess-pink bed from the Lobo money, a superfancy four-poster. It didn't look so pretty now, though. You can't climb under the covers if you don't got your legs working right.

When I lifted up her shirt she looked down, and her face didn't tight up with hurt or curl with shame. Nothing. "It ain't bad, chica, you gonna heal right up," I kept saying, making like it's true. I turned the lamp on her naked skin and touched her light like I was her mama. Star Girl had this round thick scar on her back, a twisted tree-stump–looking cut. There's white shiny skin lines like roots spreading out from where the doctors dug the bullet out. She was broke, all right. Her hands loose in her lap, like she can't hold on. And I'd seen before how her legs looked smaller because she can't use them no more, they was only hanging down from that silver wheelchair.

She shook her head again. "I'm out of it for good."

"You're out of it when I say so," I tell her, trying to sound tough as nails. Like I'm still her jefa and she's got to listen. But she don't. She only turned her head to the window and rubbed her dry mouth. It's all over, ésa, is what she's saying to me. Can't bring back the dead. Well don't I know it. She's looking outside at the blue-black night and what I see is her red eyes and them white cracked lips. There's dusk colors washing down over her face that ain't never gonna be the same.

It reminds me of something bad, that's right. Something I can't forget even if I close my eyes tight. No, I don't have *no* shame, but it don't matter. I can't ever shut my eyes tight enough to black it all out.

So I opened them up real wide. I wouldn't look away. Gonna get them for *you*, Girl, I thought to myself. You ain't never known something better than a crazy angry woman, and when I saw her busted up, staring out by the window and the night's coming down dark over her something in me went SNAP. You've been here before, something tells me. So get loca mad before that monster eats you up.

I started dreaming about that C-4 shooter all night long. His blank face was teasing me and when I wake up, I almost feel his steel-chain hands grip down on my throat. My teeth are chattering like I'm freezing. I can't even think about the business no more. The only thing in my head is how my Girl's all broke up.

"You go and kill him, right, Beto?" I asked him. When I got back from seeing Star I wrapped my arms around his neck, trying to kiss his lips and cheeks like the sweetest, nicest sheep he's ever seen. I made like he's the prince and cried on him just like a girl so he feels sorry. "You're gonna make him hurt, eh? Can you do it for me, baby?" I cooed, kissing his hands, his fingers. Acting like a geisha, but I didn't care a stitch. Inside I was feeling wild and mean and it took all my strength not to bash him on the head. You just DO IT, I wanted to scream in his ear, and my hands was itching and burning from wanting to scratch at his face till he finds me that C-4 killer.

But I couldn't. He was the boss of the Lobos now after that rumbla. It didn't matter that it was Chico who came to *me*, these days Beto was maddogging his ass down the street and all the vatos was watching him. He wasn't weak yet, like Manny got. The man was still full of fire, and it was gonna burn me bad if I didn't work him right. "Stop your whining, ésa. Keep it down," he'd started saying, waving at me with his hand when I'm telling him something. So I had to be more careful since he thinks he's Mr. Bad. Fine, we'll play it that way, I'm thinking. I'll sheep you so hard you'll walk weak-kneed all day. So Beto did what I want and that slick boy thought he was doing me favors. "Help me out, right?" I asked him again, and then smiled sweet. Yah, I'm thinking inside. You do for me. Tell your fools to drive on down to Edgeware and bring me home a dead man.

"All right, linda," he said, looking down at me and getting that big-daddy face on. He puts his hands under my shirt where it's warm and closes his eyes. "I'll show that vato where I'm from."

I should of known not to waste my breath. Beto got his homies running around asking questions and trying to get somebody from the eastside to rat out, but that didn't do me one bit of good. "Eh, ése, you know about the C-4 that tagged a Lobo sheep? You tell me, vato, our little secret." We didn't get no names. Whoever tagged my Girl was hiding out where I couldn't find him.

I got my hopes up when Beto sent these locos Montalvo and Rudy to Edgeware on a first-class mission to get me some answers about who shot my Girl. I sat up all night by my phone waiting to hear something, watching the wallpaper and the carpet and listening to some cricket chirp outside my window. I knew my bad time's gonna end once I get that call. But you don't send warriors on a job like that. Montalvo and Rudy was two baby-faced hot-blooded Oaxaca brothers who wore these red shirts and flashed their Lobos sets on the street looking for fights like blockheads so they could make a tough name for themselves in la clika. Instead of asking around cool and careful, they ran down to the Avenida de Asesinos, this dirty alley where the yellow dogs deal their powder. Them two started screaming RIFA and shooting crazy as soon as they see C-4 vatos giving them bad eyes. It's no good to me. Montalvo got hit with one in the shoulder and came home showing off his emergency-room war wound like he was a hero, and Rudy was maddogging around

cause he got so close to the Avenida. But they didn't find out
who that C-4 was.

· "You got me a name, right?" I ask them after. I drove on
over to where they lived, this cheapie flophouse on Savanna
Street full of homeboys sleeping on the floor, flojos snoring on
the couches, three tangled in a bed. There's white paint peel-
ing back from the shutters and these busted windows pieced
with electric tape. It was a grouper crash, the place where the
vatos go when their mamas yell them out of the house. I walked
up and banged on their door early in the morning and didn't
even blink when Montalvo answers it and I see how one of his
arms is wrapped up with bandages, a pink stain seeping through.
"I *know* you got me a name, son."

"Sorry, ésa," Montalvo says to me. He's wearing this bag-
lady–looking t-shirt and boxers and I can see all the red on his
skin from the Avenida. But under them scrapes he's giving me
icicle eyes to show he don't care one way or another. "Couldn't
get nothing," he said, then shrugs.

I knew I was in trouble when he looks at me like that,
forgetting who I am. That I'm la primera. Something crawls into
my belly then, sitting there cold and making me feel weak and
seasick. "You didn't find nothing because you don't want to,"
is what I say, knowing he thinks I'm just this crazy chavala who's
trying to get payback for a sorry crippled sheep. Montalvo don't
care I got Beto's ear, one woman's the same as the next to him.
The neighborhood's quiet with everybody still sleeping and I'm
trying to make my voice mean and low, but instead it grows
bigger, bending up and stretching like a howl. "You don't *want
to*," I tried to say again but then I hear I'm only screaming sounds
at him, *crying* sounds, filling up the streets and the sidewalks
and the trees with my sad noise.

Those was some black bad days. I'd look in the mirror
sometimes and see this white-faced llorona, with skinny bones

sticking out her face and big shiny eyes, like I'm sick. I remind myself how I used to be swinging around here telling locos what to do, not looking like some old ghost. You've gotta be that strong chica, I'd whisper to myself, staring at what I see. You didn't come this far to crack your head up. It don't matter Star Girl can't walk none, it don't hurt you, does it? Sit tight, woman, I'd say, and try to smile. But all my talking didn't make the bruja in the mirror run off, she just showed me her sharp bad wolf teeth.

A chica like me, she ain't meant to be crazy. I don't got time to be weak. I remember when I was a niña, tough as iron even then. Not the baby bandido hiding under the bed. I remember the one watching the world with her smart head and checking out what goes which way. There's the busboys and slick suits walking in my mami's house, there's me standing out in the hall listening. And even when Manny was beating me down, I kept my nose above water. Remember to breathe, that's what I do best. Breathe and keep living. So I didn't know why I was going all loose now. It seemed like I couldn't keep myself together no matter how hard I tried.

The only thing that made me feel strong was playing payback big. And I did it till it hurt.

"You all right, Lucía?" Chique asked me after I screamed crazy at Montalvo. I hadn't been right in the head for a while there, shivering and talking to myself, hiding out in my house. I knew she was checking up on me. "What's up, girl?" she said, standing over by the refri in her shiny black boots and mall-girl clothes and staring at my face like she sees something crazy there, like she sees my llorona. But she ain't stupid. She didn't try and touch me light on the arm, or tell me things are OK. She knew me good enough by then.

Back when Star Girl was walking, Chique knew she was always my second. I didn't hide that I loved Star special. I'd give her the lookout jobs and made her the main picker, the big dealer. But Chique was my right hand now. She was the one doing the lookouts and keeping her ear to the ground for me just like Star Girl used to. Girl didn't even wanna see me no more. Every day she's not walking she just got harder and meaner, but not like before. This was the hard you get when you lose something. She'd told me that she didn't want nothing more to do with la clika. "I paid enough, you see that," she'd said, turning her head up at me from her chair so I see that pale mouth, her stringy hair. She didn't even wanna get the C-4 who banged her. "It ain't gonna make me walk now, is it?" She wheeled herself around her place, her squeaky-sounding chair moving over the carpet. I thought, Give Girl time, give her time. We're gonna patch things up right.

Chique fit herself right into that empty space. She snugged herself by my side after the rumbla and acted like she'd always been my main gangster. And being a big head these days suited Chique good, I could tell that, turning my eyes from my wall and seeing her stand in my kitchen door waiting to hear what I've got to say. She just wanted to crawl up on top same as any other gangbanger, and with Star Girl gone she'd got this new shine in her eye. She'd permed her hair out curly and started wearing this butter-soft black leather jacket, a skin-tight skirt. Her skin glowed out like warm satin, and even though she was still pig-slop fat she was wearing it better, shifting her heavy ass back and forth down the street so you'd turn and look. The woman was even making sexy eyes at some of the vatos and acting tough with the sheep. She still had her head on straight, though. That girl could tell there was something up with me.

But she didn't have to worry about me too hard. I'm a woman who's always gonna keep standing strong. After all them days looking crazy at myself in the mirror, staring at my walls and my floors, I'd made up my mind. I already knew how I was gonna get my C-4. And having that plan set into me pushed up my bones, it put a shield in my hands. I was almost feeling good and scrappy again now that I knew what I was gonna do.

"So. Lucía. You all right?" Chique said again. She was staring at me patient.

"Just fine, ésa," I told her, flashing out a grin. "You go on and get me some Garfield babies and I'll be doing even better."

It all comes down to Garfield, that's where we fought our war. Garfield's full of mainly westside Parker kids cause it's on our side of the line but some of your C-4 babies go there too. Just walk around and look through the chain-link fence some-time. You'll see them little niños from both sides playing recess ball and laughing on the playground, stomping the flat black asphalt and screaming down from the bars like little monkeys. They're too young yet to know they can't be friends, but I'm changing that. All over the school walls there's Lobo and C-4 tags now, these big black and yellow sets tangled together and warring out over who's the main clika. It used to be that Gar-field's nothing but a money bag for me, I'd look through the fence and only see curious-cat junior high schoolers with a little pocket change. Now Garfield looked lots different. I knew if I got them greenhorns to go with the Lobos, we'd get so big nobody could hide from me. Not even that blank-faced C-4 boy.

If you wanna take over a place, you've got to piss all over it. And the first thing we did is fuck with Chico's head by crossing out all the C-4 tags and get a graffiti war started. Warming up. It was too easy, almost. We got the finest taggers here in the Lobos.

In the clikas, you got your warriors and you got your taggers. Taggers are usually third-raters cause they're the little bow-legged stubby locos that can't fight good. They got spray cans instead of pistols and go on their midnight tagging missions like they're ninjas. A Lobo tagger will paint our set up on the buildings, on the storefronts, on the stop signs, so that everybody knows who we are. You've seen it. ECHO PARK! in thick black blocky letters ten feet high blasting on down from the freeway signs. Our taggers have got their names painted proud all over town, and that's their black zebra stripes crossing out the lemon yellow C-4 tags on the walls. Around here, crossing out a homeboy's set is serious business. If a gangster walks by and sees your big old black line drawn through his name, he's gonna start hunting for you. He has to do something or else he loses face. Getting crossed out means somebody's slamming on your manhood. And rebels think that if they don't got their respect, they don't got nothing else either.

Well, that never used to matter to me none. That was all scratching and crowing, a waste of my time. "See how many tags I got, homes?" the tagger vatos would say to each other, and there'd be red and black and blue all over their hands. "I got me twenty-three last night, ése. I'm doing firme, you know what I'm saying." Stupid roosters. What did I care about that? The only thing that matters to me is money and my ladies. But I can play these boy games if I need to. The rules are real simple. You got to tag your territory or else it ain't really yours.

"Go out to Garfield and cross out all the C-4 you can see, eh?" Beto told the vatos, with me standing behind him quiet. Now that Hoyo was dead—there's this big RIP HOYO tag up by the 101—the main Lobo taggers was Tiko and Dreamer. Tiko, he knew how to butcher streets ugly by running down the sidewalk with his thumb on the spray-gun trigger. Dreamer, though, he's the best tagger in L.A. The number-one paint boy. A short dude, with this jailbird buzz cut and a slow buffalo walk, but he had these mile-a-minute hands. He was so fast with his can that even the cops knew his name. He'd tagged every big wall between here and Edgeware three times already.

Those two tagger boys started crossing out C-4 sets regular. They'd do it at night, dressing in black jeans and sweater, black cotton cap on to cover up. Dreamer would lead, and him and Tiko would sneak on down to Garfield quiet and careful with their black backpack full of cans, scope out all the C-4 sets, and then cross them out with a long black line and write up LOBOS after. They sprayed the whole school as black and red as a ladybug, and after a couple nights of missions there wasn't an inch of yellow anywhere in sight.

We had some bad rumblas then. The taggers was dog-fighting bloody over walls and right-hand vatos from both sides was circling Garfield, not even doing coke deals now but trying to jump in the junior high babies. "Hey, ése, you come over here a minute?" Gangsters would run on down after school's over and all the niños was walking home dressed in their sweaters and white scuffy sneakers. "You with us now, hear it?" the vatos would say, slapping them around a little. Most of them little boys would try and tough it out, but sometimes they'd be crying and looking around scared with their mouths hanging open. It didn't matter. Either way they swore they'd go with whatever clika was beating them.

Even I started to get some grouping done. About a month after Star Girl got shot, me and Chique went down to Garfield with Beto's boys looking for a couple of fresh-meat chicas to rough. Now that Girl was gone it was just the two of us, and I wanted a whole crowd of cholas under my feet. I wouldn't set my sights on just one or two. I'd get myself a dozen, twenty, and they'd all be scrappy and mean-hearted. Not at first, mind you. I wouldn't expect nothing of them pigeon-toes at first except some bawling and thumb sucking. But after I got through with them they'd be as tough as leather.

"Hey, *cholita*, pretty girl, you come right on over here, wanna talk to you," Chique was calling out to the sixth graders, watching out for a good one. My old homegirl Chique, she was the best jumper I ever saw. She cornered this little thing with a swingy ponytail who was walking home, later we called her Conejo because she was a round-faced bunnyrabbit-looking girl, her nose and eyes getting all pink. "Yah, I'm talking to *you*, ésa," Chique hissed at her, getting in her way on the sidewalk and then reaching down and grabbing her skinny arm. "You're a Lobo now, ain't you?"

"No, I ain't nothing," I heard Conejo tell Chique, making up this street voice, but she knew it wasn't no use.

I was standing right there in front of them and giving Chique my proud eyes, but in my head I saw how it was when I jumped in Star Girl. How we'd been warm and laughing there on the cold grass after, looking at the sky and feeling like familia.

"Yah, chica, you is," I heard Chique saying now, her breath coming up fast.

I looked off, over where a couple Lobos was messing with the little Garfield boys. They was the same as us, crowding and pushing and buzzing around like hornets. I could make out Rudy and Montalvo twisting around some scrubby-headed niño and Beto laughing at them on the side. Chevy was standing around with his hand in his pocket and hooting, "Chavala!" Even Dreamer was there, with his black shades on and arms crossed in front like a big head now that he'd done all them tough tagging jobs. And far out, outside them, there was my old tired man. He was peeking his head over the vatos and then sloping back and watching them quiet same as me. Oh yah, that's good, I'm thinking. I see you, Manny. Loser boy. And looking at him then, it seemed like so long since everything. Wacha me, right? I got what I wanted. Here's me jumping in a chola and there's him, way gone.

I'd heard that Manny was crawling around here already, that he'd started walking the junkie streets just a few months after the rumbla even though he'd got hurt so bad. I have to say he'd healed up pretty quick, cause he looked almost as strong as he used to even though you could still see how his shoulder was bent in and hunched some from Beto's knife. It almost made me sorry to see him outside, cause I know how cold that life is. He's got this sheepdog face on like he wants to help out with the Lobo jumping, but the vatos was turning their eyes from him and butting up their shoulders so he can't squeeze on in the circle. The homeboy looked poor too. He was wearing this raggedy old shirt and black wool cap pulled down to his eyes. I heard he was sometimes crashing at Chevy's and making his ends by doing little stickups at liquor stores, pushing his guns in them bodega ladies' faces the same as any old third-rater's gonna do. I knew he was hoping like hell to get back on in with la clika, that's why he's standing over there like a scarecrow. But it couldn't happen. Once you've been a jefe, that's it. You get a stink on you.

"Why don't you just head your ass on home, ése?" I screamed at him over the sound of Chique banging Conejo around, and the little one's crying now. "Go on back to your mama!"

I don't know if he heard me. Maybe he turned his eyes over my way to see me standing over my cholas and watching him hard. Maybe he don't wanna see me cause he knows he's just a beggar-looking Mexican wearing hobo clothes now. All I'm thinking is, Things sure are different, son, and I almost get soft-hearted there remembering how he used to be. But it don't last.

When I'm listening to them jumping sounds I start seeing that same picture again, there's Star Girl on the grass, smiling up at me with the fog of her breath twining up in the night air with mine. And then there's that woman sitting in her chair, and I see again how the dark sky's coming. Yah, things are different now, I think on over to him again, but colder.

I turned back to look at Chique doing her work. "Beat her good if you have to," I tell her. "Cause this little chola ain't going nowhere."

The Lobos grew bigger and spilled over with all of that new junior high blood. Soon we had almost double the number of vatos scamming the streets and fighting any C-4 they lay eyes on. Beto was strutting around with his bluffy big talk and his hitman swagger, but instead of a fedora he'd wear a Stetson. "You *know* you chose good," he'd say, making a muscle and then trying to give me his weak-mouthed French kiss. Well baby, either way it don't matter, I'd think on back to him. You could be anybody. You're worse than anybody. With me too busy dreaming on the C-4's blank face and with Beto playing king, the Lobo business had shrunk up and almost died. Now that Manny was gone Mario wasn't coming by no more, and the locals had heard we'd run out of supplies. But so what. I'll deal with that thing later, I told myself. I still had my own job to finish.

I'd got together a whole posse of chicas by then. I called them my Fire Girls. Hey, you're on fire now, girl, I'd tell them after they got jumped in and they'd look over at me with their wet eyes and scuffed-up faces then try and give me a smile. We got that Conejo, she was a big crybaby at first, a second-generation Sunday school chavala chewing on her nails and running home, but she warmed up quick enough once I showed her how good gangbanging can be. After that we snatched Payasa. I named her that cause she's clown funny with some big curly Bozo hair. And then Sleepy, this heavy-lidded cholita, and Linda and Thumper, these two sisters from Jalisco. Thumper banged her leg on the chair when she's happy and Linda didn't want no new clika name, so we let her stay the way she was. That was us, the Fire Girls. They was only twelve and thirteen years old but you want them young ones cause they can be the meanest. You just gotta kick that girlie out of them. It ain't so hard, once you scratch their dresses off and give them baggies and lipstick and taks, they take to it real nice.

A woman's clika does it different than the men. And not how you'd think, neither. I don't got no pink-dress lunch club, there ain't no softies in my gang. After we jump in a chica, she acts as wicked as a snake. She'll take on a vato if we tell her to, smack him right over the head with a lead pipe if that's what I want. No, a woman gang's different than a man's cause women need more love. The locos swing around Echo Park thinking they don't need nothing. They've got their clika brothers, right, but a man can just stand alone if he's got to. My girls, they're looking at me for something they don't got at home. Their daddies are whoring around and Mama's crying in the closet or wiping up the kitchen sink and *gritando* ugly if their niña misses a confession. Everybody's looking at the brother like he's the man of the house and who cares about little sister? Well, I do, I tell them. I'm gonna care for you good, girl, you'll be special here. You should see them open up, a woman's gonna bloom like a cut rose in water if you talk to her special. And once you hook a chica like that, she'll throw down worse than any man you'll ever know. They can be some vicious kick-ass bitches if you work them right.

That's why just after we'd jump them in by beating them down on the street and calling out Take it bitch, I'd change from a wolf to a kitten so fast that all their hurt and scared would crumple right into my hands. "We're your familia now, ésa," I'd tell my little girls, touching them soft on their shoulder like I'm their mama. "And you ain't never gonna be a sheep, all right? Now you're acting like you got some *respeto*. Don't forget it. I take care of my own, you hear that."

I'd say all the right words that they wanted to hear and then they'd look up at me with their flashlight faces, those sunny smiles, but I didn't feel their heat. I was saying the same things I told Star Girl and Chique all that time ago, but now I was talking through a cold wind. No matter how hard I tried I couldn't get that feeling like before, like when I was just a little loca myself, jumped in and brand new under them stars.

But you do what you do. Me and Chique got them started off picking pockets on the downtown streets at six o'clock when all the businessmen are walking home fast and hungry for dinner. Conejo and Linda would bump the gabachos and Sleepy and Thumper would dig down and snatch the wallets then come running back home to me flashing dollar bills. I even got my own big head meetings going, with Chique standing right by my side and my Fire Girls bringing me the money then sitting down in my living room. Hushed, watching me. They was listening to everything I'd say, lined up in a row and looking like sparrows waiting on a wire. "Do it like *this*, ésas," I'd tell them, showing them how to flick open a zipper on Chique. It almost made me feel like my old self, cause I could tell I hadn't lost my touch.

But the main job I had for my girls was for them to keep their eyes wide, their ears open. They was my lookouts. I had them scooting around the westside and even the sidelines of Edgeware and Crosby, watching out and listening hard for anything I might wanna hear. "Check out for the C-4, eh?" I told them. "You keep quiet and you'll hear some loco bragging sooner or later." Those girls was perfect spies cause they get dark in the shadows, go green around grass. They're invisible to men. If a chica stands around quiet long enough, a man just forgets her. He'll let forty cats out of their bags before he turns around and sees her watching him, her ears as big as jugs.

Well. Maybe. Even though I had them chicas, it still took me months before I got my payback. That C-4 hid out from me so tricky that even with my girls poking around after him night and day all I got was ghost stories, nothing I could sink my teeth into.

"Hear he's some C-4 big head, way up top," Thumper told me, hooking her thumbs in her pockets and poking her beak out at me. Or there's Linda, kicking the sidewalk with her sneaker and not looking me in my eye. "Lupe told me he was some C-4 vatito who moved away, jefa. Back to Arizona or something."

No, it took me months. My babies was coming back home with rumors and empty hands, and that blank-face C-4 was just teasing me with a sawtooth smile. I was dreaming about him every night then, his shadow creeping over the park, the sounds of the shot ringing, the feel of that cold wet grass over and over and the yells and screams of the rumbla while I'm racing away with wings on my feet. And Star Girl with her white cheeks out on the bench, her dry mouth like a pale flower and her eyes staring out the window. It almost got me shook up again, cause things wasn't fixing fast like I needed. Chasing that vato made my blood thin and my eyes cloud over, and that llorona started fighting me down harder than before. She'd raise up in me bigger and blacker and grin out from the mirror on late nights when I couldn't sleep good. I wanted that C-4 boy so bad I could taste it bitter on my tongue.

So when my Fire Girls told me they can't find nothing, when they'd scrape their shoes on the street and mumble into their hands, it got real hard to stay still. It got almost more than this chica could take. I'd pull out my pack and light up a Marlboro nice and slow, breathing in that black smoke deep to keep my hands from shaking the same as two leaves, to keep them from reaching out at my girls like biting snakes. Watch it, woman, I tell myself inside. Keep it cool.

"I don't wanna hear that," I'd say, slitting my eyes at them, my voice getting dark like the dusk before a bad fight. "You *find* him, eh? You go on out there and find out who my man is."

But a woman don't die from waiting. I've looked enough at the viejas around here to learn a lesson or two about long life. You've got to sit down on your ass sometimes and let the devil wander your way. And that's when you catch him. When he ain't looking.

I got my payback in the chilly autumn after a long hot summer of Lobos and Bomber rumblas. The enemies was busy hoofing up and down their turf and naming their streets, and the drivebys got random and cold blooded, even worse than before. The locals started hiding in their houses behind window bars and double-bolt locks, so the streets emptied and the air cleared of most everything except for the sounds of racing cars and shoot-outs and the once-in-a-while crying of a siren. Beto was getting himself a váto loco name even down in East L.A. from all the craziness, and I was grouping big too. Me and Chique and my Fire Girls jumped in five new fresh babies that winter, and they kept me rolling in pickpocket money and gossip news. Still. It seemed like my C-4 was gonna get the better of me, the better of my Star Girl. The Lobos and my cholas never stopped crawling around the Park and trying to sniff him out, but for a while there it looked like he'd hid out too good for even this mean perra.

I never forgot him for one day, though. I let all that fire-and-brimstone feeling sink down deep inside of me, so I'm swimming in it. I was looking up at the sky from the bottom of a lake, through all this black water. And it got so that I could see that llorona in the mirror and not feel scared no more, even if she jumps out and tears me with them wicked teeth. Well, chingado. I'm the one biting bloody now.

It was a cold California Saturday, the kind when there ain't no rain or no clouds but the air's sharp blades sticking you when you're outside, that they saw what I could do. Don't you mess with me or my own, I showed them. Cause you won't wanna pay my price. I can hurt you in the soft little place you didn't even know you had.

I remember every minute like it was yesterday. It's a late foggy morning and I'm trying to cool out by kicking my feet up on my table and rolling Marlboro smoke rings off my tongue like Dolores Del Rio. I'm all alone just the way I like it. I don't got to make nice to no jefe or landlord over chicas. I had a spell to sit there thinking my own thoughts. It was peaceful almost, a cigarette in my fingers and time on my hands, listening to the leaves rustle outside my window and the far-off holler of morning TV, but it don't last. I'm not dreaming there ten minutes when I get jangled by these vatos who start screaming down the street.

Hey man! I hear them outside. Órale! some loco yells, and it sounds like he's real close by. Their noise makes me sit up straight and bend my ear so I can hear better. Chique rushes me then, banging down my door with her two fists like the war's coming. "This better be good," I say when I open up, and she's standing there looking *chistosa*, her permed hair funky twisted from the wind and her big red lips yelling at me how we got to go down to Garfield *now*, that she found out my shooter man.

"Some Lobos got his baby brother Mauricio down at the school, Lucía," Chique tells me, I feel her hot breath on my skin and even though it's so cold her face is sweaty, but then I can't feel or see nothing. What she say? Baby brother. Baby brother, I keep thinking it over in my head. I know that name. I used to know it.

"All right, ésa, check it," she says, and it's like she's trying not to jump out her own skin. "Montalvo caught this little C-4 tagger crossing out Lobo sets at Garfield and when he gets to beating on him, the baby starts going on how the Lobos better watch it cause he's Chico's brother, and how Chico will kill all of us, that kind of shit. 'He'll kill you and your women,' he says. Like that one he took out at the rumbla. The one he shot in the back.

It takes me a minute, but then it hits me solid in the chest. The vato that started the whole thing finished it too. "We're gonna talk straight up, Lucía. I hear there ain't no other Lobo who's got it together," that's what he told me through the crack in my door and I felt full of spice and flame when he said them words. Then he's fighting Manny at the rumbla and after Beto takes over you couldn't see nothing but arms and legs bending and the blur of faces. There was the sounds of guns popping and the pounding of the Bombers running up by the benches and so I'd raced off, leaving my Star Girl to try and kill the loco that took out her Ghost man, her with them weak hands she had and she couldn't hold the gun right, but Chico don't show her no mercy. He just walks up while her back's turned and puts a clip right in her spine.

"How you hear this?" I ask Chique, filling out that C-4 blank face in my head. Halfie fuck. Greaser rubia hair like a girl, pinkie skin that can't take no sun. You're a strung-out white boy can't do your fights fair, eh? Can't walk away like a man. Got to go and bang on my chola cause you can't hold tight. Old Chico. That's the vato I've been dreaming about, and I know him too good. I knew you when, boy. When you was nothing. "How you hear?" I say again, but mostly so I hear my own voice out loud. I'm standing there in my doorway but it feels like my heart ain't even beating.

"Girl, you're gonna be the *last* Lobo to find out," Chique says, pulling my arm and making me get in my car. "I guess there was some homeboys around and word's spreading in the neighborhood like wildfire."

When I got there, after screaming on over to the school like a dragracer and jamming on all the reds, I looked around to see what my battle was gonna be. I'd have to be careful, cause once a man goes down in this neighborhood it seems like everybody hears electric fast at the same time, and I knew the C-4s would be racing over here to help out their jefe's baby brother as soon as they got wind. "Good thing, eh?" I said to Chique when we set foot on asphalt, eyeballing the playground for any badasses. But I didn't see any Bomber locos yet. There's just a crowd of Lobos far off, standing in a circle and looking down. Montalvo, Rudy, Madball, Dreamer. I see some of them have red warrior bandannas sticking out their pockets like blood roses, but now they look as still and timid as schoolteachers. And there's some sheep on the sidelines, keeping their mouths shut but playing nervous with that fried hair of theirs. I even see Manny waiting on the outside as usual and wearing his loser hangdog face.

I can't make out what they've got there. I figure it's that Mauricio beat up bad on the ground cause they ain't kicking or laughing at nothing, only keeping their shaved heads bent. Watching. It's quiet as a cloud. There's still a little baby blue morning color in the sky so nobody's out yet, and you can't hear a peep coming from the vatos. Nothing was coming from baby brother neither.

More Lobos show when I start walking up to that little circle. Beto comes around, and I see Chevy and Wanda driving up. Rocky and Tiko and Popeye are coming through the gate behind me. Even Cecilia's racing on in and beelining for Manny.

"It's gonna be hot, ésa," Chique's saying next to me, and my heart starts steamrolling cause I know I'm gonna get that C-4 back after all this time.

"What you homeboys up to, eh?" I say, my voice breezy. I'm making my way up there slow the same as a big head would instead of running and flapping my hands like a henpecking woman, and I'm still keeping a lookout for any sign of C-4. "What up?" I ask again but nobody's talking. I don't get one sign from them till I get real close and then Dreamer looks up at me, and he don't have no buffalo to him right then. He's wearing this face as ragged and thin as worn cotton, and from the pinch of his eyes I see how he's fighting down shame.

I push them open and see this red-colored beat-up kid bent up double on the ground like babies do in their mama's bellies. His shirt's scraped off, his arm's twisted the wrong way, and there's that yellow tagging paint on his open hands, capping his fingers. I can't make out his face, but that vatito looked right, dark like I remembered and he wasn't more than nine or ten even though his head's half buzzed clika style and he's got a Bomber tak scratched on his bony boy chest. He looked like Chico's. But he'd took it bad. From what I can see of his skin, already blue and purple in places, there's some stripe cuts bleeding down his ribs and slashing up his neck and face. I know them marks. He got them from getting kicked when he was already flat down. This puppyboy was whipped worse than any full-sized loco I'd ever seen except for old dead Ghost, but he still was breathing. I see his lips flutter up like they'd caught a breeze.

"This the baby brother?" I ask, and I see Manny standing behind them begging at me with his glassy eyes as big as mirrors, asking me can he have a piece.

Montalvo nods his head, looking at me careful but not like before when he was thinking I'm some bird-brained nobody screaming on his front steps. Now he's scared *he*'s the crazy

Mexican cause he'd beat some empty-handed tagger baby near dead. "Yah, he was yelling something about Chico shooting off a sheep at the rumbla."

"What's that?" Beto'd caught up by then and the homeboys stepped aside easy, but when he sees Chico's boy he shuts right down. He leans back on his heels and whistles low while the homies watched him careful to see what he's gonna do. But he didn't do nothing but keep standing there as dumb and fix-eyed as a cow, and they started coughing and twitching their heads around nervous.

"All right éses, looks like you done real good," I start saying, keeping that voice of mine nice and light.

I could tell they was getting weak on me there, that they was gonna curl up the same as that boy on the ground if I didn't make my move. But it don't surprise me none they can't take it. Like I said before, clikas used to have rules. We used to have some religion. Time was, the locos had to leave the pride-and-joy women and babies alone and keep the fighting to themselves. But not no more. Chico broke up my Girl and left her with that tree stump cutting her back open, the white shiny roots stretching down to her loose legs. My homeboys was staring at that C-4 baby like they don't wanna know what their own monster hands can do, but I can look it straight in the face any damn day then swallow it down and smile. Baby brother there with the eyes beat shut ain't gonna ruffle my feathers. He had it coming.

All of a sudden the light flickers and it looks like his eyes was gonna open, or that his mouth's twitching like a smile and I think he's gonna sit right up and laugh at me the same as old Lazarus. But it wasn't nothing but a shadow falling on his bent-up self. It flashed in my head then how Manny and me used to be the same, rock sharp and strong all the way through down to the bones, I remembered that when Manny moved quick by me and I hear his breath close to my ear and he blocks the sun from the baby on the ground. Manny was switching his hands up like he was gonna do something, gonna grab hold of that boy and beat him worse to show me he could still sing for his supper, but when I turn and look at him I see he don't have his old hot stare or the same steel jaw sticking at me prideful. He's only some burn-out veterano now, with a skinny face and glassed-out carga eyes, wearing that wool cap pulled low and some ripped-up dumpster pants. He's not the same vato I used to know. With his mashed arm Manny couldn't give a good featherweight punch these days even to save his own skin.

"Yah, you vatos done a real nice job here, but we better scoot off, hear me?" I say, pushing Manny soft with my hand and he gave easy, backing down like a hit dog and Beto's vatos close around me again.

I know it for sure then. Nobody, nobody can tough it out like this chica can. I see past Manny how the sheep was looking over at me scandalous and making their tight mouths like I'm this empty-bellied bruja. Some even got muddy crocodile tears running down their faces from crying over the little C-4. Cecilia's staring at me wicked out of that dirt-colored face of hers, thinking I'm some baby-eating witch who's stealing up her brother. And my homeboys was circling me, their lips pulling sad like they're some viejas at a funeral.

"Órale. Looks like he's hurt bad," Beto says, bending down and poking the brother with his finger but the thing down by my shoes wasn't moving an inch.

"Well fuck him then. Got it?" I start up, steel-tough sounding now and Beto gives me some cold-water eyes, the same as Manny got when he figured me out but I don't care. They can see me all they like cause I can tell we're all gonna be standing around here like lazy brains when the C-4 bigs get here, and they're gonna give us an eye for an eye cause it looks like we killed one of their babies. "Let's GO, they're coming quick, you hear that?" I'm yelling at them now, that llorona bumping up in me big. It feels dark and windy when I watch them walk away from the brother in slow motion, dragging their heels even though this is for my Girl, this is our payback, leaving a half-dead C-4 baby twisted on the ground like my Star Girl on the grass waiting for la chota to bring her back to Kaiser. The Bombers can't just bang a Lobo woman and get off scot-free. This is the one thing that's gonna make us equal.

"Come ON," I say, hitting Beto hard in the arm so that he wakes up and we scattered on out of there. I ran as fast as the vatos with the air cold on my cheeks, hearing the sheep crying behind me and leaving that busted brother with all the life bleeding out of him for Chico to find. I got this blast of heat that was singing through my arms and legs and making me feel like my old self again, knowing that soon he'd see his pride-and-joy C-4 baby and put his red wet face in his hands cause I hurt him so bad, the same as he hurt me.

I didn't care about nothing then when I was pounding my way back. I wasn't thinking about Chique or the Lobos or doing deals or even Star Girl with that dark sky over her face. I only felt cut loose and fire-hot inside, thinking how I'm the only one in this town who can do it. *Wáchale* man! I felt that steering wheel tight in my hand and I was gunning my Maverick down the street, laughing loud as a banshee the whole way home cause I knew it. Check it on out. Nothing's keeping this chola down. I'm the only woman or man in this place, the only one in Echo Park who can scratch on up to the top and stay there.

Part Three

1997

Cecilia

I don't get stir crazy no more. I don't crouch down in the dark to watch the street in the cool air after bad midnight. I don't kiss pillows or breathe in sweet musk. You can see how I'm all fixed up and righteous now with this Bible in my hand. I don't bang and I don't sex. I don't do nothing but sit here and pray and clean and eat and sleep.

I do what should come natural. Because a woman's first thing is to make babies and love them better than herself, better than the skin that's covering her bones. A woman's first thing is to sit on the park bench with the other ladies and look at her baby and smile. That's what I was all set up to do. I was pregnant with my baby girl, and I know she would have been real beautiful, a precious pink flower blooming. But I wasn't like a real woman. I had something wrong in me, something dirty. I didn't deserve her and God showed me that crystal clear. He showed me twice.

So I do a woman's second thing. I go to the church and confession my soul out till it's clean and snow white, the same as fresh-washed clothes hanging on the line. *Purísima.* I sit with the padre in that small hot booth and fold my hands careful, breathe in the dry hot air while I tell him all my evil thoughts, all the bad things I ever did, and I feel my sins rushing out of me like water, like a river, back into the dark salt sea. I pray my rosary every day. I've got it hanging by my bed so I can see the plain wood cross minding me when I wake up. I offer the silver milagros at the altar as penance. And there ain't nothing that can hurt me now. Because I live right.

I pray and I work. I ride to the rich neighborhoods on the RTD and sit with the other cleanerladies, some of them so tired they're sleeping with their heads thrown back or butting up against the dirty window glass. But I don't sleep. I wash them fancy houses and smile at the rich rubias who can't say my name, they break it ugly in their mouths and then talk too loud like I'm half deaf. Even if I want to smack them across the teeth I just smile and get down on the floor to scrub and sweat and wash all that dirt off, bending my head modest just like a woman should. I work till I can't think no more, till my arms hurt, my neck stiffs up, till I see my red hands and my red knees and my eyes sting. That's when I get my peace. That's when I get my rest, when I'm dead tired and all the ghosts stop their yelling and singing. I can get my sleep then.

There wasn't nowhere else for me to go but to these hard church seats every Sunday, praying Amen with my hands pressed together. God made sure of that. He cut me off from everybody and everything I ever loved before, so I was standing alone, just me for once, and I looked up at the sky and through the streets for something, anything to get me through.

When I saw that little boy beat so bad he wasn't going to last the night, and all of them racing off and leaving him on the playground because they were too scared for their own selves to care about anybody else, my brother even, I got freezed up ice cold inside. That morning I was on my way to the market with a list in my head and my mama's money in my purse. Bread, coffee, pan dulce, apples, milk. But then there was that rushing sound, the racing rumbla sound of all the feet running on the sidewalk and the streets and everybody yelling and screaming and laughing while they're banging off to Garfield, and I knew something bad was going down. Manny, I thought, something bad, Manny. Even though we were strangers then, I still couldn't break off my brother. That's why I followed the homeboys and the sheep to the school so that I could stand there on the playground all freezed up while I watched them leave that Mauricio for dead. I was alone there, and what am I going to do? I knew it was my job to help Chico's baby brother because that's what a woman's made for. It was my second chance. But the C-4 locos were coming and it was going to be me then, Lobo Manny's little sister beat up hard on the ground or worse. So I was the same as my weak-hearted Manny, running away coward fast back out of Garfield, and I could still hear that boy trying to breathe and live even though it wasn't no use.

No, there wasn't nothing for me after that. I couldn't shake off that freezed-up feeling, knowing how I was as wicked as the rest of them. And when I turned around there wasn't no one there to warm me up, neither.

"That's it then, you ain't gonna see me no more," Chucha said when she'd heard, and I saw again how she was a hard-trash sheep who wore tight jeans and had a wide loud brick-red mouth. This was an old-timer that bottom-line belonged to Chico. She'd never really been mine.

"It wasn't *me*, I didn't do nothing," I told her, hearing my voice break because I knew my girl was already gone. I reached my hands on out but she wouldn't let me touch. Mauricio being dead because of the Lobos meant she didn't have room for me no matter what I say. Chico had screamed and cried like a wild man when he found out about his brother, I'd heard. He promised to kill us all. He'd burn the westside to cinders. Chucha wasn't going to leave her boss man for some girl like me who was so far on the outside nobody would even say my last name. She knew where her steady came from.

"Not even gonna know you on the street," she said, folding herself up like a box and I could tell by her thin voice how she meant it. I tried to dig up all the hate I had in me, scrape it out my heart and into my mouth so I wouldn't cry. I wouldn't care about this trash sheep chica ditching me. But she still had the same brown velvet and gold-dust–colored eyes that looked straight at mine, and my mouth was empty. When she took off my ring from her little finger and put it back in my hand, I couldn't feel hard against her because she was still my only girl.

That's some cold day, being alone like that. And I'm not a person who's built to be alone. Muñeca, that's what they called me and they were right. I ain't built for it. I always had a somebody, my mama when I was a baby, Manny all them years, then Chucha. There was always a beating heart and pair of strong arms for me to love. Somebody who let me know where I am, pointing me down my road.

* * *

I could have been a hundred different things. With Chucha I didn't need to have no baby to be going someplace. I thought I could be like a real strong man who'd walk off into the sunset and make you wonder. Where's that girl going? Anything, once. Anything. But after Chucha split me, that big world shrank back up like a small hard stone. The only thing I could see then was the church, because that's where all the women run to once they lose what they used to have. They sit on the benches and pray for their husbands dead from drink or bolas and light the candles for their gangbanging sons dead from gunshots. You'll see me there now too, sitting right next to them and my mama with my eyes closed, whispering.

God loves you, Cecilia, padre John told me, and I figured I'd believe him. God loves you better than anybody. So I tied back my hair tight and washed houses and prayed all my days away by the gold shining candles, the old rose incense. But God doesn't have eyes to look at you and he doesn't have a flesh-and-blood hand that can reach out and touch you when you can't sleep. I try to make Him out in the shadows of my mirrors or in the lines of my palms, in the smoke that comes up from the candles. He hides. On Sundays I listen to the padre preach on about love and forgiveness and I pray *Señor, Virgen, no te apartes de mí* but my prayers don't float. They're these heavy stones sinking in the river, not clouds like they should be. It's my own fault. I work hard, but some days my mind fights me. While I'm trying to hear the padre or pray up past the ceiling, instead I'm seeing the old days. Back when I was the lookout out on the sidewalk late at night watching the cars' high beams curve around the corner, and those times when the homeboys looked at me like I was that princess because I was Manny's sister.

But I get better every day with trying so hard. You've got to get your faith as strong as a mountain and forget those bad things to catch God. Some people, they've got the gift. There's an Anglo lady out in Georgia who lives on a farm and she sees the Virgin nice and regular out there in the grassy fields. You read about her in the paper. She's built herself an altar with a big cross and all the foreigners come out to visit her and grab a peek of Mary. Then there's the three little *mexicano* boys out by Acapulco, they saw the Virgin wearing snow-white robes in the rock cliffs by the water and now they can cure cancer with a touch of their finger. The pope himself came out to see and blessed the spot with his own hands. And the vieja that was visited by three angels dressed in silver armor and holding spears who warned her about the earthquake in Mexico City. They say she saved two hundred people.

Those are the ones who are pure, the ones who get visions or who bleed from the hands and feet. The ones who speak in tongues. They've got God inside them through and through. If you cracked their hearts open you'd look and see nothing but solid gold.

But not me. If you cracked my heart open all you'd see is blood. I'm regular people, a normal woman, not even a chica no more. I used to be that princess and I could choose whichever vato I wanted. I'll take *you*, that's what I told Beto, and back then he smiled like he won a prize. Now I'm one of the ladies trying to see God's face in a shadow, a viejita dressed in blue on the bus, ready to bend my back over your mess.

I tell you how to do it. Scrub the sinks down with hot water and vinegar, works better than any store-bought. And wipe the floors with Pine-Sol so that they're all shiny. Dust wood with old cotton rags, wipe every corner clean. That's where I get my pride now. Polish the silver, clean out the toilet, take out the trash. Thirty dollars for a house, and I'll make it sparkle, make it smell just like fresh lemons broke from the tree branches and squeezed in my own fists. That's my pride. I make my living honest.

Even my mama's seeing how I changed so much. She used to think that I was a no-good. Puta, that's what she called me. *Puta*, spit out through her teeth like a seed. She said I'd been whoring around with gangsters and so she had her eyes bright only for Manny. Even though he shook his hand at her like a naked animal and shamed her by being a jailbird, when he'd come back home her face lit up like Christmas, and then faded back down when she was alone again except for me. But Mama thinks of me different now, I can feel it in her fingers. She must have looked around finally and seen how all the men go away, how they can't be trusted, the husbands and the sons leaving you behind cold and lonely when they're through with what you've got to give. When you're empty from all that giving. Not the daughters, though. She must have seen that. It's the daughters that come back, moving their lips silent and seeing the ghosts behind the doors. Ready to scrub floors till they're blind tired.

Mama's face didn't smooth and she still wouldn't spend a kind word on me, but I could tell. I was her hija again. She's got the same square brown hands as me, the same short cinnamon-colored bracero fingers. She keeps them clenched by her sides when she talks but they flex and nimble when she works in the kitchen. They smell like cut meat and coffee, of the brown oil soap we use. And they started touching me soft sometimes. They'd brush my sleeve or pull back a string of my hair, or cup my elbow when she walks past me close in the kitchen. It almost made things worth it, those little warm touches that let me know things were all right. That I could stay.

* * *

So I can stay right here with Mama, in this house, on this street, in this neighborhood. I can come home every night to the quiet dinners where we trade salt and small talk back and forth, and I can spend my Saturdays watching the novelas and cry too hard at the sad scenes. It ain't a bad life. I don't complain. I made my best choice, so I get to live just fine. Better than most. Better than an old kingpin even. See, because Manny, he was burning too bright. You've got to stick with the kind of life you're meant for, here with Mama, here with the other Parkers on the bus. A person can't reach too high, or else they get burned.

I ain't seen Manny again since that last time, but I can't forget it. You can't rip those pictures from your eyes no matter what. We'd heard the stories that he'd never got his place back with the Lobos and so his pride had turned him bad, made him into a trash-eater, but I never believed them. Not till then. I'd got off at my bus stop after a day of cleaning two big houses, and if my back was hurting you wouldn't know it because I was walking as straight as a line. Down the block I saw a bum sitting against a red-tagged concrete wall, cradling one of his arms close to his chest and wearing these raggy black clothes, and I wiggled my fingers in my pocket looking for a coin even though he wasn't sticking out his hands or shaking a can of dimes. But when I got closer, I saw the hard shape of the bum's chin, the curve of his shoulder, and I knew.

"Oh, no," I said, looking down. "Manny."

He turned a face up to me that was dirty and paler and scratched bloody on the left cheek, and it took a minute for them milky eyes to see who I was.

"Lookit that. Cecilia. Hey *you*, baby sister." His voice swung up like he was crooning but I heard a mean edge under them words. I bent down to touch him on the hand, and then started tugging on his sleeve.

"Come on, you can't sit here in the dirt. I'm taking you home."

"Baby sister's gonna save me, everybody!" he yells out, laughing when I start pulling on his arm, and he smelled bad, this sharp sour coming off in waves. His sleeve pushed up and I saw blue bruises striping his arm, and when he didn't move I stood back and pressed my hands together.

Manny pulls out his pack then and lights one up, but I saw how the match flame's shaking. He eyeballs me real hard.

"Well shit," he says, and he wasn't laughing no more. "I don't need no saving, Ceci. What could you do anyways. Nothing, eh? Check you out, church lady. Looking at me like some dummy."

He's right. I'm standing there like a slack-jawed fool, but I can't cough out a word. My hands grab into fists because it's still catching up on me that this is my Manny. He's skin and bones. He's got newspapers stuffed in his shoes. And he's a mumble talker too, like an old drunk who's been singing himself to sleep for too long.

"Well, girl, my little girl," he says. "Never was too sharp up there, know what I'm saying?" He spits out a laugh and wags his fingers at me and then points to his head like a clown. "But oh no, baby, that ain't me. No, SIR. I ain't deaf. I ain't blind. I know plenty about you fools. Hoo-hoo. I know what you're saying. Talking how I fucked it up. Didn't mess Mauricio like I should. Didn't beat Lucía good while I had my shot. But nobody knows, man. Órale but they forget all about it. It was me, my baby girl. ME. I made this town with my bare hands." Manny sticks out his skeleton hands to show me and then puts them back down. "So do me right, see? Vatitos maddogging me down the streets. Leaving me here. Should give me RESPECT. And a jefe can't be low-down for too long, stupids. A jefe can't be digging through the trash. No baby, not like that. I gotta walk *tall*. Eh? I gotta make my living like a *man*."

Manny finished taking a drag then he flashed his arm straight out and points his finger so I flinch, but his eyes looked far away like he didn't see me. "'Stick em up, son! YAH!' That's what I tell them. 'Stick it up, motherfuck, you gotta bad loco in your face now! Oughta be scared. I better see you shaking.'" He puts his hand down then leans his head back, and he looked almost happy now. "Ooooh, I like it. Like them old days, Muñeca girl. And oh no. It ain't over, neither. Hear me. Gonna be all set up right. Then you gonna see. And I'll show you too, my baby. I was always the baddest loco and nothing's changed that."

I was crying by that time. There's wet messy tears streaming down my face and my nose is running, and I bent back down to grip hold of his sleeve, keeping the cloth tight in my hand, but he wouldn't stop his singing. I'd pushed up his sleeve again and both of us looked down at all them bruises, blue, purple-green, new red bloody ones, and he covered them up. "Ceci," he says, looking back in my face. "That wasn't gonna be me. No way. That was *him*. There he was looking at me. He was punching the air and I could tell he was junked bad. Hmmm? I thought, Hey, man. That loco's gone for good. He's a junk boy now. Oh, you all fucked up with them drugs. Made him turn his back on me so that better-than-blood don't mean shit no more. Chingado downed me. Never never gonna forget what he did. But I see it. Okay. Why he punked me out. If you cold outside and your main locos forget you? You gotta beg for your lady to give you a look? You gotta turn. Turn it *on*. I was itching for my time, but that waiting's gonna wear you thin. Need a pick up, señor, that's right. Pick me up."

He wasn't making a piece of sense to me. "Manny, let's just go home," I heard myself say, and then I was down on my knees next to him. "We'll take you back and then you'll be all right."

But he didn't get to his feet and straight up his clothes like I wanted. Instead his head swung loose on his neck and his eyes got glassy, and he was smiling like an old end-of-the-rope veterano. "Back home. Where's back home? I ain't going to no back home. Belong right here. These my streets, girl." His voice was getting blurry and he wasn't even singing no more, just talking crooked so it's hard to keep up with his words, and when I saw that he was diving down deeper I edged away from him because it looked like death. "Now I told you, and you know that I'm gonna be styling it soon. Make her wish she ain't never even heard my name. But right now I'm taking a little *vacation*, little baby sister." He breathed up heavy and stretched his hands out like he wants a hug, but I couldn't touch him then. "See that?" His feet kicked out like a twitch. "That's my fire, Muñeca. See how it burns bright? Warm inside, like looking straight in the sun. That's the fresh thing. Hhhmmmmm. Just gotta put my head back and sleep a little. Dream that monkey down. But pretty soon. It's gonna happen. They're gonna see me and say, Hey, baby. Don't be mad. We didn't forget you. They're gonna say it. You're the real thing, ése. You're the number one."

He didn't say nothing more, just let his cigarette roll out his hand and burn dead on the sidewalk while I watched. And after that, what's to say? I don't remember leaving him, getting up off my knees and brushing the dirt off my hands, turning my back away and walking off. All I know is that I didn't take him home. I didn't wipe up his bloody face or get him some food. Didn't even say nothing to our mama when I got back to the house, just walked through the door and warmed up dinner the same as any other day. I ain't sinful how I left him there. And it doesn't mean I stopped loving the cowboy part of him that's strong enough to fight the world. But there's times when a body can't go down no old road again, they get to a place and you're stuck for good. In a ditch. Me, I got myself right back on track and here's where it gets me. Safe and sound. Knowing right from wrong. But still feeling too much so I can't forget. Bums on the street haunting me. That gangster blood banging in my heart sometimes late at night when I can't sleep and the stars keep shining white-hot into my room the same as they always did. Maybe after a while, though, all that old hurt won't feel so bad. See, because if she prays enough and works enough, a woman can forget most anything.

God, He's supposed to fill you up inside. He's supposed to give you hope. Señor, no te apartes de mí, that's what I pray when the padre puts his hands down and we stand up. Don't leave me, God, the words coming out of my mouth and landing stone-heavy on the ground. But it's hard to pray to something so big. To something so mean. The Dios we hear about in church, He's got storms in his eyes and hell-red fires on his breath. He wants you weak and scared, the same as a lamb before the kill else you're going to be burning once Judgment comes, burn so hot your skin will turn to silver and crack in blue flame. He strips you of what you had before, all your bad dreams, your bad wants, and you've got to love Him anyways with all your soul, like I loved Manny in them old times with his strong arms and his beautiful skin, like I loved Chucha laughing with me on the couch.

Got to love Him and do what He says. A woman *prays*, He tells you. She prays and bends and doesn't complain. So that's what I do but my prayers, they don't float. They don't swim. They're smooth river rocks, slipping out your fingers and down through the water. I'm sitting in church but in my heart I'm bending over the river, trying to grab up them rocks before it's too late. And sometimes I think, It is too late. Too late for you, Muñeca. Because that's what you still are. I hear the sermon march on and feel my mama's warm fingers beside me, but I'm seeing all them old faces rushing up and I'm saying to myself, Too late, Muñeca, you're too far gone. I grab up any river rock I see then. Amen, the padre says again, and I know I've got to stand up for all I'm worth. Stand up and throw them stones hard at the sky.

Water and vinegar, soap, dry clean cloth, and candles. River rocks, *santos*, milagros. Here's my confession, padre. The one I don't tell you. I don't got Jesus' blood on my hands, I don't see angels, and the God with the hot-fire breath doesn't fill me up the way He should.

Maybe I've got my own God right here, and He doesn't look like the padre's. He doesn't look like my mama's. He won't kill you dead with lightning bolts come Judgment Day, and he won't tear out your red heart and show you how it ain't worth nothing. He's got this nice wide face, smiling. He knows who I am, deep down. I'm the viejita crossing her legs on the bus, folding my hands careful in confession, and I pray with my lips moving quiet while I wash the floor. I smooth my tight hair back with water. But that ain't the last word. I made some things in this life. I made me a baby and I made me a good friend. You can't get them things for cheap. Maybe I got my own God sitting right here, waiting till I bloom like that flower I once had turning inside me. Then he'll show me my good thing, waiting so patient behind the dark trees in the park.

Or maybe I'll make it myself. That's what I think when I'm feeling good and brave, on the days when I can throw stones at the sky. That I'll carve it up from the dirt and the water and the soap, the candle wax. Bless it with my own breath. It doesn't have to be beautiful, it doesn't even have to be pure. It just has to last me. It just has to be my very own.

Lucía

See that street? Alvarado Street, the straight black road lined
with the bodega stores and the little cholas hanging by the
corner? It belongs to me. And Elsinor, Benton, Reservoir streets
with the old peel-paint houses and the rusted chain-link and the
pickups by the curb? All mine. If you say my name out loud there
every Mexican walking by is gonna stop and look at you careful. They all know who I am. I'm the one who's got her vatos
and chicas kicking it up and down the sidewalks selling sugar
to the daddies driving by looking for some game. Hey baby, you
wanna bite? Give them a couple a dollars and they'll get you
smoking real fine. Because of me this neighborhood's *jamming*.
I gotta watch out cause of la chota, they stick it in me hard by
jacking my Fire Girls up on the walls for pat down and they stay
busy by beating up my Lobos. But I got my businessman hat back
on and nobody's stopping this jefa now.

I've just gotta be careful. I'm watching my back these days. I ain't gonna loca out for anybody no more. I killed that llorona and buried her deep in the ground. I knew she was dead for good when I saw Star Girl that one last time. After I banged that C-4 baby brother. "Girl, I did it for you," I told her, but she didn't care none. She's rolling around in that wheelchair and taking them poor government checks. She don't want nothing to do with my clika. Just kept saying the same things. "Ain't gonna make me walk now, is it? Ain't gonna bring back my Paco." Girl still had that dry mouth and those loose hands and I felt like I was looking at her from a long ways off. I didn't even feel nothing, no cold wind making me crazy, no hot blood boiling up. I saw how I had to close that door. Her or me, I could see that clear as day. Her or me. And I wasn't gonna let her bring me down. I won't spend the rest of my days staring out some window. Cause I've already paid my price.

I can see how it is, and it don't pain me. It don't give me no shame. I've left losers behind before, and now I can do it without barely blinking an eye. I look at you and the first thing I think is, How much are you gonna cost me? It all comes down to dollars. How much are you gonna take? Any time we jump in a new Fire Girl, I let them know it straight up. I own you, ésa. You cost what I say. So my Fire Girls, they're working out good. I've got a whole posse of them brown baby girls now, slanging and picking and trying to get on my right side. Most of them are gutter chicas, somebody else's thrown-out trash. But they're worth something to me. Pennies, dollars, whatever they bring in. You do for me, and you're treated real nice, that's what I tell them. And they're jumping, these cholitas with their big eyes. You give them a little love and they'll jump as high as you want.

Chique's still hanging by. She's a tired black-leather ruca these days who can't run the way she used to but I let her kick it for old-time's sake. "Hey you remember?" that's all she says now, she's wearing out like all the rest except for me. You can see them vieja lines already around her eyes and she breathes heavy even when she's walking up porch stairs. "Hey you remember when we was fresh and young and banged around here like tigers?" she says and I throw her a couple dollars to keep her quiet. "I don't remember nothing," I tell her. "So shut up." Chique pipes right down and stuffs that money in her pocket but what I say ain't altogether true. Turtle girl, you remind me of them good times, don't you. Something about you.

I got myself one special cholita around here. She's this Tijuana-born-and-bred illegal who slipped on over with her brother when she was just fourteen and I found her skinny like a winter tree, begging out on my streets with her empty hands cupped open. "Get your ass outta here," I yelled at her then smashed a bottle sharp on the ground, but she stayed put. Turtle. Named her that cause she snaps shut. She must have some ugly Mexico in her cause she don't never say nothing about her old days. Once I cleaned her off I saw that chola in her, fresh and mean. Now I give her my mama smile and she puppydogs my heels but she don't show you her cards. Turtle girl don't talk back and she don't say much of anything else, neither. She just looks at you with them black Indian eyes she's got. Yah, she reminds me of something. The loca is meaner than a barracuda and I can send her on some tough missions—reds, whites, carga, snow, don't matter. She'll come back with more money than three chicas put together. "You get any trouble?" I ask her, and she just shakes her head no. "Nothing I can't handle," she says, simple as that, and it almost makes me proud. I see them scrapes on her hands but she don't brag. Gets the job done. Maybe someday I'll make her a big head same as Chique was, the same as Star used to be. Cause I've got my eye on the future. But I try not to think about her much. Every time I get to feeling too warm or too proud or too sorry, that old cold front comes creeping back up my spine. How much are you gonna cost? I look at them Indian eyes and I know she's gonna cost big if I let her. And you're not gonna see me there again, hearing rancheras in my head and talking crazy in the mirror cause I let some chica get under my skin. She reminds me of something, but I don't know what. And I ain't gonna try too hard to find out.

I've already got enough on my mind. We're back in business and it's better than ever. Beto and me are busy heading up these two clikas, the Lobos and my Fire Girls, and once we got Mario back on the job we started pulling in the steady cash again. Mr. Slick Boy Mario with his sugar and silk shirts didn't wanna do business with me. When I called him up for supplies he just laughed that old laugh. "No chavalas, no chavalas," he said. "I don't deal with bitches." And so I had to hand him on over to Beto. I told the little scarface to show Mario a wad of stick-up cash and get me some load. Now we're hooked into Echo Park, Lincoln Heights, El Sereno. Some Long Beach and Cerritos. And I run these streets like a clock with my little pencil and that calculator in my head.

I've still got to let Beto think he's the Man. He's doing his job fine now but anytime he gets weak there's some other sweet-smelling vato I've got waiting on the side. "You know you picked right," he still says to me and I wink pretty at him but I've got my eyes wide open. I'm always on the lookout for the next jefe once this one burns out. Right *there*, ése. Right there soft till I say when, that's what I tell them little vatitos who want their shot. They look up at me with their wine-red mouths and they don't never get tired, do they? The young ones are the best, working so hard. They hope and hope that I'll set them up good, but I never make no promises. I just ease my head on back and close my eyes and see how long they can go for the ride.

Those locos line up for me whenever I want. Nobody asks me no questions now. They see how I stood there tough and strong at Garfield, and they know what I can do. I can make them a king if I feel like it. Even if Beto's acting like he's boss man, I'm the one here giving the orders. After Garfield, everybody knew jefa's my real name.

It ain't like I don't got my problems. The C-4s still give me a good kick in the ass. Even though junked-out Chico got banged off the top last year and now they got some new patrón named Hi-C—he's this mean mother who bloods his boys ugly when they get out of line—them C-4s still don't give me no rest cause of what we did to that Mauricio. If you see yellow you still gotta duck your head low. But my biggest pain is the cops now, la LAPD. All of these gabachos started moving back into the Park. Take a look around and you'll see them blondies with their full pockets walking around here, mixing in with the Mexican peoples. It don't seem fair. Stay on your side, right? They're itching for a taste of what we got to sell—cheap houses, sunshine, a little snow. And any time you got gabachos, you got trouble. Four months ago some white dudes trying to show off to their women had the balls to try and buy over at the Avenida de Asesinos but they got spanked. Some C-4s opened up on them and killed a rubia. Made it all over the TV. And even though we've got a hundred dead brown babies in these parts and there ain't nobody crying about them, after the gabacha girl got hit there was black-and-whites driving down my streets thick as locusts. These days even if you're just standing around minding your own, they'll come up and jack you up hard against the wall, spreading you out and kneeing you in the ass, in the gut, feeling you up and in between to see if you're packing some.

Sometimes you'll see a real badass homeboy crying when he gets jacked, his face all red and the tears streaming down his cheeks cause he's so mad and scared that he's gonna get sent back. And my Fire Girls, they break down even worse, say Yes sir and No sir and I think they're gonna get down on their knees like in church. They lose their pride once them Blue Suits show, because they think about all they could lose. But not this chola. I've been there a couple of times, but I always stand real still. You can't see nothing on my face and I don't say a word. I let them pigs do what they want. They can't get nothing on me. I'm just a chica, and they don't know what they got on their hands.

That's how I was, too, when I heard my mami's dead. I stood there icy cool and nothing showed on my face but tough. They say her landlord found her dead three days, sitting up straight in her chair and a bottle of spilled red wine was right there on the floor. Died drinking, all alone. No more peso Johns standing around, no more hija waiting out in the hall, just her and that bottle she loves so much. Well hell. That don't pain me, like I say. The woman's been dead a long time. You get what you pay for, right? It's the same old story you hear every day.

You know how I hear it? On the street, like I always get my news. Usually I'm standing there watching over my homies and I'll get some snitch crawling up, a try-out or a border brother giving me a piece that he thinks I can use. This vato's stealing from you, they'll say. Or C-4s got in on this deal. But this time it was Cecilia. That sister thought she was showing me some mercy when she came walking up to me on my corner. She was wearing her cleanerlady slave dress and I saw how the skin on her hands was wrinkled, like they'd been sitting in water for too long. But she couldn't touch me. I know you, that's what I thought when she's coming up and I see that cross around her throat, her puckered hands hanging down. You slanged with the best of them, sheepiegirl. It wasn't too long ago that you was banging around here like any other chola. And now you're making like that Virgin Mary cause your pretty C-4 sheep's gone and broke your heart, eh? Yah, I see you good enough. I see how you got you head on wrong. I still got my ace. I could snap my fingers and all your church ladies would be running you out of town.

      "The padre told me she went nice and peaceful, Lucía," old Muñeca said like it made some difference, and my heart didn't twist, my eyes didn't burn. I know you, I thought over and over, and I kept this still-water look on and listened to the sounds of cars driving by, the daddies sticking their hands out of their car windows and asking for a dime. "She's with God now," I heard her say, but I wouldn't let my cool skin heat up for some burn-out sheep. I didn't even tell her how I knew that if my old mami's anywhere she's roasting in hell. I was covered up in the steel I got all over, shiny and hard, and things don't get through. Can't touch me. There was that picture of my mami dead three days right in my head, and Star and my old Manny, and I felt it all the same as the weather. Even when Cecilia looked at me curious, raising one eyebrow and asking me questions I couldn't hear, even when I stood there thinking calm about how I could do most anything I wanted to out there on my turf, how I could bang her hard in the face, scream at her like that old llorona, or drag her screaming by the hair, it only felt like some light rain or a wind blowing from far off. So I didn't do nothing to that girl. "You going to have a funeral, Lucía?" she asked, pushing me, but I didn't do one thing. I let her walk right on out after she gives up cause I won't say a word. I only stared at her right in the eye and kept my mouth locked tight. I let her walk on out without touching a hair on her head.

* * *

You can see that I'm the only winner around here. I'm the only one who can do what it takes. See that street. That street's mine. And that chola on the corner. Mine too. All of this belongs to me. I ain't gonna be going loca for nobody no more, no woman sitting in her chair and no cholita with some Indian eyes. I ain't gonna be popping out no babies or letting no babies get in my way. I know when to run and when to bite and I know how to smooth-talk vatos even when it makes my tongue burn. I'm a woman that can meet any man's price. I know how to make things pay.

Keep breathing, girl. That's what I always tell myself. Keep breathing and stay alive. That's what I'm thinking even when I start getting pulled back under. I have my bad days. Sometimes when Turtle looks down, when she's playing with her hands or fooling with her shirt while I'm telling her what to do, she looks real young. You can see her baby face without them old eyes glaring out. Hey, you listening to me? You hear what I'm saying? I'll bark but I can feel that black water rising up to my chin, cold wet on my mouth. She was skinny as a winter tree begging on my corner and wouldn't run, reminds me of something. You hear me? I'm hissing at her and she snaps her face up turtle tight, so that some shadow or some shine I thought I saw shifts back and hides from me. But I ain't safe like I think. That old monster I usually stare down wicked and break to my own use comes back dark and windy, and the black water closes up over me. I see it then.

There, you mine now, I said out on the cold wet grass under them bright stars and I was feeling brand new like I just got born. And I was that cherry in a pink dress sitting on the steps and waiting around for some man to come and save my life. And when I stood up, smelling that sick sweet air and looking right in her red eyes, my hands was shaking like leaves in a bad storm.

Acknowledgments

Allison Draper, my editor at Grove Press, was insightful, witty, kind, hugely helpful with editorial suggestions, always ready to take my calls and press me a little harder; she helped make this book possible.

My mother, Thelma Diaz Quinn, a veteran Spanish teacher in the Los Angeles public school system, proofread for Spanish-language errors and made enthusiastic sounds over the phone when my spirits lagged.

Virginia Barber, my literary agent, thoughtfully and gently led me through the process.

My grandmother and grandfather, Maria and Walter Adastik, my father and stepmother, Fred MacMurray and Dawn Rouda, and my stepfather, John Quinn, all contributed moral support and excitement and a bottomless supply of love.

And finally, I have to thank my husband, Andrew Brown, who was always patient and loving, even when I called upon the great aim of ART to get out of doing housework and grocery shopping and kitty-litter duties. Baby, you're the best.